About the author

The author grew up in Yorkshire with her large family and a horde of pets. Keen on travelling, her first job was with Lufthansa in Germany.

After bringing up three children and a few more pets, she began writing in the nineties. Her special area of interest is history and after discovering her family roots with the Dalriada in Ireland, particularly this era. Her debut fiction novel titled, 'The Missionary' is a historical novel about St Patrick. It was published by Pegasus in 2021.

This is her second novel. It centres around Fergus Mór, the founder father of Scotland and takes place in fifth century Ireland and Scotland.

The author is presently based near Lake Constance, Germany.

THE SCOTS OF DALRIADA

Fergus Mór

Rowena Kinread

THE SCOTS OF DALRIADA

Fergus Mór

Vanguard Press

VANGUARD PAPERBACK

A CIP catalogue record for this title is
available from the British Library.

ISBN 978-1-80016-461-1

Vanguard Press is an imprint of
Pegasus Elliot Mackenzie Publishers Ltd.
www.pegasuspublishers.com

First Published in 2023

Vanguard Press
Sheraton House Castle Park
Cambridge England

Printed & Bound in Great Britain

Dedication

Franz and
Penelope, Anthony, Roger
Nicola and Jonathan

Acknowledgements

There are many people I would like to thank for helping this book to end up in print.
My family for always being supportive and for putting up with me.
My sister, Nicola, for teaching me everything I know about horses. Any mistakes of course, are hers not mine.
The book blogging community, I would love to name you all but am afraid I might leave someone out. Thank you for your help.
My fellow author friends, there are too many to list but most especially and above all, Deborah Swift, I want you to know how much you have helped me.
The whole team at Pegasus for their patience with someone with still a lot to learn. Many thanks particularly to Chandray.
I would like to thank Jutta for her stories about her black stallion, Lockhead, and his crumbly hoof. Yes, there really is a Lockhead, although he's not a war horse!
Special thanks to DeeDee for the captivating cover design. It was great working with you.
Finally, and most importantly, thank you dear reader for buying this book and being supportive of the publishing industry. If you enjoyed reading 'The Scots of Dalriada' please consider writing a review on for example, Amazon or Goodreads.com.

List of main characters in order of appearance.

Fergus (Mór — the Great): king of the Dalriada, founder father of Scotland.
Loarn: his brother.
Angus: Fergus' youngest brother.
Erc: their father.
Mista: their mother, Erc's second wife.
Fionn: Mista's brother.
Brother Aedan: the boys' teacher.
Cartan: believed to be the boys' half-brother; in fact, an uncle.
Daire: king of the Dalriada till 455 A.D.
Eochaid Muinremuir: Erc and Cartan's father.
Carthn: Eochaid's wife and Erc's mother.
Marca: Cartan's mother and Erc's first wife.
Niall: high king of Ireland.
Caelan: Cartan's son.
Mairead: Cartan's wife.
Feradach: a warrior.
Gair: a warrior.
Brión: king of Connacht, Niall's brother.
Fiacre: Niall's half-brother.
Oran: Niall's second-in-command.
Mahon: a warrior, Lorcan's twin.
Lorcan: a warrior.
Laeghaire: high king of Ireland.
Crimthann: king in Munster.
Nathi: Fiacre's son.
Sloan: a bailiff.
Ryley: a commander in Laeghaire's army.
Mhairi: Fionn' and Mista's cousin.
Donald: laird of Islay.
The Dalfiatach: a tribe in northern Hibernia.
The Ui Neill: a tribe in northern Hibernia.

Cenel Eogain: a tribe in northern Hibernia.
Mongan: one of Erc's sons by Marca.
Tigernach: one of Erc's sons by Marca.
Becc: one of Erc's sons by Marca.
Patricius: Christian missionary in Hibernia.
Miliucc: king of Dalriada before Daire.
Sullivan: a warrior.
Rowan: a warrior.
Tlachtga: druidess, a healer.
Grainne: Fionn's wife.
Slevin: Fionn's son.
Shanley: a soldier
Laird Mac Dougall.
Flora: wife of above and Donald's sister.
Conan: Mhairi's brother.
Rhianna: Laird Douglas' daughter.
Beth: Rhianna's maid.
Ceredig: laird of Strathclyde, Rhianna's first husband.
Tormey: Lorcan and Mahon's cousin.
Douglas: laird of Aran.
Hamish: head stable lad at Brodick.
Birga one tooth: druidess, surrogate mother to Cartan.
Morag: maid that works for Cartan.
Mac Arthur: owner of a shipyard on Islay.
Logan: captain of a boat.
Murdoch: commander of Mac Dougal's army.
Wulfhild, known as 'the Wolf': healer in a forest near Alt Clut.
Domangart: Fergus' son and successor.

Glossary of terms.

Acushla: an old term of affection from, 'a chuisle mo chroí' (pulse of my heart).
A ghrá: my love, my dear.
A stóirín: my little treasure.
Bairn: child.
Bernicia: the Anglian territory of Bernicia was approximately equivalent to the modern English counties of Northumberland and Durham, and the Scottish counties of Berwickshire and East Lothian, stretching from the Forth to the Tees. In the early seventh century, it merged with its southern neighbour, Deira, to form the kingdom of Northumbria.
Bodach: a man, especially a peasant or an old man.
Borama: cattle tribute.
Brat: cloak.
Broch: watchtower, usually made from drystone.
Brogs: shoes — later called 'brogues'.
Caitiff: a contemptable or cowardly person.
Caledonia: is a Roman name of Celtic origin for most of the area that has become Scotland.
Cantyre: old name for Kintyre.
Castle Rock: former name for Edinburgh.
Cenel: a race of people; a division of a tribe.
Corinium: present day Cirencester.
Courser: a courser is a swift and strong horse.
Damnú air: damnation (informal).
Destrier: a war horse.
Doaty: stupid, simple.
Fudir: slave.
'Goidi l': The Gaels called themselves Goidi, modernised today as Gaels.
Gowl: stupid person.
Gwynedd: North Wales.
Herbarium: a herb garden.

Ionar: a short jacket.
Léine: a shirt or tunic made from cloth.
Lia Fáil: believed by many historians to be the Stone of Destiny otherwise known as the Stone of Scone.
Máthair: mother.
Rouncey: an ordinary, all-purpose horse.
Roydammna (literally, those of kingly material): the tanist (heir to the throne) was chosen from among the heads of the Roydammna.
'Scoti': a racially derogatory term used by the Romans to describe the Gaelic-speaking 'pirates' who raided Britannia in the third and fourth centuries.
See: The place in which a cathedral church stands, identified as the seat of authority of a bishop or archbishop.
Seneschal: The steward or major-domo of a great house (historical).
Slighe: a highway.
Tackesman: the rents for farms were not paid in money, they were generally paid in a meal, cheese, and cows. The tackesman converted a good deal of this produce into money before he paid the rents to the landowner or laird.
Tanistry: ancient Celtic law of succession to throne.
Truis: trousers.

Contents

Chapter one
416 A.D. Erc's family home, Dalriada, Ireland

The force of the sword knocks his own out of his hand and he falls to the ground. Sharp stones tear into the skin on his knees. He tries to stand up quickly, but the air has left his lungs and he feels the icy tip of his opponent's sword touching his neck.

"Don't lie there boy, get up!" The master claps his hands. "Come on now, you'd be dead on a battlefield!"

Fifteen-year-old Erc stands up. With a dirty hand he wipes the blood trickling down his left knee away, lifting his sword, takes up his stance again. They have been training with sword and shield for over three hours now and he feels ready to drop down dead and die. His opponent is eighteen-years-old but that is the whole point of it, Erc easily beats any of his contemporaries. Forwards, slash, step sidewards, watch the shield, plunge, weight on your right knee. Again, and again. Something distracts his opponent. Without hesitating, Erc leaps forward and places the tip of his sword just above his opponent's heart. The master claps his hands, and they all turn to see where the distraction had come from.

Erc's father, Eochaid Muinremuir, the 'Valiant', as he is named, and his mother, Carthn, are standing in front of the ringfort, watching. Erc walks over to them. He wonders what they want. *Had his father been judging his performance? Would he finally be allowed to accompany him in battle? But then surely just his father would be present, why was his mother here? Had he committed some wrongdoing?* He racks his brain wondering what he might have done, whilst he approaches them.

"Erc," his mother, Carthn speaks, her voice lilts with her Pictish accent. "We have pleasant news for you, your cousin, Marca Ingen Eochaid is coming to visit. You are to be betrothed."

"What? Me? Who? I cannot remember a cousin Marca. Aren't I too young?" he asks, blushing deeply.

"She's a distant cousin, from your father's side of the family. You will like her. She was already married and has two children, so she is fruitful and will produce many sons for you."

"What? Already married? How old is she?"

"Thirty years and one."

"That's twice my age!"

His father coughs and taking him by the elbow, leads him away.

"Let us walk a little."

They walk down the glen towards Lough Neagh.

"It's—" Eochaid coughs, this talk embarrasses him. "It's sometimes advantageous, especially at your age, to—ahem—gain some experience with—er—an older lady. She will—show you what to—do."

Erc, cheeks already rosy, flushes now from his neck upwards, crimson.

"But what is the rush, father? I'm only fifteen, surely I don't need to get married yet, or er—produce sons? I want to gain experience on the battlefield first!"

"Yes, yes, well that will come and soon, I promise you, but the matter is a little more delicate, er—you see, Marca's man fell on the battlefield, and now she's er—she's with child again."

"Why is that a problem?"

"Her man died er—twenty months ago."

"What?"

"Her father, my brother, asked me if I would agree to you marrying her. You see, her reputation is at stake. She is a good woman though; she will not dishonour you. She won't make the same mistake twice."

"But—"

"Yes, I know, look—the first child will receive your name, but then you can have many more children together."

"Do I have a choice?"

"No, she's coming later today. I would like you to be agreeable."

"Very well then, but now I need sometime for myself. I shall ride out."

"Yes, be back for dinner."

***

"You're dripping!"

"It's raining."

"Everyone is asking for you."

"Everyone?"

"The nobles, your wife-to-be, her father—"

"Well, I'm here now."

Erc retrieves the brace of pheasants slung over his shoulder and thrusts them roughly into his mother's hand as he pushes past her. His sheepskin brat is wet, and the wool hangs down in dirty ringlets. His hands are filthy. He strides into the great hall full of long tables and people banqueting. With a glance, he sees an empty place at the top table, saved for his person, next to his wife-to-be. He sits down on the wooden bench without acknowledging her, and beckons to a serf, shouts for beer and food. A mug of beer is placed before him. He knocks it back in one go, letting the beer run down his chin. He slams the mug on the table and shouts for more, whilst wiping his chin with the back of his grubby hand. His mother starts to rise from her seat, but his father pushes her back down. Marca pretends not to notice. He reaches for a leg of lamb and chomps it noisily with his mouth open, grease runs down the side of his mouth. He knocks back another beer, letting it dribble again. *If she doesn't like it, she doesn't have to marry me, I won't insist.*

She is still pretending that nothing is amiss. He glances sideways, *she looks all right I suppose.* He begrudges this, he would prefer her to be ugly with warts on her nose and rotting teeth, for then his behaviour would be justified. He looks again, *actually she's quite pretty and doesn't really look like thirty. More like twenty-five. That's still old.*

People come to congratulate him, friends, and family; they thump him on the shoulder and grin. He turns permanently red and wishes the floor would swallow him up.

A druid approaches and requests the pair to follow him. A sort of ceremony commences and minutes later they are man and wife.

He drinks more beer and goes outside to pee. Marca sees him go out and follows him.

She takes his hand and whispers softly in his ear, "Come now."

She leads him to a guest chamber and even before they enter, he has an erection. *Damnú air! that's not supposed to happen.*

This time she lets him know she has noticed. She removes her clothes and drapes herself across the bed. With her finger she beckons him to come to her.

"Won't it hurt the—er—baby?"

"No."

He removes his ionar and truis and joins her on the bed. She smiles, takes his member in her hand, and directs it to the right place. He cannot hold back, and lets go of himself thrusting back and forth until two minutes later he's spent. He lies back exhausted. She leaves him ten minutes, then turns on her side and begins to move her hand up and down along his penis, squeezing.

A dhiabhail! he thinks, as he becomes stiff again. He enters her, without help this time, and moves up and down purposefully. Five minutes later he has another release. Ecstasy. This time she lets him rest longer, and then she shows him how to please her.

For a couple of months, he enjoys her bed at night, but they have nothing in common, apart from the sex. Little things begin to bother him. *She has teeth like a horse,* he finds himself thinking, *she laughs like one too*.

During the day he continues practising warfare. He is more determined now, angry. He doesn't know why. His master is pleased.

"Erc makes progress," he tells Eochaid. "Soon he will be ready."

Marca's belly is swollen. Erc frequents her room less often.

One day his father awaits him in the courtyard. "The time has come," he says. "Tomorrow, you shall accompany me to Tara. High King Niall is expecting us."

***

A hundred new recruits stand in the courtyard waiting, nervous. A few apprehensive attempts to chat, say hello. They eye each other up. Most are of his age, or round about. High King Niall, Overking of Ireland, rules over the many Underkings, Chieftains of the clans, small territories, and baronies. He stands on a balustrade in front of the entrance to Tara, his royal palace. Steps lead down to the courtyard, but he remains where he is, scrutinising his new recruits, a humble gaggle of scrawny adolescents. He speaks, a sort of battle cry against the villainous, dishonourable, unscrupulous, renegade tribes in the south, constantly snatching land and livestock that doesn't belong to them, terrorising innocent farmers and their families, burning their homes down and killing them, merciless. It was his job as high king to protect his people, and they, the recruits had been chosen from many, to help him. It was an honour to be selected. A deafening cheer, fists raised high, the young soldiers, naïve, are ready to give their lives for their king.

A brief training, four weeks in all, and then a long march southward. On the way admiring glances, they make an imposing heroic parade.

The warriors are divided into groups of forty, each with a leader. Five groups of forty have an older, experienced warrior, a captain. Small armies of four hundred men have a commander, five in all. High King Niall is at the head of two thousand men. He rides in a chariot, the commanders likewise. There are more chariots and a cavalry. The foot soldiers are divided into swordsmen, they are the majority, and archers, those with bows and arrows who go up front and fire their missiles when ordered. In the camps there are women, who cook but do not fight; druids who heal and advise; craftsmen who sharpen swords on stone wheels and make arrows.

Erc is a swordsman, his leader a calm, seasoned fighter, his commander is his father. He fights with no respect for his own life; his courageous deeds do not go unnoticed. Soon he is named Erc 'the Ferocious'.

When the fighting season ends, he returns home with his father. Marca has birthed a son. She has called him Cartan. She doesn't ask Erc if he agrees to the name or even likes it. He doesn't really care. His mother and father dote over the child.

"Such a strong, winsome lad," they say. "Our first grandson," they swoon. Erc regards them strangely, *why do they say that?* he wonders. *Do they really believe this?* He shakes his head in disbelief.

After three months, he enters Marca's chamber again. She knows all the right buttons to touch, and he has no problem ejaculating again and again. When he leaves her room though, he somehow feels uneasy, manipulated. He goes hunting and returns home with a dozen rabbits. He gives them to his mother to prepare for dinner and then sits by the fire to warm his bones and waits, he doesn't really know for what.

His father finds him and draws up a chair to sit next to him and speaks.

"You fought bravely, Erc. Your leader and captain both praise you, I'm proud."

"The Southerners are not good warriors. They lack training and their swords are blunt."

"Hmmn, you are modest. It is advantageous not to be too cocky, many soldiers overestimate their skills."

"Or underestimate their foes. You need not worry Father, I won't be reckless, I saw the bodies, as you did."

"I want to speak to you about another matter. The farms in the north, they are yours."

"I don't know what to say, are you sure?"

"Yes, you've proved yourself more than worthy. They are tenanted and will bring you income. You can build your own house and settle there with Marca and your children."

"Thank you, Father, tomorrow I shall ride out there and look the land over."

"That's settled then."

***

Erc chooses a promontory; the locals call it Fairhead; it is an ideal place to construct a fortress. It's on the utmost North-eastern headland of his land, within the territory of his tribe, the Dalriada. On a fine day there are magnificent views all the way to Caledonia. He decides to build it as a bastion. To the north and east steep cliffs provide a natural obstacle to any invaders. Around the south and west perimeter stone ramparts could be constructed. He would hew a souterrain through the rock to the cove below the castle. It would remain secret, a hidden passage for emergencies.

Chapter two
424 A.D. Tara, Meath, Ireland

Erc is glad when the winter is over, and the fighting season begins again. He has visited his land and farms in the north, spoken to the tenants and collected the rent, an annual tribute of a portion of the harvest. With grain he has paid labourers to start constructing a fortress for his family home. It is seven years now since they started preparing the land with massive ramparts made from stone and earth. Marca has given him six sons already and the accommodation at his father's house is getting cramped.

He rides with his father, Eochaid, to Leinster and they report to High King Niall in Tara. New recruits arrive to replace those who are dead. Erc is promoted to captain of five groups of forty warriors.

"Come with me," Eochaid tells Erc. "The commanders and captains are meeting Niall in his headquarters to discuss how to go forwards this year."

They enter the castle and walk along corridors and past closed chambers, through the great hall and further until they reach Niall's command centre. The door stands open and Niall sits at a table with four commanders. Eochaid joins them whilst Erc takes place standing around the perimeter of the room with other captains. The last captains arrive, and the door is closed.

"I have an urgent message from my brother, Brión." Niall starts without wasting any time for preliminaries after the long winter break. "Fiacre, my half-brother, a jealous rat, has summoned his followers together, and has laid siege to Brión at Rathcroghan castle. He has managed to call a tidy army together by all accounts. Brión doesn't know exactly how many men he has, but at least six hundred, maybe more."

"Well, it was to be expected, I suppose. He made no secret of not being happy with the decision to position Brión as king of Connacht," Oran, Niall's second-in-command speaks.

“That may well be, but I cannot tolerate insubordination. The problem is that there is trouble in the south too. The Britons, and even Saxons, those uncouth wretches, will simply not leave us in peace. However often we fight them, chasing them back across the seas; as soon as we retreat, they are back again, grabbing spoils and riches from our well tested farmers; like persistent weeds sprouting up between rows of vegetables, scarcely you think you are rid of them all, when new ones start cropping up all over the place.”

“How long can Brión last?” Oran asks.

“He has food but no water. The water spring is out of reach, below the castle.”

“Ale? Milk?”

“A little, not enough for all, not for long.”

“Hmmn, he doesn’t know exactly how large Fiacre’s army is, you say?”

“How many men does Brión have with him, in the castle complex?” Eochaid butts in.

“Maybe a hundred,” Niall replies.

“If Fiacre has only six hundred men, we could split the forces.”

“And if he has more? He is a mighty warrior with a keen head for devising clever strategies; and his men are well trained and outfitted.”

“Hmmn, we could send some scouts to find out how many men he really has—Erc?”

“Yes, Father.”

“How long would you need with—say four men?”

“A week at the longest.”

“Do you have the right men?”

“Yes, Sir. Gair is from Connacht, he will be invaluable. Feradach is courageous but not foolhardy; then the twins, Mahon and Lorcan, they are strong and trustworthy.”

“That sounds excellent, the less known about the matter the better, we all know there are spies among us. When can you leave?” Niall asks, the decision already taken.

“As soon as dusk falls; we need provisions for a week and five horses. Bay mares, their colour will merge with this filthy weather, and they won’t whinny like overexcited stallions,” Erc replies.

“You shall receive all you need, and we’ll await your return eagerly.”

***

Thunder growls and the clouds burst open pelting rain down with a velocity that hurts with contact to his skin. Erc turns his head sideways in the other direction, trying to avoid head-on contact, at the same time urging his horse on quickly along the beaten paths. The forest becomes so dense that no light penetrates the foliage; the ground is slippery from the deluge. Leafy branches, heavy with rain, hang low and Erc lays his torso flat along his horse’s neck, ducking the overhanging obstacles. His men follow him. Just a lighter shade of black tells them it is still dusk outside the forest. When this too dims and they can see nothing in front of their horses’ ears, they slow down. They pull their horses up, the clamour of their hooves ceases, and they hear that the forest is alive with sound. A scurry of feet, leaves that rustle, owls hooting. Gair puts a finger to his mouth.

“Those aren’t just animal noises,” he whispers. “Our presence is known. Stay here, I will go and try to find my people, see what they can tell me.”

“Be back before dawn, we must proceed,” Erc tells him.

“I’ll be here before the first chords of the morning chorus strike.”

Erc and his men dismount, Feradach holds Gair’s horse whilst he scutters silently uphill through the forest. He is soon out of sight. The horses are uneasy, sensing the presence of the unknown. The men stroke their horses’ muzzles and whisper softly in their ears, until they settle down and stop fidgeting with their hooves. They wait three hours before Gair returns.

“My people have fled to the hills,” he tells them. “Fiacre’s army is bored, waiting for Brión to surrender. They are also hungry and are plundering the farms, taking all, leaving nothing but destruction and dead bodies. Brión is holding out, waiting for Niall to come to the rescue. My family and many others feared for their lives. They have deserted their farms, carrying all they can with them. They are waiting now, in caves high up in the hills, until the war is over, and they can return to their homes."

"Do they know how many men Fiacre has?" Erc asks.

"They say eight hundred."

"And weapons?"

"Those without swords are armed with farm tools; pitchforks, their prongs sharpened so that they gleam in the sunlight, spades, whatever is to hand."

"Good work Gair! We shall return to Tara now; Niall is awaiting us."

***

Erc has been travelling for six days on the king's mission and has been on the saddle nearly as long. He is filthy, splattered with mud, and his bones ache from sleeping on the cold, stony ground.

"Tell me, how is my brother? Is the situation as bad as he says?" Niall asks Erc without preamble.

"Worse," Erc replies. "He cannot hold out much longer. Without help he will die and all with him, within the month."

"And Fiacre? How many men does he have?"

"Eight hundred; all armed."

"Call the commanders and captains together, Erc! We have waited long enough, now is time for action. And Erc—well done, you and your men will be rewarded."

"Yes Sire, thank you my king."

***

Niall splits his army. With Oran, his second in command and a thousand men, he rushes to the south-eastern coast in Munster. Savage overseas people are ravaging the land, greedily taking heaps of booty. Niall and his men arrive and fighting fiercely put them to flight across the sea. When Niall withdraws, the barbarians reappear, a little further down the coast. Niall's army repulses the second incursion. Once again as his soldiers withdraw, hordes of foreigners emerge eagerly from the currachs that carry them across the waves. Every time Niall fights the rebels back, they re-emerge. Aching from wounds and battered, Niall returns with the remainder of his army to Tara. He needs time to recuperate. *I'll wait for the other half of my army to return from Connacht, then we'll go back south and slaughter the vile savages once and for all,* he thinks.

Meanwhile, Erc has been sent with the rest of the army, under Eochaid's command, to free Brión from Fiacre's siege. They arrive at Rathcroghan to find Fiacre gone and Brión and his men in good health.

"Fiacre has retreated with his army to Damchluain," Brión tells Eochaid. "We were waiting for you to arrive. Now we can go together and kill the villainous rebels."

The vast army increases when local yeomen, determined to defend their property, join them. They march towards Damchluain. From an elevation, two miles away, they see why Fiacre has chosen the site. A long valley is banked on each side by compact forest hills.

"The second we enter that valley, they will sweep down upon us from both sides," Eochaid says. "Neither can we use our arrows with the target hidden from view."

Erc is mounted on his horse, sitting next to his father; he surveys the lay of the land.

"Could we divide our forces," he asks. "And making a large sweep approach them from behind, through the rear of the forest, forcing them into the valley themselves?"

"What do you say?" Eochaid asks Brión.

"We would have to advance under the cover of night," Brión replies. "So they cannot see where we go."

When night falls the army moves; half go left, half go right. The strategy is devastating for Fiacre. His men fall like dice from a beaker and Fiacre is taken prisoner. Erc, Gair, Lorcan and Mahon are bringing Fiacre to Tara when Feradach comes riding up as if a wild boar were chasing him.

"Erc," he calls from a distance; he is panting, out of breath. "Come quickly, your father—Eochaid is injured!"

"What? Is it bad?" Erc turns his horse around and gallops back after Feradach, who leads the way.

After just five miles they reach the camp where the wounded are being tended to. Erc enters a tent and sees his father on a pallet, pale, his breathing laboured. A few men stand around the pallet, one gives his father something to drink.

"What happened?" Erc asks.

"A stupid coincidence, the fighting was almost over, a short lack of concentration, just as long as the blink of an eyelid, and a stray arrow; it pierced his lung—" The soldier lets his sentence trail; the consequence is clear. Erc kneels next to his father, tears swell up in his eyes, he shivers.

"Father," he says, his voice breaking.

Eochaid turns his head and focusses on his son, "Erc—look after Cartan—promise me—he's *my* son!" With this last effort to speak, he dies.

Erc thinks he's misheard. He looks up to the soldier next to him and raises his eyebrows in question. The soldier shrugs his shoulders and expresses his sympathies. A cloth is pulled over Eochaid's body. Erc stands up abruptly and leaves the tent. Mounting his horse, he rides to re-join his men bringing Fiacre to Tara. His men greet him when he approaches, but seeing the expression on his face, they don't ask questions. They ride in silence to Tara.

At Tara Fiacre is brought to Niall. He orders Fiacre to be imprisoned in the dungeons. Niall calls for Erc and praises Eochaid.

"A valiant soldier," he says. "I will accompany you home to your family. He will receive an honourable burial."

"You honour me, my king, but I would prefer to go alone, if that is acceptable."

"Yes, go home and sort things out. Come back when you're done."

Erc rides home and confronts Marca, even before he informs his mother of his father's death.

"Is it true? Is my own father Cartan's sire? Tell me!" he demands.

"Yes," she replies simply. "It is true!"

He is angry. She hadn't even bothered to lie, for his sake if not for hers. So his father had made his widowed niece with child and then forced him, Erc his son, the child's half-brother, to become the child's father and his mistress' man. *Had his mother known?* He guesses, yes. Now many things seem to make sense.

After the funeral he leaves Marca with his mother, and riding north, spends all his time and energy working on his prestigious abode. Niall had said he could have as much time as he wanted, so he takes it. Two years ago, the ramparts had been finished, they were ten feet high and six feet deep. Then last year he had hewn a tunnel through the rock, three hundred feet down to a cove below the castle. He is proud of his work. He hadn't dug it out single-handedly, but only his most trustworthy men had been allowed to labour in the souterrain, he wanted it to remain unknown.

In spring, work had begun on the living quarters and outbuildings. Now he is present, the work progresses rapidly. The lower parts of the buildings are constructed with stone, five feet high. The rest of the walls are wooden, the rooves thatched. The entrance is through an archway, secured by heavy oak doors. Vicious iron spikes adorn the stone arch; no unwanted visitors can enter. It has taken years to complete, but it has been worth it. He calls it Dunseverick.

Chapter three
455 A.D. Dunseverick, Ireland

"Race you to the Giant's Stones!" Fergus calls to his two younger brothers, Loarn and Angus. "First one there gets my sweetbread."

His two siblings need no further incentive and race down the grassy slopes, their knees almost buckling beneath them. They charge through the sheep, who scurry away bleating in protest, and sprint up the trodden path towards the cliff tops and Bengore Head. The wind is strong, and they fight against it, battling on courageously.

Fergus lets them have a head start and then begins to run after them at a leisurely pace. It's a good six miles to the Giant's Causeway and he knows they will have spent their energy soon. The cliffs drop dramatically into the stormy sea below them; it's coloured deep blue today, the waves topped white. The seagulls call to each other, screaming against the gale and circling in wide loops, looking for the tell-tale silver streak of fish. His brothers are stretching their arms out wide now and letting themselves be blown to and fro by the wind, giggling and laughing.

"Not too near the edge!" Fergus shouts.

The wind scoops up his words and blows them away. Angus runs dangerously near the cliff top. Fergus shouts again, then sighs and picks up his pace. He reaches Angus just as a squall of wind sweeps his little brother's slight frame towards the precipitous edge. Fergus leaps on him from behind, pinning his body to the ground.

"Ouch! What did you do that for?" Angus complains.

"I told you not to go near the edge!" Fergus shouts at him, angry but relieved that his brother is unharmed. "Come on now, we'll go together."

"Aren't we racing any more?" asks Loarn.

"No, Mother gave me enough sweetbread for all of us. First, we have to collect a bag full of mussels though, each one of us."

They continue at a more sedate pace until they reach Bengore Head. The cliff tops soar a thousand feet above the raging sea below. The boys crawl on their stomachs towards the edge so that the gale force winds have no chance of whisking their bodies away. It rushes towards them, tearing at their hair. The skies are blue with white cumulus clouds and the visibility reaches across the western sea to Caledonia. Seagulls hover above them calling and screeching to one another. Loarn points to the sea stacks rising high out of the sea, the waves crashing against them, thrusting white and turquoise fountains soaring into the sky. Although lying next to each other, they have to shout to make themselves heard. Fergus aims his finger at the islands, far away yet clearly in view, off the coast of Caledonia.

"When I'm older, I'm going to conquer those islands."

"Because of the horses?" Loarn smiles; the islands are in Argyll, territory of the Epidii, the horse-folk, and Fergus is passionate about horses.

"Well not because of the ginger heads!" Fergus refers to their belief that all people from Caledonia have red hair.

"I'm going to build you the fastest boats ever, so that pirates can't catch you," Angus declares seriously from between them.

"We shall be the pirates." Fergus grins wickedly. "And what shall my ship look like? Like the ones you've drawn, with wooden planks and two sails?"

"Yes, it will have a flat bottom which will let you navigate shallow water but a high bow and stern to protect it from heavy storms. The hull will be narrow, so it'll cut through the waves like a dagger—but the stability is still a problem. Brother Aedan says I'm to try again. He is worried about capsizing, he can't swim!"

Angus giggles because all the children he knows can swim, and Brother Aedan is an adult.

"The ship's going to be much faster than that currach over there," he says, pointing to a vessel cutting through the waves at about twenty knots, as if a triple-headed sea monster and not just the wind were behind it.

They continue along a grassy path that curves around each headland and gradually descends all the way down to Hawks Hollow. A glance and a nod, in unison they drop to their stomachs again and crawl to the cliff's edge. Heads hanging over the top, they look down to a rocky outcrop where an enormous nest nearly six-feet wide is wedged in the cliff, fifteen-feet below them. A brown, greyish sea hawk, huge, two feet long, is sitting in the nest regurgitating food into the beak of a fledgling. The boys gaze in awe. A series of sharp whistles, yewk, yewk, yewk, and a shadow passes over them. They look up and see the male hawk, circling above them and using aerodynamics spirals down toward them with a frenzied cheep, cheep, cheep. Startled, they jump up and holding hands run away quickly, as fast as their young legs will carry them. The hawk has arched wings and follows from above, eyeballing them. Not until the hawk's calls become distant, do they dare to slow their pace and finally bend over double, panting.

"How much further?" Angus asks.

"Not much further now. Look there are the arches!" Fergus points to white limestone arches, covered with tufts of green grass, protruding out into the sea. Emerald water swirls beneath them, eating away at the rock pillars. Soon they can see giant boulders resting in the sea below them. Their hexagonal shapes stretch out towards the Isle of Rathlin, six miles distant. The boys reach the Shepherd's Steps. The flat rocks, wedged into the cliff face to ease descent, are slick with spray from the waves and green weeds. "I'll go first," Fergus says. "Angus follow me, and Loarn, you take up the rear."

Concentrating on his siblings, Fergus slips and falls down a few feet.

"Are you all right?" Loarn calls.

Fergus gets up and looks at the scrape on his knee. "Yes, just a graze, nothing serious."

There are one hundred and sixty-two steps; he has counted them many times. They are very steep but in face of danger, they are careful and make it to the shore unscathed. Angus races ahead to the giant volcanic stones, determined to win the race that no longer is. They stretch out far towards another country, but a mist has descended out of nowhere and hangs over the sea obscuring the view.

"It was sunny at Bengore Head," Loarn comments, half complaining.

But they grew up here and they all know how quickly the weather can change.

Fergus leaps up onto a rock and stretching a hand out to pull Loarn up, and says, “Come on, let’s eat the sweetbread first, and then pick the mussels before the tide turns.”

The seawater has worn away the surface of the rocks creating hollows, now full of tiny crabs and seaweed. They hunker down beside a rock pool and unpacking the bread begin to eat. A mysterious invisible alarm has alerted Angus and within seconds he is sitting beside them, anxious not to miss out on his share. The feast is devoured quickly.

“Tell me the story about the giant again,” Angus begs.

Fergus sighs theatrically but repeats the story. “A long, long time ago there was a giant called Fionn, who lived here peacefully with his wife, Oonagh. Then one day, Benandonner, a ferocious giant with red hair and a beard who lived in Caledonia, challenged him to a fight. Fionn accepted the provocation and threw rocks into the western sea to make a causeway all the way to Caledonia so that the two giants could meet. Fionn crept secretly across the rocks at night so that he could spy on Benandonner and see where his weaknesses lay. He wanted to know how he could defeat him. But when Fionn reached the other side of the sea and saw how big Benandonner was, he fled back to Oonagh and wanted to hide. Then Oonagh disguised Fionn as a baby and tucked him in a cradle. When Benandonner came and saw the size of the ‘baby’, he thought that his father, Fionn, must be a horrendous mammoth-sized monster. He was so frightened that he ran all the way back to Caledonia, destroying the pathway behind him, so that Fionn could not follow and devour him.”

“And he was really called Fionn just like our uncle?” asks Angus.

“Yes, maybe our uncle was called after him; he’s tall and strong, after all.”

“Not as tall as a real giant though.”

“No not that tall, but I like him, he’s fun!”

“Me too! Last time he came he took me hunting with Flash.”

“His peregrine, oh you’re so lucky!”

“He gave me his leather glove to put on my hand and Flash landed on it. He’s heavier than he looks. He’ll take you too, if you ask.”

"Yes, he's much nicer than Cartan. I don't trust him at all, he's always sneaking around."

"I'm glad he's only our half-brother. Last time he came, he pushed me off the stone rampart. On purpose. Mother happened to be watching and told Father and he told Cartan off."

"You were lucky not to be harmed," Fergus tells Angus. "Brother Aedan says I'll have this scar for life!" he points to a ragged scar above his left eyebrow.

"I can't believe that he just attacked you like that," Loarn says.

"He said I fell upon him with my knife, for no reason at all, he was just defending himself!"

"Yes, well nobody believed him. You of all people, and not even half his age!"

Something catches Fergus' attention. He narrows his eyes and scans the horizon.

"Hurry now!" he says, throwing two empty canvas sacks to his brothers. "The tide is turning. Remember Angus; just pick the mussels that come off the rocks easily, they're ready. Leave the others for another day."

The boys run and jump, back along the causeway to the cliffs. Wading knee-deep into the sea they begin to prise the black, shiny mussels off the rock face. There are so many. Fergus finishes first; his sack is full to the brim. He heaves it over his shoulder and brings it to the foot of the Shepherd's Steps. Then he runs back to his brothers. He is hurrying and slips on the rocks covered in seaweed. Cursing, he stands up again. Loarn's bag is nearly full, but Angus is wandering too far out into the sea.

"Angus, come back!" he yells. His voice is barely audible over the crash of waves. He curses again, this time under his breath, and strides out through the sea to his brother. The water is only knee-deep, but the waves swirl up to his waist. Reaching Angus, he grabs hold of his hand and starts pulling him back towards the shore. Angus looks surprised but doesn't protest. The wind and waves crashing against the cliffs make talking pointless. Loarn has filled his sack and placed it next to Fergus'. Now they help Angus fill his, just before the tide becomes too high.

The Shepherd's Steps zigzag up the cliff. They are treacherously slippery but going up is safer than descending. The last two hundred feet are practically perpendicular. They lift the sacks up first and then follow themselves, step for step. By the time they reach the cliff top, the bay is covered by the sea, and the sky is becoming grey. The boys set off, walking home to Dunseverick castle. Angus doesn't complain but Fergus and Loarn see that he's tired.

"Give me your sack!" Fergus says. "I'm going lopsided with just one."

Angus looks at him gratefully. He's not fooled but realises that he wouldn't manage the whole way back with his full sack heavy with mussels. They no longer run, they no longer drop to their bellies to look at the hawks, they simply place one foot in front of the next, intent on getting home before night falls. They've gone two miles when they see a rider on a horse cantering towards them. They hurry to hide behind some bushes, hoping they haven't been seen. The rider comes nearer looking to his right and to his left. Angus, curious, peeps above the bush.

"Uncle Fionn!" he cries. "What are you doing here?"

Fionn pulls his horse up and walks towards them smiling. "I thought you might like a lift home."

"Oh yes," Angus cries. "Can I ride up front?"

"Up you get then." Fionn leans down from his horse and giving Angus a hand, pulls him up in front of him.

"What about you two?" he asks.

Loarn puts his mussels down and straddles the horse behind Fionn. Fergus gives him the three sacks of mussels to wedge between their bodies and then accepts a hand up from Fionn to sit behind Loarn.

"I'm glad you've come Uncle Fionn, Angus was flagging. How come you're here? And how did you know where to find us?"

"That was easy, Fergus; your mother told me that she'd sent you to collect mussels. And why I'm here? You know King Daire died a month gone, with only daughters. I've got a surprise for you all: the Roydammna has elected Erc as king of the Dalriada!"

"Our father?"

"Yes, you are young princes now."

Chapter four
455 A.D. Flight to Finlaggan, Islay, Caledonia

The sun has fallen behind the forest hills and night is approaching rapidly. The last grey streaks in the sky turn inky black, the moon begins to rise. The horse clatters under the archway into the courtyard, Fionn pulls her up. Fergus and Loarn slip off the horse's back, whilst Fionn lifts Angus down, places him on his feet, and gives the boys their sacks of mussels. Fionn pats his horse's neck.

"I'll take Niamh to the stables and rub her down," he tells the boys. "You wash those mussels now and yourselves a bit, and then hurry indoors, your mother's waiting for you."

"Shall I help you, Uncle?" Fergus offers.

"No, you're all right lad, thank you; better you help your brothers tonight."

The boys carry the mussels to the well and start drawing water up to rinse them.

A small, light figure, dressed in finery, enters the courtyard, and watches them.

"What are you doing?" the figure asks.

The boys, intent on their task, hadn't heard anyone approach. They look up startled. It's Caelan, Cartan's eldest son, younger than Fergus but older than Loarn and Angus.

"What have you got there?" he asks again.

"Mussels," Angus replies, scooping some up in his hands and carrying them over to Caelan, dripping.

"Aagh you're dripping all over me!" Caelan yelps and runs a few steps away. "You've ruined my léine, and just look at my brogs!"

Angus looks at Caelan's leather brogs with a shiny golden buckle. They are a little wet. "Sorry I just wanted to show you the mussels—"

"What's going on here?" Cartan's voice thunders from behind them and the boys jump, startled.

Fergus and Loarn automatically place themselves each side of Angus, their arms, and shoulders touching.

"He's ruined my clothes!" Caelan accuses Angus, pointing at him.

Cartan narrows his eyes and focusses on Angus. Before Cartan can open his mouth, Fergus and Loarn both nudge Angus.

Angus bows low before his half-brother.

"I apologise sincerely, Sire, it was a misunderstanding, I—"

"Are you calling my son a *liar*, boy?"

"No, of course not, I just—"

"You are an uncouth wretch. I'm not surprised, being educated by that foreign imposter. What's his name? Brother Aedan. Ha, that I do not laugh! Well, I shall speak to your father and arrange for you to come home with me tomorrow. I shall soon teach you some manners and my druids will knock some sense into your gammy head!"

"Thank you, that won't be necessary," Fionn's deep calm voice comes from the direction of the stables and he takes long, quick strides towards the boys.

Putting an arm around them all, he ushers them towards the kitchens.

"The mussels—" Fergus asks.

"Leave them!" Fionn's voice is husky with controlled emotion "They are not important now."

They enter the kitchen. Mista, their mother, Erc's second wife, rushes towards them and embraces them in a tight hug.

"Thank goodness you are all safe," she ruffles their hair.

"Mother, you won't let Cartan take me away, will you?" Angus is worried.

Mista looks up sharply to Fionn. He shakes his head slightly and makes a sign that they should leave the kitchen, where they can be overheard. Mista nods fractionally to indicate that she has understood.

"Of course not, whatever gave you that idea? Come now—"

She puts her finger silently on her lips to signal to them not to speak and pushes the boys out of the kitchen and down a narrow corridor to a chamber at the back of the castle. They all enter, Fionn last, closing the door quietly behind him. Mista lets out a long deep sigh.

"Already?" she asks Fionn quietly.

"Aye, he's not wasting any time."

The boys' eyes widen as they look from their mother to Fionn and back again, not understanding what is going on.

"Have I done something wrong, Mother?" Angus is bewildered.

"Sssh, no, you've done nothing wrong, my love. This has nothing to do with any of you—or rather yes, it does, but you've done nothing wrong. Your half-brother, Cartan, is an evil person; resentful, jealous and a troublemaker. He disapproves that your father remarried; worse still that I am the daughter and granddaughter of two high kings of Ireland; but to top it all, we have three healthy sons. Not daughters, who are unimportant in the question of succession, but you three beautiful, intelligent, and beloved boys. You know the law of tanistry in our country. The Roydammna, the males of royal blood, elect the king amongst themselves. The king holds this office for life, and the Roydammna chooses the man whom they deem as the worthiest of this dignity. The trouble is that the group of eligibles becomes larger each generation, and this leaves the leadership open to ambitious men, like Cartan, who are prepared to murder their own siblings in order to achieve their goal."

"Cartan is a despicable murderer, a coward, an obnoxious worm!" Fionn interrupts.

"He resents his position," Mista intervenes. "He is simply never *satisfied*. He married a princess from the Ui Neill tribe. Not because he loved her, he made no secret of that, but to further his ambitions for power. His—your father was actually relieved when he left the Dalriada for the Ui Neill. He gave him land and farms when he married, as was his due. His father-in-law also gave him farms and land. Cartan is a rich and influential man now. He has a small army and as a landowner he is a noble. But he wants to be king and will try to eliminate any co-contenders to the throne."

"But Father was only just made king today!" Fergus protests. "He won't die for years yet, surely?"

"Hopefully not, no. But you are not safe here. Cartan is already conspiring to harm you. He has powerful friends and will try to organise 'accidents' for you."

"He's a *scumbag*!" Angus stamps his foot. "Is that why he pushed me off the ramparts?"

"Yes, and injured Fergus!" Loarn bursts out indignantly.

"What can we do, Mother?" Fergus asks.

"Your father, Fionn and I have already discussed this. We've known for several weeks now that there was a good possibility that he would be elected king once Daire died. And all three of us are of one opinion about Cartan. We have no illusions about his character or the intrigues he is plotting. We all agreed that it would be best for you to leave this place. I have written to Mhairi, Fionn's and my cousin who lives on Islay. Her husband, Donald, is Laird of the Isle and owns much land. They have agreed to look after you and protect you for as long as necessary."

"Islay in *Argyll*, the territory of the Epidii, the horse-folk?" Fergus asks.

"Yes, my love, at least you can surround yourself with horses." Mista smiles, acknowledging Fergus' passion.

"But you, Mother? And Father?"

"It breaks my heart, my loves, but I have to do what is best for you. I shall try to visit you in a few months. I hope the situation here settles down soon."

"So we're just to go *alone*?"

"No, Fionn will accompany you and Brother Aedan, you must continue your studies; and four of your father's most trusted men will also go with you."

"And when?"

"Now, immediately, your things are already packed. Your father wanted to say farewell to you, but if Cartan is already causing trouble, it is too dangerous. If Erc leaves the hall, Cartan will become suspicious. Fionn will lead you down a souterrain to the cove below the castle—" Mista takes a deep breath; her voice is raw with emotion. A dagger pierces her heart and shreds it in pieces as she gives each of her boys a fierce hug. "Look after your brothers," she whispers in Fergus' ear. "Help Fergus," she tells Loarn. To Angus she whispers, "Don't give up on your dreams. I want to sail on one of your ships one day, my angel." Tears are running freely down her cheeks.

"Don't worry, Mother. We'll be back soon," Angus tells her.

Fionn leads the boys out of the door and as they leave their mother, she closes the door silently behind them. Her whole body heaves and trembles violently.

Choking on her tears she collapses to the floor and weeps uncontrollably, '*Have we made the right decision?*' she asks herself. '*Will I ever see my boys again?*'

***

Erc waits until the line of well-wishers diminishes, then excusing himself saying he must pee, stands up and leaves the grand hall. He goes down the corridor and enters the last chamber on the right.

Cartan waits half a minute, mumbles he must pee also, and then follows Erc silently down the corridor. He sees Erc enter the chamber and rejoices that he has left the door ajar. Flattening his back against the wall, he advances, going as near as he dares, and cocks his ears.

Erc sees Mista on the floor, her body heaving and emitting animal-like noises. He kneels before her and gathers her up in his arms. He strokes her hair out of her face and wipes her tears away.

"I'm too late," he states "they've gone already."

"Yes." She sobs, her body shudders again.

Erc places kisses on his wife's cheeks, her forehead, her neck. He hugs her and stroking her hair promises her, "We'll visit soon."

Cartan's ears are popping. *The boys already gone?* That was sooner than he had expected. He exits the corridor quickly and goes to the courtyard, the stables, his men's quarters. Thirty men have accompanied him here. He gathers them together and orders them to spread out and find the boys.

"Fionn will be with them," he says. "They cannot go alone, and some of Erc's warriors too, no doubt, for protection. Hurry," he cries. "They cannot be gone far."

As his men mount their steeds and spread out, Cartan returns to the hall to continue his play of innocence.

Erc has already returned. Mista is not present.

"Is your wife unwell?" Cartan feigns concern.

"Women's troubles, she'll be right as rain tomorrow." Erc grunts.

"Oh, such a shame, today of all days, your day of triumph. I'm sure Mairead would bite her teeth together to be present at such a time, wouldn't you, my dear?" Cartan says turning towards his wife.

Mairead blushes and lowers her head. Erc is no longer listening; he is attending to his visitors, listening to their pledges of loyalty.

***

Meanwhile, Fionn, finger on his lips, and crouching low, whispers to the boys, "Keep to the shadows and follow me quietly."

They advance towards the hidden entrance to the secret tunnel. Erc had dug out and built the souterrain even before the construction of castle was begun, and only a handful of men knew of its existence. The entrance is on the sandy promontory at the very head of the peninsula. Nothing grows there save long grasses, and usually one had no reason to approach the area. Not even the boys know of it, Erc wisely realising that the temptation to play there would be too great. They reach the end of the promontory, 'Fair Head'. Fionn looks for a heap of stones, thrown as if by chance in an irregular circle, kneels on the grass and pushes sand away with both hands until he finds an iron ring. He pulls on it and a rectangular wooden trapdoor opens. The boys are bursting with questions but stay quiet for now. Fionn signals Fergus to hold the door open whilst he enters, then he beckons the boys to follow him. They are on a small stone landing, steps, hewn out of rock, spiral steeply downwards. Fionn tells Fergus to hold the door open, just a finger wide, whilst he removes a torch from the wall and attempts to light it. He hands the lit torch to Fergus and bolts the trapdoor behind them.

"You must stay silent," he warns the boys. "The steps are steep and perilously slippery. Hold onto the rope railing and follow me carefully, I'll light the way, Angus, stay behind me and Fergus, you take up the rear."

The steps are long thin wedges and Fergus' feet are large for his fifteen years. He climbs down the stairs next to the wall where the steps are widest. The rope rail is looped through iron rings hammered in the rock. It hangs loosely and is more a guide than a secure handrail. It is too low for him; he is tall for his age too. He gropes blindly, feeling his way along the wall slick with moisture, the stone floor slippery underfoot. It is icy cold, sometimes it feels slimy. Fionn's torch emits gloomy shadows, dancing and flickering up and down, like murky clouds in a moonless night. They progress down and down, in spiralling circles, seemingly unending. Feeling dizzy, Fergus slows his pace.

An excited cheer from Angus followed by a muffled noise, signals his arrival at the bottom of the stairway and Fionn's hand clapped over his mouth. Fergus' feet reach the last step, and he joins Fionn and his brothers on a more or less circular landing. The walls are made of rock. Fionn warns them again to be quiet. He holds his torch up high and they see dark-brown bats hanging upside down from the ceiling. They all turn around on the spot, in circles, for the space is small. Fionn finds what he is looking for and points to a wedge of rock that can be pushed aside. With joint effort they move it to the right and slip through the resulting gap. Behind the slab of stone is a narrow corridor. Fergus must walk sideways; the cold wet rock brushes his cheeks. The path twists and turns constantly. Sometimes it is so narrow that Fergus must suppress a feeling of anguish verging on panic rising from his groin. *If Fionn can get through, so can I*, he encourages himself in a mantra, stepping over a boulder on the floor and contorting his body backwards around an overhang. After fifty feet they exit the corridor into a cove. Fergus feels relief as fresh, cold air hits him and he hears waves lapping onto the shore. Despite the darkness, he makes out the shape of a five-bencher. Erc's warriors and Brother Aedan are waiting.

"You are early; the tide is still coming in," Feradach, one of the warriors speaks softly.

"There were circumstances—" Fionn doesn't finish his sentence, they are all petrified as they hear shouting from the cliffs above them.

Hurriedly, they push the boat away from the shore. When the waves lap around their loins, the boys jump onto the boat; just a little deeper, the men follow. They snatch up their oars and heave to, as powerfully as they can, against the tide. Twenty paces out, they dare to look up to the cliff top. They hear no voices but see men riding, searching along the cliffs.

"Ah, they have not thought of the sea." Fionn sighs, easing.

"Well, with the dark night and the tide coming in, that's no wonder," Gair, a second warrior, short in stature but broad in the shoulders, speaks.

"Careful, the tide is sweeping us back ashore!" Angus squeals.

The men curse under their breath and concentrate on pulling their oars. They regain lost distance, but the sea is rough. They are sweating with effort and their breathing is laboured. The boys take position next to the men and pull on the oars rhythmically with them.

"Head for Rathlin!" Fionn gasps. "If we can make it to the eastern shore, we will be safe there until the tide turns and dawn breaks."

A stretch of water that, under normal circumstances, would take the oarsmen scarcely thirty minutes to cross, takes three times that long. But they make it to the east side of Rathlin and pull their boat ashore. It is an island inhabited with thousands of seabirds. Fionn grabs rugs from a wooden chest on the boat and throws one to each of the boys. They are hunkering on the beach and now the adrenaline is subsiding they are beginning to shiver.

"We can't make a fire," Fionn apologises. "It could be seen from the mainland. In three hours, the tide will turn, and dawn will break. Try to get some sleep."

Chapter five
424 A.D. Tara, Meath, Ireland

It is September, and the hard, physical labour has diminished Erc's anger. He rides to Tara and re-joins his comrades. They are sitting around in the cold, miserable. Erc wants to know what has happened in his absence.

"Where is High King Niall?" he asks. "I suppose I should report back to him."

"No one knows," Gair tells him. "When we returned from Rathcroghan, we departed again almost immediately, for Munster. Niall wanted to banish the invaders from overseas, once and for all. Oran said that he should build watch towers along the coast, he said there will always be outlanders invading our shores. But Niall insisted that with his army complete, he could cast them out forever. So we all marched south and fought and defeated the enemy. Those taken prisoner were brought to Niall, but he didn't want them as slaves, he ordered them to be drowned."

"It was gut wrenching," Mahon says. Despite having the stature and appearance of a fully grown grizzly bear, he has a soft heart and shudders. "Some of them were only lads. He had them led to the sea; they begged and squirmed, called to their mothers and prayed to their God, but Niall remained unmoved. They were thrown into the salt water head first, and then warriors knelt upon their backs and held their heads down until all life exited them."

"Not an honourable fight. They could've been slaves, there's enough work to be done!" Lorcan interrupts.

He is Mahon's twin by birth, but from appearance couldn't be more different. He is tall, six-foot-six, but there the likeness stops. Mahon has black hair, not just on his head, but his chest, his back, shoulders, arms, legs; he is covered in it, like wiry fur. He is broad shouldered and his muscles bulge. He has olive-coloured skin. Lorcan is pale skinned with watery-blue eyes; his hair is blond, almost white. He has a long neck prolonged by shoulders that seemingly don't exist, and long dangling extremities. That appearances can be deceitful applied doubly in their case. Walking Lorcan could easily stumble over his own feet, but he could jump on and off a horse as nimbly as a squirrel racing up a tree; he could ride standing up on a horse's back, wielding a sword and bellowing battle cries like a hurricane raising the roof off a house. Mahon is solid like a five-hundred-year-old oak tree. No man or object can budge him or get past him if he doesn't choose to let them. His voice is, however, high-pitched, like that of a woman, and he is scared of sudden noises. Both men had endured a childhood of ridicule and mockery. In the army, Erc had soon discovered their talents and respected them, and now both are devoted to him.

"And then?" Erc asks. "You are here, most of the army too, I think. I haven't seen Oran though."

"Ah," Feradach continues. "Well, you see, some savages still escaped in their boats. As they sailed eastwards, Niall decided to follow them."

"Alone? Surely not!"

"No, but only a hundred men had room on the boats. We were ordered to return to Tara and settle any troubles arising here. A hundred men pursued the barbarians to Gwynedd and slaughtered them there. Niall decided to proceed north to Caledonia with just thirty men; he sent the rest home."

"What did he want in Caledonia? Where is he now?"

"The men who returned said that Niall had been dazzled by the riches in Gwynedd, and someone had told him that the gold came from Caledonia. He wanted to scout the land, hoping to attack and get booty on the way. He sent some of his men with boats up the coast northwards, and the plan was to meet them at the end of the Cantyre peninsula and then return home."

"But where is he then?"

"That's it, nobody knows! His men sailed around the coast of Cantyre for a whole month, waiting. When nobody turned up and the locals started battling against them, they returned home."

"So they're here now, I see. And who's in charge? Ryley? Or maybe Hogan?"

Erc's companions pull faces and look at each other.

"Who's going to tell him, lads?" Gair asks.

Erc furrows his brow concentrating, whilst his men look at him expectantly. Then he realizes.

"Laeghaire?" His men nod. "No wonder you were all looking so miserable when I came. But how? Surely no one would elect that dobber?"

"Who said he was elected?" Gair enlightens him.

"What? He just decided himself. But why didn't anyone protest?"

"With Oran absent, no one really had the courage. Anyway, at first everyone thought Niall and Oran would return within a matter of days."

"How long have they been missing now?"

"About six weeks."

"That's a long time, especially if the men had already waited four weeks in Cantyre. But bugger! That means I have to report to Laeghaire now. I'd better go and get it behind me. Here—" Erc says, digging into his saddle bag and throwing a leather pouch of firewater into their midst. "Leave some for me, I'll need it when I get back."

***

Erc enters the royal palace and goes to the great hall. He finds Laeghaire speaking to his bailiff.

"What do you mean 'they refuse to pay the borama'? They can't *refuse*, it's my *right*, they *have* to pay!" Laeghaire stamps his foot like an impudent child.

"The Munstermen do not recognise you as high king, Sire. They say they will pay the cattle tribute only to Niall or a successor lawfully elected by the Roydammna," the bailiff answers.

At that moment they notice Erc. The bailiff looks relieved to see him. Erc approaches Laeghaire and takes a deep subordinate bow. Laeghaire smiles, mellowed in his wrath.

"Ah Erc, returned, I see. Well, you're just the man I need, did you hear? These two-timing villainous bastards from Munster refuse to pay my borama! How am I supposed to feed my army? Tell me that! What shall I do?"

"I've been away many months Sire, who is king in Munster? Is it still Crimthann?"

"Aye."

"Do we know how large his army is?" Erc asks.

"He can easily get a couple of thousand together," the bailiff answers. "Nathi, Fiacre's son, wants revenge for his father and will join forces with him."

"Hmmn, well we could wait for High King Niall's return, but we all know what he'd do, he'd go out and confront Crimthann with his army," Erc says.

"*I'm* high king now and *I* make the decisions." Laeghaire spits his words out. "Erc, I appoint you commander to replace your father, prepare the army, we shall leave as soon as possible."

Erc hesitates a little. "It'd be better we speak with the other commanders first; we need a strategy. Sloan," he addresses the bailiff "can you try to round up more soldiers from the North? We'll need all the men we can get."

"Aye, I'll do that, give me three days."

"We'll need that long to prepare," Erc agrees.

***

Three commanders and Laeghaire lead the army, two thousand three hundred men, through the forests, westwards to Connacht. Brión is sick of the Munstermen who lead petty wars and skirmishes against him. They are like a persisting boil in his backside. Only too willingly has he agreed to meet Laeghaire with eight hundred of his own men. *They won't get off lightly*, he hopes.

Laeghaire rides a young black stallion, not yet fully trained and much too nervous to face an army. He, himself is dressed in finery, as if he were meeting a delegation of royal kings from overseas. Particularly, his brogs, with a gold buckle, studded with jewels and with a three-inch heel to make his measly frame appear taller, give rise to contemptuous, scornful sneers behind his back.

Meanwhile, Crimthann and Nathi's scouts have kept them well informed. They rally their forces together and march once again towards the glens of Damchluain.

Laeghaire's scouts also keep him well informed.

"What crackbrained dobbers!" Laeghaire grins from ear to ear; revealing wet, red gums and yellow teeth, as he hears where Crimthann is advancing to with his forces. "Didn't they get enough last time!"

"Crimthann did not fight alongside Fiacre," Erc replies, "but he most certainly knows of their defeat. It could be a trap. What do you think Brión?"

"I'm not sure. What sort of trickery could that be? Either he's there or he isn't, and our scouts say his army is on the way."

"That's settled then," Laeghaire replies, "they will arrive in a couple of hours; we'll attack them as last time, as soon as night falls."

"But Sire." Erc looks at his fellow commanders, hoping for support. "Our attack will not be a surprise this time. They will have some sort of plan."

"Erc is right," Ryley ventures. "We should think this through carefully, and try a different strategy this time."

"Rubbish, they're white-livered bodachs, the lot of them, we'll attack tonight!"

"But Sire—" Ryley dares to protest.

"*Tonight*, as soon as night falls!" Laeghaire determines.

When night falls, Laeghaire's army marches silently forwards towards the glen of Damchluain. As in the previous battle, the army breaks up, half going right and half going left. They make a generous sweep behind the forest hills and as dawn breaks, they are in position ready to advance upon Crimthann's army. Erc rides next to Laeghaire and Brión, their warriors are positioned behind them.

As the sun rises behind the dark hills, Laeghaire gives the signal to attack. The army surges forwards, but this time the Munstermen are awaiting them. With a hullabaloo of ear-battering war cries and thousands of arrows darkening the sky, the enemy appears, shooting forth like a volcanic eruption.

Laeghaire's stallion rears in fright and is struck in the chest by an arrow. It collapses and Laeghaire falls to the ground. Erc does a spot turn on his horse, bends low, and stretching his hand towards Laeghaire, hoists him up behind himself onto his own horse. More and more enemies appear, darting forth like lizards from between their rocky crevices, until they are surrounded by the enemy on three sides.

"Retreat!" Laeghaire screams. "Retreat!"

Erc spurs his horse, and they race back the way they came, weaving through trees, ducking low branches until they reach the safety of Rathcroghan. As they clatter into the courtyard, by some miracle unharmed, Laeghaire jumps down from behind Erc.

"You saved my life," Laeghaire says. "I owe you a favour."

"I will remind you," Erc replies solemnly.

He hopes their losses will not be too disastrous and worries for his comrades.

"I need a drink," Laeghaire states, striding towards the castle. "Come with me, let's celebrate!"

Celebrate! We've probably just lost half our army! Good men, their widows will grieve, and their children grow up without their fathers!

"I must see to the horse first," Erc answers Laeghaire lamely, feeling a coward for not speaking his mind.

As Laeghaire disappears inside Rathcroghan, more soldiers begin to enter the courtyard. No one has a proper overview of the situation. Erc takes his horse to the water trough and then leads it to the stables and rubs it down.

"Ah, here you're hiding!" Gair appears with his own horse. He is splattered with blood but says it is not his own. He shakes his head.

"A bloodbath," he curses. "A bloody carnage!"

Feradach, Mahon, and Lorcan enter the stables, leading their horses behind them.

"You're safe!" Erc rejoices. "What do you know?"

"Brión is dead," Feradach tells him. "Nathi is hastening to Tara to release his father."

"And how many of our men have fallen?" Erc asks.

"More than a thousand. Crimthann had his entire army in the forest on the right-hand side of the valley. Our army, halved, was completely outnumbered. Those of our army, who went left, found the forest deserted. They arrived on the battle scene too late to be of any help," Feradach answers, his voice trailing off in despair.

The men look at each other glumly. No one speaks; they are battling with treasonous thoughts.

"Laeghaire is a fool." When Erc finally breaks the silence, they just nod silently. "At the moment he's drinking in the castle; I'd better go and tell him the news; we must return to Tara."

He finds Laeghaire in a chamber behind the hall. He is lounging in a chair, a flacon of wine in one hand. Seeing Erc, he stretches the flacon towards him. Erc ignores the gesture and reports to Laeghaire in terse sentences. Laeghaire yawns.

"Back to Tara tomorrow then," he says. "Tell the men!"

***

Erc and his men return to Tara and upon their arrival are astonished to see Oran.

"You live, we thought you were dead!" Erc speaks for all.

"I thought myself dead seven times but each time I found myself still breathing."

"And High King Niall?"

"He is dead. Shot by an arrow in his back, between his shoulder blades, from the opposite side of a valley in Caledonia. We were thirty men left. We struggled to bring his corpse back to Ireland. We fought seven battles on the way and at the end we were seven men."

"We have suffered great losses here too. Crimthann and Nathi rallied forces at Damchluain and lured us into an ambush."

"Who was in charge?" Oran asks.

"Laeghaire."

"Ah—and now?"

"Isn't Nathi here yet? He was on his way," Erc answers.

"No, but he won't be long then. In that case, we'd better release Fiacre," Oran says. "Let him clean up and give him some decent food."

"We'll do that." Erc nods to Gair who hastens towards the castle dungeons.

Gair unlocks the prison door and releases Fiacre from his chains.

“Ah, this means my son has defeated Brión.” Fiacre is jubilant. “Niall shall pay for his disloyalty towards me.” He stands up and rubs his ankles, red and sore from the fetters.

“Niall was killed in Caledonia; his body is being brought here now. Your son will arrive soon. Follow me. I’ll bring you to the palace. A maid will bring you warm water and clean clothes. The cook is preparing food.”

“Good. Tell the maid to bring me wine.”

A short time later, Nathi arrives with his army. Niall’s men make way for him. Nathi enters the palace and seeks out his father. He is washed and changed into clean garments. He is relaxing in a chair, a flask of wine in his hand. Nathi musters his pale features and haggard body.

“Father, are you well?”

“Aged ten years in a matter of months, but aye, thanks to you, my son, recovering speedily.” Fiacre takes another gulp of wine then offers the flagon to Nathi. “And you? How do you fare? Injuries? How do things stand?”

“Uninjured and scarcely any losses to the army. Niall was in Caledonia and his fool son took charge. Such an idiot! I pity his commanders; they lost a thousand soldiers!”

“I heard Niall has fallen.”

“Yes, his body is being brought back to Tara now. He will get a royal burial; he has ruled for many years. Afterwards the Roydammna will select his successor.”

“You.”

“There is no one else. I sent Crimthann back to Munster. He is happy there, as long as our tributes aren’t extortionate. I would like you to go to Rathcroghan, as King of Connacht.”

“It is my rightful position.”

“Yes.”

***

The Roydammna, the male descendants of royal blood, gather together and unanimously elect Nathi as their lawful high king.

Two days before Samhain, the pagan New Year, Nathi's court prepares to visit a sacred idol known to them as Cenn Cruaich. The pagans have worshipped the gold figure surrounded by twelve stone pillars since the time of Érimón. It stands on Magh Slécht in County Cavan and is propitiated with the sacrifice of a firstborn male child in exchange for a good harvest.

Erc doesn't believe in idol worship. He has no interest in witnessing either the futile death of an infant, nor the ensuing grief of its mother. The participation isn't obligatory. Erc saddles his horse and taking his leave, travels home to Dunseverick for the winter.

Chapter six
455 A.D. Arrival in Finlaggan, Islay, Caledonia

Fergus awakes to the sound of footsteps crunching on the pebble shore. He concentrates; they are adult footsteps, and they are stealthy, trying to be quiet. Immediately alert, he opens his eyes wide open, but stays lying down, not daring to budge an inch. It is still dark, and he recognises only shadows.

"Damnú air, bugger, and blast!" Recognising Lorcan's voice, Fergus smiles and sits up. He can just perceive Lorcan's silhouette hopping around in circles on one foot, whilst holding his other foot in his hands. "Who the devil put this rock right before my big toe?" he demands.

"Who d'you think, leprechauns? You gowl!" Fionn shouts at him. "The whole island is awake now with you hollering about, never mind the boys, who I told you to let sleep a while!"

"It hurts, my toe is bleeding! I swear that rock wasn't there before," Lorcan complains.

Fergus grins at his brothers who are now awake and sitting up, beaming from ear to ear. They all love Lorcan. The best and most accomplished horseman they know, on his own two feet a catastrophe. If there were one single cowpat in eight square miles of sweet-smelling meadows, Lorcan would be sure to stumble in it.

"Well, now Lorcan's managed to wake you all up, we might as well get going," Fionn says.

The boys throw their rugs into the boat and jump in after them. A strip of pale grey on the horizon announces the coming dawn. The men position themselves on each side of the boat, and pressing their weight forwards, push it off the shingle beach into the dark grey water. When the boat floats they heave themselves on board and taking up the oars, row powerfully out of the bay. Once they reach the open sea, they hoist the sails and picking up speed, race towards Islay.

There is a brisk wind, and the waves roll up and down six feet high. The boat dips and rises with the swell of the stormy sea. Loarn turns white and beads of sweat appear on his forehead.

"I feel funny—" he says, breaking into a cold sweat. He leans overboard, heaves, and throws up. He wipes his mouth and sits up again. "Ugh, I feel terrible—"

Fergus puts his arm around Loarn's shoulders and looks at Brother Aedan.

"Cartan hasn't poisoned him, has he?"

"No, no, don't worry, it's just seasickness," Aedan replies. "Loarn, look towards the horizon and let your body move with waves, it will help." The boat climbs up the next wave and dips down again.

"Ugh." Loarn leans over the side of the boat like a shot rabbit. His complexion turns green. Just the occasional twitch as his body heaves weakly to throw up more gall fluid, reveals that he still lives. "I think I'm dying," Loarn groans.

"You'll be all right once we get there." Fionn smiles.

"How long do we need?"

"A while yet."

"I'm never going to sail again!"

The men laugh. "All sailors struck with seasickness say that," Fionn tells him, "but it's difficult to avoid the sea here!"

"It's not funny, I mean it!"

Loarn is so adamant that the men chuckle again. "It won't be so bad next time." Lorcan tries to console him.

After several hours, the boat enters Loch Indaal and the surrounding hills provide shelter from the wind. The churning sea calms, and the men lower the sails to row into Bridgend harbour. Feradach jumps from board onto the dock and Fionn throws him a spring line. Feradach secures the line to a dock cleat and then knots a second rope from the stern cleat to the dock.

Fergus rubs Loarn's back, then putting his arm around his brother's shoulders, helps him from board onto solid ground. Loarn's legs shake but he stands.

"You'll be as right as an apple tart in a few minutes." Fionn comforts him.

Loarn gives him a weak smile. Gair and Mahon stay on board with Brother Aedan to keep watch, as the others leap from board onto the dock.

The men look around the harbour. They want to hire small boats to take them up the River Sorn to Finlaggan, where Fionn's and Mista's cousin, Mhairi, lives with her man, Donald, Laird of Islay. The small port is busy. Whilst fishermen empty their nets into large iron vessels, women are gutting and packing herring into wooden barrels, salting, and curing them to preserve the catch. The stench, an assault on the most seasoned of noses, and the bloody fish guts slipping about on the stone paving, knock Loarn's stricken stomach upside down. Afraid of throwing up in front of everybody, he turns away abruptly and walks towards a blacksmith hammering a metal sword. Behind him is his work shed and stables.

"Couldn't we ride to Finlaggan instead of taking a boat?" Loarn asks Fionn.

"We could," Lorcan supports him. "There's a paved road to Ballygrant. We could leave the horses in a stable there and walk the last two miles. Your cousin will have a boat to pick us up."

"Huh?" The three young brothers look puzzled.

"Fionn," Fergus asks. "Where are we going?"

"Ah, didn't I tell you? My cousin lives on an island in the middle of a loch, we thought it would be easier to protect you there."

"But you said we were going to Finlaggan!" Loarn's heart sinks as he thinks of water.

"Finlaggan is the name of the loch *and* of the place where we are going. It's on an island called Eilean Mór, my cousin lives there. The castle has been the dwelling of the Laird of the Isles since ancient times. The only way to reach the castle on the island is by boat."

"Oh."

"It might be useful to have our own horses nearby though. We could split up. If Lorcan rides with Fergus and Loarn, the rest of us could take a boat and pick them up on the east bank of Loch Finlaggan," Fionn suggests.

The men are standing around listening and nod. "Aye, let's do that," Feradach speaks. "Come on Angus, let us go and inspect the coracles whilst the others are choosing their horses."

Feradach and Angus walk along the harbour side as Lorcan moves towards the stables with Fergus and Loarn. They go past the fishing boats and come to an area where flat bottomed skiff-type boats are bobbing up and down on the waves. They're tied with ropes to iron rings set into the harbour wall.

Angus points to the coracles. They look like upturned baskets, woven with willow and covered in animal hides. The whiff of pine tar hits Angus' nose and he breathes in deeply savouring the smell. Some men are painting a coracle. Feradach speaks to one of the men working. He speaks Brittonic, the native language, and the fisherman answers in a lilting voice. There follows a little haggling and then they slap hands on the deal.

"The two coracles down there on the left," Feradach tells Angus.

In the meantime, Brother Aedan has spoken with the harbour master to arrange to leave their longboat protected in the port, and now Gair, Mahon and Fionn join them also.

Angus jumps down from the harbour wall into one of the coracles, and with an acrobatic balancing act, nearly capsizing the boat, sits down at the end with the paddle rudder.

"I can, can't I?" he pleads. He smiles and looks from one to the other with the charm and innocence of a twelve-year-old. Not one of the hardened warriors can deny him the request.

So they take place at the oars and let themselves be manoeuvred out of the harbour, and upriver along the Sorn.

"Bit of a grand name, *River* Sorn," Feradach mumbles. "It's not more than a burn."

"Main thing, it carries enough water to get us there," Fionn answers, pulling on his oars.

"Look at tem mountains!" Gair calls from the boat behind them and points to the north-east. "They look like a fine pair of brollach mór! Just up your street Feradach!" Gair cackles like an old woman and Mahon joins in.

Angus looks at the steep-sided hills with distinctive conical shapes. As realisation dawns, he blushes fiercely. This sets the men off laughing again. Tears run down Gair's cheeks, and he slaps his thigh. A sudden jolt stops him abruptly. With no one paying attention, the boat has hit a rock sticking out of the water, and Gair tumbles into the river with a gigantic splash, soaking everyone. The men laugh until the tears run. Gair dives under the boat and pushes it over, tipping them all in. Brother Aedan cannot swim but the water is only two feet deep. He sits on the river bed; his head sticking out above the surface and laughs like horse whinnying. The men fool around like a bunch of adolescents. Gair upturns Fionn's boat and makes sure everyone gets a good drenching. Finally, they pull themselves up onto the river bank and let the sun dry them. The laughter releases the tension pent-up in Fionn's body, and he takes deep breaths. He hadn't realised that the responsibility for the boys had affected him so much, but now they are safe, and he feels calmer.

They go back to the coracles and continue rowing upriver towards Loch Finlaggan. The sun is beginning to descend behind the mountains. The sky is pale turquoise streaked with blinding gold and grey; and there it is, clearly visible for all, on a low rising on an island in the Loch: Finlaggan, a castle with four towers built from dark-grey stone. It looks foreboding, a dark, gloomy silhouette against a sky turning rapidly black. Thunder clouds begin to gather in the distance. Angus gazes at his future home and wonders what his destiny holds for him.

***

Lorcan strolls towards the blacksmith, Fergus and Loarn follow him. He stumbles on a cobble but regains his balance and continues walking without batting an eyelid. He cannot speak Brittonic, nor the blacksmith Gaelic. Lorcan points to the stables and gestures to the boys. The blacksmith gets the gist and laying his tools down, wipes his black sooty hands on his greasy leather apron.

He strides towards the stables and beckons for Lorcan and the boys to follow him. He opens the stable doors and walks slowly down the gap between the boxes. A variety of horses push their heads over their box's lower door, curious about the visitors and in particular whether they have anything edible with them. Lorcan pulls an apple out of his pocket and gives it to a grey rouncey, about twelve hands high. He strokes the horse's muzzle and signals with his hands to ask if he can enter the box. The blacksmith nods and watches whilst Lorcan checks the horse over.

"What do you think, Loarn?" he asks. "This one suit you?"

Loarn approaches the horse and strokes it.

"Yes, she looks fine."

They choose two more horses for Fergus and Lorcan. They swoon over a stallion with a bay coat so shiny, that they have to blink. It stands at a proud fourteen point two hands and has a jet-black mane and tail.

"Ah," Fergus sighs. "Just look at his arched neck!"

"And such a refined head," Lorcan adds. "A destrier?" he asks in direction of the blacksmith.

"Aye, but no!" he says wagging his finger. "Laird."

"Ah, it's not for hire, it belongs to the Laird."

Lorcan understands. "It's just as well, I could never afford it." He looks gloomy.

"Three horses? Where to?" The blacksmith asks suspiciously.

"Laird Donald, Finlaggan," Lorcan answers.

"Good." The blacksmith is satisfied, and they haggle over an amount of silver.

Fergus and Loarn have ridden since they were three. They jump onto their mounts bareback and hold the reins loosely in their hands. Lorcan throws his leg over his own rouncey, and the blacksmith bids them farewell. Choosing the right mounts has taken a lot of time and now they need to get a move on. They press their knees gently together on their horses' bellies, to signal them to move forward. After the first few yards they squeeze their knees again, urging them into a gentle trot along the paved road. They have gone a mile when Fergus spurs his horse on, until he is adjacent to Lorcan.

"Is the road paved all the way to Finlaggan?" Fergus asks.

"No," Lorcan replies. "It goes to the north of the Islay, passing two miles east of Finlaggan. But we can leave the horses in Ballygrant and walk the last mile or two to the shores of the loch."

"That's grand," Fergus replies. "Just think of all those heavily loaded waggons and carts! The wheels can turn as easily as those in watermills, no more getting stuck in the mud! Why don't we have roads in Ireland?"

"Who would make them?" Lorcan asks. "The road passes through everyone's property."

"But it's the same here, surely?" Fergus protests.

Lorcan thinks about this. "Aye you're right," he finally says. "Maybe the folks here don't squabble as much as the Gaels. I can't imagine some of the folks back home giving up their land without a fight."

"It would be better for everyone though, at the end of the day, all the farmers and everyone else too would profit from paved roads."

They turn round a corner and at that moment see a farmer leading a horse, pulling a cart laden with wooden logs.

"You see!" Fergus says as they greet the farmer. They continue their way to Ballygrant.

More and more folk pass them along the road. Everyone greets them friendlily with a couple of words, or they tip their hand to their head. One man on a horse stops and speaks to them in Gaelic.

"Are you on your way north?" he asks.

"Neh, just to Ballygrant. We'll leave the horses there, then we're going to Finlaggan. What about your good self? I can tell from your dialect that you are from Dalriada. Are you a trader?"

"Neh, neh. I'm settled here now, with my mistress and three bairns. We have a farm three miles down the road. Good, fertile land; there are quite a few of our fellow county men here now. More and more come every year, that's what I thought you were planning."

"What, the Britons let you stay here on their land without a fight?"

"Some of us are married into the families here, but yes, there is enough fertile land available that no one cultivates."

"But we Dalriadians, we're always protecting our borders! The Dalfiatach and the Ui Neill are constantly fighting us to steal our property, not to mention those thieving Cenel Eogain!"

"I came here at first as a trader, and I came in peace, as the others also. You will have seen the brochs along the coastline, they are always manned. If a fleet of long ships, heading for our coastlines, is spotted, the guards send a signal. By the time the ships land ashore, our soldiers are waiting for them. So Islay protects its shores from hordes of outlanders wanting to steal, destroy and murder; but the people are tolerant to families ready to work hard and make an honest living."

"What are brochs?" Fergus asks. "I don't think I've seen any."

"Ah, then you have come straight from Bridgend. I thought I recognised some of the blacksmith's horses. Brochs are watchtowers. They are made of stone and situated along the coastline at good vantage points. You can't miss them, they're quite high, over twenty feet. Our soldiers have a good view from the top of the towers to the seas below, far into the distance."

"What type of signal do they make, a fire?"

"Neh my lad, they blow on a hunting horn," he says.

Fergus would like to ask more questions, but Lorcan says they must get on. They bid the man farewell.

Passing through Ballygrant, they immediately see the tavern where the blacksmith said they could leave the horses. It's on the right-hand side of the road and all travellers must pass it. They enter and Lorcan orders ale. He drowns a mug of warm beer greedily, wipes his sleeve across his mouth and sighs with self-indulgence

"Ah, that was good, I must've swallowed a whole bucket of dust on that road!"

The boys drink a little more slowly and screw their noses up at the bitter taste of the local beer, but they are too thirsty to let a single drop waste. Lorcan speaks with the landlord, and they reach an agreement to leave the horses in his stables.

"Right lads, are you finished? Time we were off!" Lorcan says.

They set off along a narrow bush trail in single file. They push away branches of overgrown brambles looming over the path with their long, sharp thorns, and try to avoid the barbs from tearing at their skin. It is dusty and hot; their skin is sticky with sweat. The nearer they get to Loch Finlaggan, the more midges, thunderbugs and mosquitos swarm around them. Fergus wipes across his face irritably with a dirty hand.

Lorcan slaps his own arm and yelps in triumph.

"Got the bastard!" he says, flicking a horsefly away with a snip of his fingers. "Looks like we're in for a thunderstorm, but we'll be at the castle shortly."

And then suddenly they are there, at the edge of the loch. A wooden plank is nailed to a post in the water, a small boat is tethered to a second pole. They get in the boat and start paddling towards the island as the first fat blobs of rain fall. Fergus and Loarn look towards the sombre building materialising before them.

"What awaits us?" they ask each other.

Chapter seven
433 A.D. Tara, Meath, Ireland

Erc sits on a bale of straw in the barn and gnaws at some dried stock fish and a chunk of bread. A mug of ale rests next to him. The barn door is open, and he watches round balls of ice, the size of rabbit droppings, pelt down from the sky, crash onto the cobbles in the courtyard and bounce up again. Spring is late this year. For that reason, fighting has been delayed and now two thousand soldiers are hanging around the palace grounds more bored than is good for them.

The leather bridles, saddles and girths have been cleansed with saddle soap and polished until they shine like dogs' noses. The swords and knives have been whetted razor-sharp. Arrows have been whittled and bows newly strung. He is running out of jobs to keep his men occupied. Already they are drinking too much, betting away their pay with game dice, and fighting. *If it carries on like this, it will look as if we've been to war before we even set out.*

The ladies at Tara look down at the men from their wooden balconies and gaze at the sky, longing for more temperate weather. As long as the outbuildings and palace surroundings are full of men, for the most part riffraff, they dare not wander down into the palace grounds or ride their horses out. They walk around the balustrades alone or in pairs and inspect the goings on below.

Erc waits to see if Mista appears. He can't stop thinking about her; he lies awake at night longing to touch her, to feel her skin, or to gaze into her eyes. He sighs, *why is everything so complicated?* At first, he had thought his marriage to Marca was a disaster; but now she was dead, he could only remember the good parts. She had given him eight sons, all healthy and strong. For the youngest, already five-years-old, she had given her life. Now he had got to know Mista though, he had discovered what it felt like to be in love. Every waking moment, knowing her nearby, his heart flutters like a fledgling learning to fly. But she is a princess, and he, but a warrior.

Cartan, the reason for his marriage to Marca, already sixteen years old, strides into the barn, banging against the door and interrupts his thoughts.

"Have you heard the rumours?" he asks as a greeting.

"Which ones would those be?" With nothing else to do, the soldiers tended to grossly exaggerate or even invent, all manner of tales.

"The druid's prophecy, it's come true!"

Erc raises his eyebrows and waits, indicating that he doesn't know which prophecy in particular Cartan is talking about. Cartan rolls his eyes in impatient frustration.

"'Eggheaded strangers with hooded robes and crook headed staffs will land on our coastline and beguile our people with a foreign doctrine'."

"And which part is true? I'm not bewitched, nor do I see any eggheads wandering around."

Cartan tuts with impatience. *His father was aggravating him purposely.*

"No, of course not, not here. But they have arrived in our territory, in Dalriada. A former fudir, they say, with thirty men, their scalps shaved on top, in hooded robes and with shepherds' crooks."

"Are the crooks their only weapons?" Erc asks.

"I've heard no different."

"Scary."

Cartan sits down on a bale of straw, opposite his father. "Actually, I came for a different reason."

Erc waits. He suspects that Cartan will bring up the subject again; he was an uncompromising adolescent, obstinate like an ingrown toenail. He would never take no for an answer, but asked again and again, hoping Erc would finally relent. Well, he wasn't going to make things easy for him.

Cartan breaks the silence. "Can you speak to Laeghaire about me?"

"We've chewed this out before, and you know my answer."

"Yes, but sons of other nobles have already been made leaders, two are captains already."

"This is only your second year, you need more experience, your leader will speak when he thinks you're ready."

"You were leader in your second year."

"Different times."

"But—"

Erc sighs. "To be a leader you need to earn the respect of your men. If you receive favours instead of being a leader by merit, then your men will not trust you wholly, nor follow you blindly."

"They will obey me; I shall make sure of that."

"And Mongan? Tigernach? Becc? If you get favours, your brothers will want the same."

"I'm the eldest. The privilege befits me."

"I will speak for you if you insist, but I recommend strongly that you wait, for your sake, not mine."

"Speak for me and put Mongan in my troop, I shall take care of him."

"Your brother, Mongan, is with the cavalry, you are a swordsman."

"He fights well with the sword."

"He is a gifted horseman. I shall speak for you if you insist, but leave your younger brother out of this."

Cartan leaves, the hail ceases to drum down on the cobbles. The sun appears from behind a cloud, low in the sky; a blinding bright light, reflecting on the wet stones, obscures his sight. Erc squints and stands up.

High King Nathi had died three years ago in battle and Laeghaire had succeeded him. He must find Laeghaire now and speak out, or he would surely lose his mind.

***

"You owe me a favour."

"I don't deny it. What shall it be? Land? Cattle? A position for one of your sons? I need a bailiff."

"Mista."

"Mista? What? Do I have some valuable horse that I have forgotten about?"

"Your daughter."

"My daughter?"

"Blonde hair, nearly white, blue eyes, a fair complexion."

"Ah, Mista—yes; with by near forty offspring, I tend to forget a few. Her mother was a Pictish slave, a princess by all accounts, very young and very beautiful, a shame she died. Very well then, but no dowry, I have too many daughters."

"A dowry is not necessary. I can speak to her then?"

"Yes, but no betrothal before Samhain. I need you here for the fighting season."

With a bounce in his step Erc goes to look for Gair, Cartan's commander. Gair looks up when he sees Erc coming.

"He doesn't listen then?" he asks.

"No, I didn't think he would. Pig-headed gowk!"

"Ah, the joys of fatherhood. Very well then, I'll make Ryan captain and give Cartan leadership."

"Keep an eye on him for me? Follies of youth you know; I don't want the blood of his men on my hands."

"I'll watch out, don't worry."

The unpleasant duty fulfilled, Erc turns away and heads for the royal palace. *And now for my reward!* he thinks happily.

***

He finds Mista in the scullery kneading dough. Clouds of flour billow up in the dim light as she thumps the dough back and forth with angry fists. She doesn't notice Erc when he enters, so he stands opposite her silently, waiting for her temper to soften. She looks up, suddenly aware of a presence, and sees him gazing at her. He's tall, has long, thick, straight black hair that hangs down his back; he wears a linen ionar and leather truis that reveal his sensuous muscular body. Her heart begins to race.

"You've spoken to him?" she asks hopefully.

His arms crossed, his face grim, he nods silently.

Mista's countenance falls. "I knew it!" she cries, smashing her fist into the bread dough. "That mean bastard, he begrudges me *any* happiness!"

"He said yes."

"What? Oh—I'll kill you!" she throws the lump of bread dough energetically straight at his face. It hits him square on, before plummeting to the floor. She laughs at his astonished expression, his black eyes staring out of a mask of brown flour. She runs around the table and leaps onto him. She wraps her legs around his hips, and with one hand on his shoulder, pounds his chest with her other fist.

"Pulling a face like that!"

"Like what?" Erc asks innocently. "Do you mean like this?" He pushes a strand of hair out of her face and tilts her chin upwards. He kisses her tenderly on her lips and she responds eagerly. He steps to the table and puts her down, propelling more flurries of flour all over them.

"But not until Samhain," he tells her, kissing her again.

***

Later, Erc returns to Gair, Feradach and the twins, his loyal companions, and fellow warriors. They sit around the camp fire, drinking beer and discussing the latest rumours.

"Is it true then? Has the fudir returned?" Erc asks.

"By all accounts, aye it's true," Feradach answers. "A man, called Patricius, who was a slave to Miliucc, near three decades ago."

"He went straight to Miliucc, yer king in Dalriada—" Gair adds.

"So it's true!" Erc interrupts. "He's gone to *my* tribe! Do I need to worry? Should I return to Dunseverick?"

"Neh, the scouts say he's come in peace. Miliucc didn't believe it though; he thought he was coming to take revenge. He barricaded himself in his own house and set fire to it. It burned down to cinders, himself as well."

"Goodness me, that's a bit extreme! What on earth did he do to this Patricius, that he was so afraid?" Erc asks.

"No idea. But everyone knows how badly he treated his slaves. He was a cruel bugger and mean too!"

"Cartan said Patricius had thirty men with him, wearing hooded robes. Where are they now and what are they up to?"

"Last I heard, they were heading south in our direction, but they mean no harm. They're teaching people about their God. Can you imagine? They only have one. They say He's more powerful than all our gods together."

"Hmmn, there's always something new to learn. But no matter, if Miliucc is dead, I must return to Dunseverick. I'm a member of the Roydammna and we need to elect a new king!"

***

As Erc rides north to Dunseverick, Patricius and his men travel south towards the Royal Palace at Tara. There are no roads in Ireland, a warren of trails criss-cross through the forests and glens. Erc doesn't pass their convoy, but a multitude of scouts are watching Patricius' every step and keeping Laeghaire informed. Laeghaire has no idea who Patricius and his men are, or what they want. But as long as they remain peaceful, he allows them to continue their journey.

Patricius has returned to Ireland with a mission. Pope Celestine has bidden him to convert the heathens to Christianity. Patricius speaks Gaelic and knows the Gaelic customs. He is aware that the druids will be bitterly against him, or indeed against anyone who might diminish their own power. He wants to persuade High King Laeghaire to convert or at least to accept Christianity. With his protection, Patricius can act without fear of assault.

***

Erc arrives in Dunseverick. He hugs his younger children and confers with their guardians and teachers. He speaks to his stewards and other household members. The next day, he rides towards Antrim to meet the other members of the Roydammna. Miliucc is dead and although he has sons, it is the turn of a different family to be honoured with the post of king of the Dalriada. The choice falls quickly and unanimously on a man called Daire. A brave warrior who has served his tribe loyally and is known for his prudency. Duty done, Erc returns to Tara.

***

His comrades are full of tales about Patricius.

"You'll never guess," Gair tells him. "He dared to light a fire on Slane *before* Laeghaire lit the one on Tara. And then he performed all sorts of wonders! Laeghaire has given him land on the hill of Slane and he and his men are building a church and a school there."

"A church?"

"Yes, a building where people can pray to Patricius' God. And a school where people can learn to read and write."

"What is that?"

"He and his men read strange signs written on vellum, and they say anyone can learn, so we know they're not just making things up."

"Well, if anyone can learn, then I'd certainly like to do that."

"Me too!"

***

When Erc meets Mista, she is bubbling over with excitement. She tells him everything she has heard about Patricius, with embellishments and details that make the hairs on the back of his neck rise.

"Come here," he says, trying to grab a kiss between her eager babble. She gives him a hasty kiss before continuing, "Patricius and his men believe in just one God. They speak about Him every evening and read gospels out of a book to anybody who comes and listens. More and more people come every day," she says. "I go too. It's fascinating and—Erc, will you come with me and listen to what they have to say too? I think I believe, and Laeghaire has allowed anyone who wants to, to convert to Christianity. Oh, please come with me Erc, and tell me what you think."

"Gladly Acushla, I'm always open to new ideas, you know that. But Laeghaire has already given us orders to march south. The Munstermen are refusing to pay their borama yet again. The bailiffs returned with their tails between their legs, unable to execute their duty. Now the army must go and battle against them. They don't stand a chance against us, and it saddens me, that now we must burn their homes and cast them and their families out. Those stupid gowls never learn, instead of paying a few cattle they will lose everything!"

"Oh. Must you go soon?"

"Tomorrow, at dawn, and tonight we have much to prepare. But when we return, I'll listen to Patricius, I promise."

The next morning, Erc sets out south with a thousand men intent on quashing the recalcitrant Connachta. Cartan is not with him. Driven by the devil, Cartan has determined to destruct Mongan, a scourge, an ulcer that corrodes his brain. *'A skilled horseman'* his father had said. *Everyone knows that Erc prefers Mongan, his second born, to himself,* he thinks. *But he is the eldest, and if his father ever became king of the Dalriada, like the people said he would, then he, Cartan should be his successor, and not a usurper like Mongan*. He broods over schemes to eliminate his brother. It must look like an accident, Cartan must on no account be held to blame. His narcissistic entity digs for cloven-footed traps. He dares not confide in any person, as yet he holds no one in his power. One scheme is dismissed after the next. At night he turns over restlessly under his blanket, his brain on overdrive. Finally, he remembers something that the druids had told him many years ago. He hits on the perfect murder, now he must just await the right opportunity.

He goes to where the cavalry is located and searches his brother out.

"Hello Mongan," he greets him. "How are you faring? Oh, is that your horse? It's very fine indeed!"

Mongan narrows his eyes and tightens his nostrils. Cartan has made his life miserable up till now. Always getting him into trouble with the druids, by getting up to mischief himself, and putting the blame on Mongan. And unbelievably they always listened to Cartan; he could never fathom out why! And now suddenly he was here, being friendly.

"No, it's not my horse, it belongs to Laeghaire," he answers, hoping that Cartan would thus withhold from hurting the stallion.

"But you ride it, huh? A fine brute! Look I know I haven't been much of a brother to you in the past, but we're both in the army now and either one of us could be killed any day, so I would like to make amends. How about us having supper together sometime, maybe Tigernach would join us?"

Mongan studies Cartan's face for any sign of deceit, but sees just open goodwill.

"Uh, well not tonight, maybe tomorrow, I'll ask Tigernach."

"Fine," Cartan answers. "I'll try to trap some quails and we can roast them over a fire."

Mongan seeks out their younger brother Tigernach. They have always been close, and both were wary of Cartan.

"Hmmn," Tigernach says. "This sudden change of attitude is a bit strange. Are you sure he means well?"

"He seemed to mean it, but I'm not really sure, you know what he's like."

"Well, we'll go together, and both pay attention. Don't eat or drink anything he doesn't consume himself."

The next morning Cartan rises early, and taking a wolfhound with him, spends all day in the forests and glens. He looks for quails, Mongan's favourite food. They are ground birds that like to remain in dense cover. The wolfhound sniffs with his nose to the ground, and Cartan strides after him, beating the bushes with a stick and holding a net ready in his hands. They disturb a quail breeding. It scurries away, but Cartan is quicker and casts his net over it. He wrings its neck quickly and places it in his shoulder bag, then returns to its nest for the eggs. A second bird is caught and killed. At the end of the day Cartan finds a third quail, but doesn't kill it. Instead, he reaches in his pocket for a handful of hemlock seeds, and feeds the bird who gobbles the seeds up greedily.

Satisfied, Cartan returns to camp. The third quail has now digested the seeds. Cartan wrings its neck, and snips a toe off the quail's small sturdy foot. It isn't noticeable. He makes a fire. He plucks the feathers from the birds, cuts them open, salts them and rubs them in pig fat. Then he spears them on an iron rod. They are just beginning to roast when Mongan and Tigernach appear. They have brought beer with them and sit around the fire with Cartan, drinking and making idle chat whilst the quails, roast.

Cartan is particularly nice and compliments his two younger brothers on their progress in the army.

"Father was just telling me the other day, what a skilled horseman you've become," he tells Mongan. "Tigernach, you fight so fiercely, I bet I wouldn't stand a chance against you!" He laughs.

The smell of the quails roasting makes their mouths water. When they are ready Cartan takes them from the rod. "Which one would you like?" he asks his brothers innocently, knowing that the quails look identical.

Mongan and Tigernach shrug politely. "No matter." They smile.

Cartan gives Mongan the quail with the missing toe "I think this one is slightly fatter," he says, smiling, because it is common knowledge among the brothers that Mongan adores quail. "Come Tigernach, which one of these two do you want?" Tigernach takes one and they all chew their fowl happily. The meal finishes and Mongan and Tigernach take their leave.

"It was good to be together," Cartan says. "We must do this more often."

Mongan hardly makes it back to the cavalry's quarters. He feels weak and drags his legs. "I'm really exhausted," he tells Tigernach, "but Cartan was nice, wasn't he?"

"Aye," Tigernach agrees, before continuing on his way to the archers. "He's up to something."

Mongan collapses on his straw mattress. The weakness he had felt in his muscles turns to spasms, and cause him intense pain. He tries to get up and find help, but he can't. He tries to call for help, but manages just a weak gurgle, not even as loud as a snore. His mind is clear as his muscles deteriorate. The pain is excruciating, but he is alone. His eyes are wide open in terror, but he has become blind and sees nothing. As paralysis begins to reach his heart and lungs, he gasps for air, drawing long laboured breaths, leaving his chest raw and burning. He endures hours of agony and torment. He is alone, he is helpless, he dies.

His absence isn't noticed until early the next morning, when his comrades are in the stables mucking out the horses and feeding them.

"Where's Mongan?" Sullivan asks his fellow soldiers.

"That's funny, I haven't seen him," Rowan answers. "He's always so reliable."

"I'll go back to quarters; I don't think I saw him this morning either. Maybe he's sick."

Sullivan goes to the men's accommodation and finds Mongan lying on his side on his pallet, and for a moment thinks he's still asleep. Then he notices that his hands are spasmed together like claws, and his eyes express terror but are unseeing. He shakes Mongan's shoulders gently, and realises he is as cold as the frost on a winter morning.

He races back to the stables and scarcely through the door cries, "He's dead!"

"Are you sure?"

"As sure as my eyes are black! I'd better go and get Lorcan."

Lorcan, commander of the cavalry, hurries to the men's quarters, but can only confirm that Mongan is dead.

"Fetch Tlachtga," he tells Sullivan. "Something's not right; he was as fine as a summer meadow yesterday. Did he say he wasn't feeling well to any of you?"

"No," the other men repeat one after another.

"He didn't eat with us last night though, he said he was going to meet his brother, maybe *he* knows something," Rowan says.

"Brother? Which one?" Lorcan asks, his heart sinking in his gut.

"I don't know, but here they are now, both of them."

Cartan and Tigernach enter the accommodation and rush up to Mongan's body. Tigernach kneels down beside him and weeps. Cartan stands, stony faced, pale.

"What happened?" he asks. "He was fine last night! Has he had a seizure?"

"I don't know," Lorcan replies, studying Cartan's face. "Tlachtga is on her way here now."

They wait until the druidess, a healer, arrives. She comes within minutes, and kneeling beside Mongan, examines his body.

"What did he eat last night?" she asks.

"He was with me and Tigernach," Cartan says. "We roasted quail over the fire and there were some quail eggs and bread; but we all ate the same."

"And to drink?"

"Beer," Tigernach answers. "We brought it with us, and all drank from the same pouch."

"And you both feel fine?"

"Yes," they both reply together.

"Hmmn, it's unusual. It could be his heart, but his hands are clenched like a claw. That would speak for a seizure, but usually it is just on the right *or* the left-hand side. Both sides are affected. Also, he is young and fit and has no history of any illness. The symptoms look like poisoning, but if you all ate the same—" She wrinkles her brow and lets the sentence dribble to an end. "Where is his father? We must bury him."

"Fighting in Connacht. I'll go to fetch him myself," Lorcan says.

***

Erc returns, grim and heartbroken. Mongan is buried and a week passes in mourning. He sends a messenger to Tigernach bidding him to his chamber. Tigernach repeats everything he knows.

"What on earth induced you to eat with Cartan?" Erc asks.

Tigernach goes hot and flushes red. "I know what you think! But we were careful; we took our own drink and ate only what he ate!" The words burst out of him angrily, as if he feels the need to justify his actions.

"And the quail?"

"There were three of course, but all identical! And anyway, Cartan asked us which one we wanted!"

"Which one you wanted?"

"He knew we were suspicious, but he caught the quails especially as a treat for Mongan. You know how he loves them."

"Aye," a tear rolls down Erc's cheek as he thinks of his firstborn. "Strange business though. I've spoken to three different druid healers. They all say the symptoms are typical for poisoning with hemlock. Quails themselves are immune to the poison, but the flesh from just one poisonous quail can paralyse a man, killing him within hours."

"What? I didn't know that! Did Cartan know?"

"I don't know; it could've been just chance."

Tigernach thinks over the sequence of the fatal night's meal. "He wanted to make up for not being a good brother to us," he said. "We were suspicious, but he seemed to mean it genuinely. We enjoyed the evening together as brothers. He can't have known; I even chose one of the birds myself. It could be Cartan dead or myself. Is it certain that a bird was poisoned?"

"We will never know. Cartan said he threw the remaining carcasses on the fire. There are no remains to examine."

"Nothing will bring us Mongan back, Father, but I believe Cartan is innocent."

***

Mongan is buried and although Patricius cannot give him a Christian burial, he prays with Erc and Mista in the church upon Slane. Erc finds comfort in prayers.

"I believe in your God," he tells Patricius. "Will you baptise me?"

Both Mista and Erc convert to Christianity. "Will you wed us?" they ask.

Four days after Samhain, Patricius marries Erc and Mista, in a Christian ceremony, before God. Cartan is present, as are Tigernach and Becc.

As Patricius finishes with the words: "Those whom God has joined together, let no man put asunder" his brothers cheer, Cartan fumes.

How dare my father remarry! he broods. *And even worse, to High King Laeghaire's daughter!* He sees his claim to the throne shrink faster than a puddle on a hot day. *They mustn't have a son* he worries, at the same time wondering how he can hinder it.

Chapter eight
434 – 450 A.D. Dunseverick, Dalriada, Ireland

Cartan leaves the wedding breakfast early. Despite the rain, hurtling down incessantly from a leaden-grey sky, he takes his horse from the stables and rides into the forest. The weather matches his mood, cold and dark. He follows a muddle of paths, crossing and turning their way through the dripping trees, until he reaches a small, round thatched hut. Ducking his large frame under the doorway he steps over the threshold and sees Birga one-tooth sitting in the gloom.

"They're united then," she mumbles barely intelligibly, exposing her gums and namesake tooth.

"Yes," Cartan replies, shaking the rain from his garments and sitting down next to her.

She has aged, yet again, he thinks sadly. He takes her gnarled hands in his and massages the knotted finger joints gently. Birga one-tooth is a surrogate mother to him. His biological mother, Marca, hadn't been unkind, nor had she ignored him. In a constant state of breastfeeding his younger brothers, or satisfying his father's needs, she had simply never had time to consider his requirements. Five druids had lived in their household until his mother had died, and then his father had thrown them all out. Rarely at home himself, his father had failed to realise the importance the druids had had for his children. They had belonged to the family. Teaching, healing, advising, consoling. And so they had lost not just their mother, but five further family members in one blow. Cartan, the eldest, had suffered most. Especially the separation from Birga had pained him. An eleven-year-old, he had started wetting his mattress again at night. The new guardian saw this as a weakness that needed to be beaten out of him. For over a year he endured a daily battering; embarrassed, hurt, and ridiculed. Until he found Birga again. She gave him a remedy. The wetting and the thrashing stopped, but something had changed inside him. His heart was as cold as a frozen lake, and his psyche as detached from the outside world, as a fallen leaf from a tree. Just one thing kept him going. Revenge.

Birga one-tooth pats his knee, and removing one hand from his grasp, gives him a bag of herbs.

"As soon as she shows the first signs of child, add them to her food," she says.

"How will I know?" Cartan asks.

Birga one-tooth thinks. "A woman," she says. "Morag. Brown hair, buxom, works in the kitchen. Give the herbs to her and say they are from me. She will understand. It's best that way, you can be far distant."

"Thank you, Máthair."

"You must marry yourself; you know that."

"I'm working on it."

***

Mista has stomach cramps. She urinates and finds blood. She knows what this means. She is desperately sad but puts on a brave face. *Many women lose their first child,* she consoles herself, *next time all will be well*. The cramps get worse, and she takes to her bed. She is in terrible pain and moans. She breaks into a sweat and finds herself soaked to the skin. She cries for help. The maid comes and tends to her. She does what she can, but Mista squirms and writhes her body back and forth. She screams in agony.

The maid is worried and goes to Erc. Erc sends for Lupus, a learned monk, a companion of Patricius, and a physician. The pain lasts all night until early the next morning. Mista falls into an exhausted sleep.

Lupus isn't happy.

"Was your mistress sick?" he asks the maid.

"Yes."

"And where is the vomit?"

"I got rid of it, of course!" The maid is indignant.

"Your mistress is very sick, make sure she keeps to her bed for at least seven days. And no heavy food! Just broth."

Lupus tells Erc that he should let Mista recover. He should wait six months before sleeping with her again.

***

Patricius sails along the river Bush with fellow monks. Erc has given the church estate to build a monastery and an orphanage, and they are rowing towards the designated plot to examine the lay of the land. A baby is bawling loudly not far from shore. No dwellings are to be seen.

"Stop! Row ashore, let me out!" Patricius commands.

He jumps out of the coracle hurriedly, ignoring the fact that his sandals and monk's habit get sodden. He strides towards the loud cries; two men hasten after him. They find an infant, tiny, lying in the grass beside his dead mother. Patricius picks the baby up, it cries louder still.

"Bury the mother!" he orders the two men who followed him. "I must return to Dunseverick instantly, for the boy to survive." He returns to the boat and with the rest of the crew, rows quickly back to the castle.

A mother, with a two-month-old infant and plenty of milk, feeds the babe. He is bathed and warmed by the fire. Patricius christens him in the chapel at Dunseverick and names him Olcán. Erc and Mista look after him.

***

A knock at the door. Patricius enters, pushing two dirty, wet, bedraggled waifs in front of him. They stand heads drooping down, reluctant, miserable, dripping wet puddles onto the stone flagging.

"Another two!" Erc exclaims, as Mista ushers the children in front of the fire.

"Warm water, blankets, and food!" Mista orders the maid. She busies herself removing their sodden rags and bathing them in a tub of warm water. They shiver despite the warmth. She gives them each a bowl of warm milk. They sit cross-legged in front of the fire and reward her with large, unbelieving eyes.

"Where did you find them, this time?" Erc asks Patricius. "In the woods? Beside the river?"

"I don't find the poor lambs, they find me," Patricius answers. "I can't just leave them alone to die, can I?"

"No, but you can't bring them all here either. How many is it now? Thirty? Forty? I have lost count."

"Just until the monastery is finished," Patricius pleads. "It won't be long now, another six weeks perhaps. Then we can give them a roof over their heads, warmth, and food."

"You do so much good for our country Patricius, why? We didn't treat you kindly."

"I survived, I live, the Lord gives me strength. Who could ignore such misery?"

"Of course they can stay here until your monastery is finished. I have neither room nor means to let them stay here forever, and even more waifs will come, of that, I am sure. I would like to give you a yearly allowance to help your cause. It won't be sufficient, but it will help."

"May the Lord bless you."

"I shall inform my tackesman tomorrow. Come now, eat, and drink yourself, before you go back into the cold."

"Thank you, but how could I possibly eat, when I know my men are waiting for me, starving?"

"Oh, you impossible man! Very well then. I shall go to the pantry and raid it my very self, and bring back as much as you can carry!"

***

Mista is with child again. She doesn't tell anyone; she wants the first trimester to pass before being too happy. But the signs shine out like the sun sparkling on the lough, a fuller face, an air of complacency and morning sickness. Morag makes a small game pie, Mista's favourite; she adds the herbs to the filling. Another miscarriage leaves Mista debilitated. For many months she is infirm, quiet, in a black place. Erc is worried.

A third miscarriage, Mista is but a dark shadow of herself. Patricius visits Dunseverick often. He prays with Erc and Mista. When nothing helps, he asks Lupus to stay with them, in the castle. Lupus insists that Mista neither eats nor drinks anything, that someone else hasn't tasted beforehand.

Morag visits Birga one-tooth.

"They know," she says. "A learned man has come, a healer, one of Patricius' followers. I can no longer help."

Mista is with child again. She is afraid. The first trimester passes. Her cheeks become rosier, and she regains her former strength and confidence. She gives birth to a healthy boy. Patricius christens him. He is named Fergus.

***

Birga one-tooth calls for Cartan.

"We can do no more about Mista. Have you found a woman?"

"Alas, the right one hasn't surfaced yet."

"The king of the northern Ui Neill has many sons but just one daughter. Her name is Mairead. She is rich and as yet unbetrothed."

"What is wrong with her?"

"Nothing—in particular. She is tall, six feet, big-boned and flat-chested."

"Can she bear children?"

"I know why not."

"It is no problem then."

"Maybe, a small one. Her father dotes upon her and she has persuaded him to let her marry a man of her own choice. She has romantic notions and as yet no man has sufficed."

"Ah, then I must think up a strategy to win her heart."

Cartan is happy about Birga's information. The tribe of the Ui Neill is five times larger and more powerful than that of the Dalriada. Princess Mairead would receive a large dowry. He would be rich, could afford a representative home and his own army. He sends scouts to watch her movements, see her habits. He is rewarded. The scouts report that Mairead likes to go out riding, alone. A plan forms.

***

The rain stops and the sun glistens on the fields. Mairead rides through an avenue of intertwined beech trees. It is like a tunnel and—Mairead thinks, *very romantic. If only she could meet her prince, a dark, handsome, chivalrous knight, like in the tales she loved to listen to.* Her daydreams are savagely interrupted by a band of three wild outlaws who, suddenly emerging from the woods, pull her down from her horse and drag her screaming into the undergrowth.

"Help! Help!" She yells at the top of her voice, as a man throws her to the ground and a second man holds her arms down. "Stop, leave me alone!" She thrashes her legs about desperately and the third man holds them down. "Get your hands off me," Mairead screams, frightened out of her wits but putting up a good fight.

"Get off her, you vermin!" Cartan appears on the scene and charges the nearest man with his shoulder. A second man jumps on Cartan from behind and the first one punches Cartan in the face, before Cartan manages to shake off the man on his back. He swivels around and the man falls flat on his face. Cartan jumps on top of him, pushing his weight into his back. The man spits mud, Cartan presses his hand on the man's head, squashing his nose to the ground. "Ya bleeding tick, ye!" Cartan swears as the man splutters for air. "Off with ya now!" Cartan gets off him and the man flees into the woods. Cartan turns around brandishing his sword, and faces the other two men. They hesitate, then seeing the determination in Cartan's eyes, run off. Cartan brushes the dirt off his garments and makes a small bow in front of Mairead. "Cartan, Prince of Dalriada, at your service, Mistress. May I escort you back to your family?" He stretches his hand out towards her.

She takes it and he pulls her up. She smiles at him coyly from under her eyelashes.

The strategy is a full success. Within three months a marriage ceremony, performed by the druids, takes place. Cartan becomes a rich man. His wife brings a hundred tenanted farms into the marriage; his own father gives him another thirty. He builds a home, protected by a high ditch and wooden palings. He accumulates an army. He has good connections which he uses. He is respected by all. When Mairead gives birth to a son, whom they name Caelan, all could be well. But Cartan is not satisfied with his fortune. He resents his dull wife, his own mother's lowly birth, his father's second wife, Mista. And above all, their son Fergus, his half-brother. It is as if he is worm ridden. And the worms are devouring him alive from inside.

***

After Fergus, Mista gives birth to Loarn, and two years later, Angus. Her happiness is complete. She has a loving husband and three healthy, adorable children. Patricius is a good friend. He visits the family often. He christens the children and introduces Erc and Mista to Brother Aedan, a monk, to teach the boys and help with their upbringing.

***

In the meantime, the continent is in unsteady times. The Roman empire continues to be besieged on all fronts. Hordes of Goths, Vandals, Sueves and Saxons are appearing from the east, the south and the north, ravaging the countryside and the peoples, leaving destruction and confusion in their wake. Illness and plague follow and Ireland isn't spared. Traders and pirates bring the pest and black diarrhoea with them. A third of the population dies.

Patricius and his disciples help the ill and needy where they can. New wells are dug to provide fresh water, and the folk told to boil water before use. The black diarrhoea reaches the Dalriada.

"The people are dropping dead like day flies," Lupus reports to Mista.

"It is that bad then?"

"Yes, it is very infectious. It comes from unclean water; the rivers are contaminated. I have come to inform you. Stay in the castle and instruct your servants."

"How can I help?"

"Keep yourselves safe and spread the word."

A messenger arrives.

"King Daire has the black diarrhoea, the druids cannot help him."

Lupus leaves Dunseverick to seek out Patricius and hurries with him towards Antrim, King Daire's ringfort. The druids don't want to let them enter Daire's chamber, but his soldiers hold the druids back, so that Patricius and Lupus can pass. Daire is delirious, his temples glow with heat and glisten with sweat.

“Quick,” Lupus orders a soldier. “Help me to remove the soiled sheets and his garments! Fetch water from the well and boil it!” he commands another. “The sheets and garments must be burned,” he tells a maid.

Lupus crushes charcoal and mixes it with a little water. He spoons it carefully into Daire’s mouth. He wraps icy poultices around Daire’s calves, whilst a maid cools his forehead with a cold cloth.

“If he survives the night, he has a chance,” Lupus tells Patricius.

He spoons more charcoal down Daire’s throat, and continues to cool his body. The bloody flux decreases, and Daire’s temperature sinks. Lupus stays by his side and treats him, a further seven days. Gradually the fear for Daire’s life recedes. He is pale and very weak, but in full command of his senses.

“How did you know how to help me?” he asks Lupus. “My druids were at the end of their knowledge.”

“The tribute is not mine, my Lord. The ancient Greeks and Egyptians knew these things, and wrote them down for all people to profit from their mastery. I have merely read their works and acquired their skill.”

“Write? Read? I don’t know these words, what do they mean?”

“If you wish, we can teach you.”

***

“Have you heard?” Brother Aedan is keen to impart the latest news. “Patricius has baptised King Daire!”

“Another Christian in our midst,” Erc replies, “and an important figurehead, many will follow his example.”

“Yes,” Aedan agrees and continues excitedly, “and he has given the church land. Patricius wants to establish a central seat of Christianity in Ireland. He will build a church and monastery.”

“And where shall it be?” Mista asks.

“Armagh, close to Emain Macha!”

“But that is an ancient pagan ceremonial site, the druids hold it sacred! Is that wise?”

Erc chuckles. "Very wise, Acushla, Patricius is even cleverer than I thought. The area is regarded sacred by all, no matter which god we pray to."

"When he is not travelling, he will stay there himself," Brother Aedan says. "It will be his see. Pope Leo gave Patricius funding when he visited him last year, and relics of the apostles Peter and Paul! It will be grand when the church is finished, we must all go there to worship the Lord. The boys should accompany us."

"Yes," Erc agrees. "Now then, what are the plans for today? The weather is fair, and your mother confided to me this morning that she would like some partridge," he addresses the boys. "Who would like to come hunting with me?"

"Me!" All three shout enthusiastically together.

"Very well then, I'll burden myself with all three of you rascals!" The boys jump up cheering. "All right, all right, steady down now. Put your warm brats and your brogs on! Brother Aedan you'll excuse the boys from classes today?"

Chapter nine.
455 A.D. Finlaggan, Islay, Caledonia

The boys, uprooted from their home and family, are sitting at the breakfast table, with their guardians and defenders. Mhairi fusses around, bringing them huge bowls of porridge with honey, ham, eggs, and haggis. A commotion at the door makes them look up.

Grainne, Fionn's wife, pushes past the guards, clutching their five-year-old son, Slevin, tightly in her hand. Fionn jumps up, knocking his stool over, and runs to them.

"Grainne, pulse of my heart, what are you doing here? Whatever's happened?" He holds her at arm's length and scrutinises her swollen black eye, her eyebrow split open, her clothing torn and dirty.

"Who did this to you?" His voice sounds like rumbling thunder. His eyes descend downward and he puts his hand on her swollen belly. "Is the baby unharmed?"

Having Fionn finally close to her, and feeling protected, the tension drops and Grainne bursts out crying.

"Hold me tight," she whispers. "Don't let me go."

Fionn wraps his arms tenderly around her and feels Slevin's little arms hugging his leg tightly. He lets go of Grainne for a second to reach down and sweep Slevin up in his embrace. Hugging them both, he pushes them towards the breakfast table and sits them down. Mhairi brings warm milk and more plates. Grainne drinks a little milk but doesn't eat.

"I cannot eat until I've told you everything. But first you must promise to hear me out, listen to me and not act rashly."

"Speak, Beloved, don't keep me in suspense! Tell me what's happened, I shall kill whoever's done this to you!"

"No, you mustn't dear, promise me that first!"

"Tell me it wasn't Cartan!" The look on Grainne's face tells Fionn the opposite. He folds his arms in front of his chest, and with a face the colour of soot, growls "Tell me!"

"He came in the night, with five of his warriors. We were fast asleep and heard nothing. The first thing I noticed was a foul smell breathing into my face. I was startled, I opened my eyes and there he was, towering over me with Flash in his hands."

"Your peregrine!" Angus yelps from between them. The boys and guardians are all riveted to Grainne's tale.

"Yes. Before I even had the chance to sit up, he took Flash's neck between his hands and screwed it. Just like that. A short squawk and he was dead. Cartan threw him away onto the floor, like a dirty rag!"

Angus cries out in anguish as Grainne continues, "I sat up quickly and saw his warriors centred around the room. Two of them held Slevin firmly between them."

"'If you don't want your boy to end up like his father's bird, tell me where Fionn is'! Cartan demanded. I struggled to get up and go to Slevin, but he held his sword against my stomach. I—I hesitated, just a second. Cartan punched my eye and my eyebrow split open; blood ran down my cheek. He spat on my face and drew his sword threateningly across my stomach. I couldn't breathe. Slevin wanted to protect me and kicked his feet against the soldiers holding him. One of them laid his arm around Slevin from behind and held the tip of a dagger on his throat. So I said you had sailed across the western sea—" Grainne stops to draw breath, and looks at the faces glued to her lips.

Fionn looks grim. Suddenly Grainne bends over double in pain. Mhairi springs up from her seat and puts her arms around her.

"Come now, time to lie down and think of your bairn," she says, ushering her away. Grainne looks back over her shoulder, tears running down her face. "You are in great peril! I had to tell him, Fionn. He knows you're all here, I'm sorry!"

As Mhairi leads her to a chamber, she leaves, stunned silence in her wake. Fionn looks at Slevin and hesitates.

Fergus, quick to catch on, says, "You were brave Slevin! Do you want to explore the castle now? Come on, we'll show you the towers." He leaves with his brothers and Slevin.

A soldier, who had escorted Grainne and Slevin from Dunseverick, steps forward and gives Fionn a letter.

"It's from your sister," he says. "She's devastated at the trouble she's caused you; she said I was to tell you, that she deeply regrets getting you mixed up in all this."

Fionn beckons him and his comrade to the table, and tells them to sit down and help themselves to food. First, he reads the letter from Mista, written on thin vellum.

He curses loudly and asks the soldiers, "What can you tell me?"

"Your wife an' son arrived on horseback very early this morning," the older soldier answers, a wiry man, medium height, with black hair. "They went straight to Erc. About half an hour later he called for a dozen soldiers. Shanley here," he says pointing to his companion, "an' I was to accompany your son an' wife here to you. We came straight away; the crossing didn't take long."

"But you must know more!" Fionn's head is pounding. "What about the soldiers I left to protect them?"

"I was just comin' to tha'. They're all dead; their throats slit open! Erc sent soldiers to your farmstead to bury them. And they'll look after yer farm till yer return."

"Don't forget the horse," Shanley reminds his elder.

"Aye. You know the night yer left? Well, the next morning the stable master came and told us all. Niamh had been poisoned in the night when everyone was asleep. He found her in the morning, dead in her box. Lying on her side she was, with still a bit a yew between her teeth. What wiv the stables locked an' all, nobody knows how it could've happened. But Shanley here, he says he saw Cartan sneaking around. Earlier on like. Can't prove it mind yer."

"Six men against a woman and child, I ask you, what type of man is that? He's out of his mind, a raging fool, and a coward at that. A peregrine and a horse! Well, he's got it coming to him, just wait till I get my hands on that villain!" Fionn thumps his fists on the table and snorts like a bull in the arena.

He begins to pace up and down but stops abruptly as Fergus and Loarn re-enter the room and sit down at the table. Fionn arches his eyebrows.

"Angus is playing outside with Slevin. If you're going to discuss our future, we want to be present," Fergus says.

"You're too young!" Fionn replies.

"In a few months I would've been sent to Tara as a warrior," Fergus argues. "If I'm old enough to fight, then I'm old enough to hear what you have to say!"

"He's right," Gair intervenes. "They've a right to know what's going on, let them stay."

Before Fionn can reply, Mhairi enters the room with Donald.

Fionn jumps up. "Will she be all right?" he asks.

"I cleaned her up. The physical wounds aren't too serious, they'll heal."

"And the baby?"

"I don't know. I gave her a sleeping draught and she's asleep now. I hope if she rests a few days, they'll both be all right. She mustn't get upset or excited at all. What did Mista say in her letter?"

"She begs me not to return to Ireland. She says I'd be playing straight into Cartan's hands. That's why he let Grainne live after she told him where we are. He knew she would come here immediately and tell me!"

"She's right, you know that, don't you?"

"Aye, but it's damn hard to sit here and do nothing."

"Can't Erc do something? Surely, he will protest to the king of the Ui Neill."

"He's sent two messengers to protest," Shanley tells them. "He doesn't think it'll lead to anything, though. With Fionn's warriors dead, there are no witnesses, except Graine, of course and Slevin. Slevin's just a bairn, so it's Cartan's word against Grainne's. Erc says Cartan will probably make his warriors give him a false alibi."

"So, he'll get away with it, yet again? What does that man need to do, until his king finally looks up and takes notice?"

"Erc was so angry, he said he'd kill him himself, son or not. But he's well protected now he's married into the Ui Neill, their tribe is five times larger than the Dalriada."

"What about the boys?" Mhairi asks.

"We'll have to split them up for safety," Fionn replies. "Cartan will dispatch spies everywhere. They'll be looking for three lads together. We can hide them better separately."

Fergus looks at Loarn; they've never been separated before.

"First our home and parents, now each other," Fergus has venom in his voice. "I swear here and now that I'll kill Cartan one day."

"Aye," Fionn agrees. "If you get to him before I do. Now, what to do with you?"

"I want to learn to fight better!" Loarn says.

"That's fair enough," Donald replies. "The best warriors come from the Isle of Lewis, Mhairi's brother lives there. He's called Conan and would protect you with his own life. He's a fierce warrior; he leads his men to fight the Picts and to help the Britons against the Saxons! What d'you think?"

"Aye, he would help, but—" Mhairi replies.

"But what?"

"Well—it *is* a very long way away, for visits and so on—" She finishes lamely as she sees Loarn's initially eager face begin to fall.

"Well then, how about my sister Flora? She lives with her husband at Dunstaffnage, that's on the mainland, not far from here, a day's travel at the most. He's Laird of the Mac Dougall clan and they live in a stone fortress. I'm sure he'd apprentice Loarn to one of his valiant warriors. And they're renowned for their bold soldiers, they've hearts of lions!"

"Brother Aedan, what do you think?" Fionn asks.

"Well, neither Fergus nor Loarn are designated for a clerical life, they will both be warriors *and* leaders too, I think. They no longer need me to help them study; their Latin is adequate and they can read themselves. But although they are both tall for their age, they are but fourteen and fifteen. They should be given time to develop and grow stronger before they are led into battle."

"And Angus?"

"Ah, Angus. He dreams of designing and building ships. He will become a leader too but not on land, a leader of a fleet of boats on the high seas. He must study geometry and astronomy further, a year or maybe two. Then he can be apprenticed to a joiner, a shipbuilder on the coast."

"I'm thinking," Fionn says, "that if we may, Mhairi and Donald, I would like to stay here with Grainne and Slevin, and God willing, our new bairn. Grainne will feel safe here and Brother Aedan could teach

Slevin alongside Angus. And I also will feel at peace, to know them here, safe, when I have business to attend to elsewhere."

Donald considers Fionn's words and nods.

"And I have the perfect hiding place for Fergus!" Lorcan beams at the faces around the table. He glances at his twin, Mahon, sitting across from him, "Our cousin, Tormey! He serves Laird Douglas on Aran, near Goat Fell. He has a fine horse breeding and training centre, one of the best, you must've heard of him!"

"Of course, the horse fair at Brodick! It's held every year; I bought my two best horses there! As cool as the snow on the mountain tops, they are, unflappable as a pair of dead moths, worth their weight in gold in battle!" Laird Donald is passionate. "Hmmn, I might visit you in summer!"

"But will Fergus be safe?" Fionn asks. "I'm sure your cousin is loyal, but what about the Laird, who's side is he on?"

"Douglas?" Donald replies. "Don't worry about him, he's a good friend of mine, I'll give you a letter to take with you."

"But where can you live?" Fionn insists.

"I'll ask my cousin to apprentice Fergus. He'll sleep in the stables. No one will suspect a stable lad to be a young prince!"

"It sounds good to me," Fergus says. "Anyway, it's not for long, I'll be fighting as a warrior soon. When do we set off?"

"First thing tomorrow!" Fionn says, snapping out of his reverie. "We have a lot to prepare first, but we can't afford to dawdle. Only the devil knows Cartan's next move." He looks as sick as a dead parrot.

The faces around the table are downcast. Mahon stands up and thumps Fionn so heftily on his back, that he plummets forwards and has to brace himself with his hands on the table, so as not to crash his face onto the wooden surface.

"He'll meet his just end, don't you worry!" Mahon says in his soprano voice.

***

Light from a crescent moon, floods in through the open window and falls like a curtain onto the stone floor of the tower room. Fergus, Loarn and

Angus are sitting cross-legged on their mattresses and chatting to each other in low voices, so as not to wake Slevin, who has already fallen into an exhausted slumber. The brothers want to make the most of their last night together. Nothing will ever be the same again.

Sudden blood-curdling screams screech out into the night, echoing against the bare, stony walls. The boys jump up, Slevin wakes.

Eyes wide open, terrified, he asks, “What was that?” The boys look at each other.

Fergus says, “Wait here, I’ll go and look.”

He exits the room and creeps down the spiral staircase. He hugs the walls; the stone steps feel like ice on his bare feet. Arriving at the bottom of the stairwell, he hears hushed voices. Whispering. He can’t determine who’s speaking. He sees figures in the gloom but cannot discern who they are. He creeps forward. An arm grabs him from behind and pins his arms behind his back.

“Ah Fergus, it’s you!” Lorcan lets go of him. “Don’t worry, Grainne had a nightmare. I was just checking that nothing else had woken her.”

“Is it the baby, will she lose it?”

“I don’t know, but for the moment it was just a bad dream. Go back upstairs now, we have an early start tomorrow.”

Fergus goes back up the dank stairwell, the stone steps are well worn and sagging in the centre. The boys look at him expectantly.

“Grainne had a nightmare,” he tells them. “We’d better try to sleep.”

His head touches the pillow and the next thing he notices are sounds, jagged and incomprehensible, piercing the fog of his stupor.

“Get up!” Loarn shakes him. “We’ve got to leave.”

Immediately alert, Fergus jumps up and pulling on some clothes, rushes downstairs. Everyone is at breakfast, even Grainne. She looks pale but is eating some porridge. Everything happens quickly, hurriedly. No one likes long farewells. They exit the castle and follow the path past the small stone chapel and the kitchen gardens. Soon they reach the pier. On the left, small boats are rocking on the water. Quick hugs and promises to write, then Gair and Lorcan get onto a boat and Fergus and Loarn step in after them.

They row to the opposite shore and walk to the tavern. Silence prevails, there is nothing left to say. At the tavern, Fergus and Loarn have to take leave of each other. Their eyes are dry, but their hearts are heavy.

"Good luck!" Fergus whispers.

"You too," Loarn replies.

They mount their horses and whilst Loarn and Gair ride north to the port at Askaig, Fergus and Lorcan ride southeast to Port Ellen.

Chapter ten
455 A.D. Brodick, Aran, Argyll

Fergus and Lorcan trot on their steeds briskly along the road and enter Port Ellen within the hour. They dismount, and leading their horses to the local stables, arrange for them to be returned to the blacksmith at Bridgend. They walk around the harbour looking for a ship, traders possibly, who would let them sail with them to Brodick or at least halfway to Campbeltown in Cantyre.

There were three large vessels, all at the far end of the harbour. The first was due to set sail for Ireland. The second was underway to Frankenland, but said they would stop in Campbeltown. The third wasn't due to sail for two more days but would take them to Brodick directly.

"I think we should go now," Lorcan tells Fergus. "We'll get another boat from Campbeltown. Who knows if Cartan doesn't already have spies questioning incoming boats."

"Oh, that's why you said your name was Aled! I wondered why."

"We can't be too careful; in Aran we'll tell people you're my orphaned nephew."

They set sail in a drizzle that seems to linger in animation. The temperature is moderate, but visibility is poor. As they enter the north channel they are engulfed in a cloak of fog.

"Climb up to the crow's nest, lad!" the captain orders Fergus. "Shout down if you see owt!"

Fergus climbs up the mast and clambers into the lookout. Grey mist swirls about him. It's cold at the top and eerily quiet.

"I can't see *any*thing!" he shouts down to deck. "Just fog."

"Well stay on the lookout and give us a shout if you see land, rocks or any other ships."

Fergus crouches down in the crow's nest, shivering. The captain gives orders to his mate to steer backboard nearer to the coast.

Fergus feels tense. Everyone is silent, listening for the slightest sound that might foretell danger. Minutes turn to hours. The mast sways gently back and forth in a rocking motion. Fergus finds himself dozing off and forces his eyes open. Not even seabirds can be heard calling to each other. Fergus concentrates on looking backboard in case they get too near to the coastline, where rocks soar out of the seabed. For a moment, he glances starboard and wakes up sharp. Huge, black shapes shoot out of the fog, almost upon them.

"Ahead!" he screams. "Starboard, ships! A fleet of longships!"

Below on deck he hears the captain shout, "Backboard, backboard!"

The sail is hastily lowered, and the sailors row urgently backboard. Foghorns blare, deafening. Fergus is frightened, his heart races, he is convinced that the massive ships will collide into them and crush them to pieces. A ship, twice their size, answers their horn, Fergus' eardrums ring. The ship brushes past them, almost touching, the sailors pull their oars hastily back on deck. A collection of relieved sighs. Fergus' heart is still beating wildly. He stays where he is, the danger may not yet be over. He feels jumpy and scared. He's not ready to die, not today, not tomorrow either, he has things he wants to do first.

Another fifteen minutes, and then suddenly the fog disperses. The sky is blue, the sun shines. They see the coast and row towards Campbeltown.

Fergus and Lorcan stay overnight in Campbeltown. The next morning, they walk around the harbour and find a trading boat willing to give them passage to Brodick. There are no open stretches of sea to cross, they keep within good sight of the coastline and approach Brodick relaxed. It is a fair day, clouds frolic across a blue sky, blessed with sunshine.

"That's Goat Fell," Lorcan points to a small summit in front of them, "and that's Brodick Castle."

Fergus gazes at the peak, forested nearly to the very top. Below are luscious green glens. The castle is built from pale brown stone. The sun casts it in a warm, friendly light. As they come nearer, they can determine horses grazing in the sun.

The ship docks in the harbour; Fergus and Lorcan take leave from the crew. They walk through the small settlement towards the castle. People greet them pleasantly and one man even recognises Lorcan.

"Guid efternuin, Lorcan is it not, are you up to visit Tormey?"

"Aye, me nephew has lost his parents, I thought Tormey might find some use for him."

"Well, good luck with tha', there's always enough to be done, is there not."

The man continues his way and so do Lorcan and Fergus.

Once out of earshot Lorcan says, "Well that went well, tonight when the tavern opens, everyone will know who you are!"

They follow a stony road, lined with flowering hedgerows, which ascends uphill towards the horse centre. They pass fields with black cattle chewing grass; black-faced sheep are spotted around on the upper hills, bleating.

"It's so peaceful here," Fergus comments. "And everything looks so clean. Are the cattle left alone in the fields? I can't see anyone guarding them."

"You can't steal cattle on an island this size, there would be nowhere to hide them," Lorcan answers. "Wait until late spring when the drovers herd them to market. That's a sight not to be missed."

"Are they sold here or on the mainland?"

"Here, but drovers come from the mainland, even from as far as Castle Rock. There are lots of hungry mouths to be fed in the large towns. The drovers buy the cattle for their masters, landowners, or butchers and such. They load them into boats to get to the mainland. A time-consuming action, you can only take a few cattle on each boat, and they have to be tightly secured or they'd jump out in panic and drown. Then they have to be unloaded again and herded to wherever they're going. It can take several days or even weeks."

"Do the drovers earn much?"

"A fair bit. A set sum is usually agreed on beforehand, depending on the number of cattle they deliver safely. But it's dangerous on the mainland; the drovers' routes are well known and there are always wayfarers, out to steal the cattle."

After a couple of miles, they reach the stud and training centre. A large block of stables is spread out in an 'L' shape below Brodick castle. Horses are grazing in small fields, separated from one another with wooden fencing. Several foals stand close to their mothers.

Adjacent to the stables are two sanded schooling areas, enclosed by wooden posts joined together with sturdy rope.

"It's *huge*!" Fergus is amazed. "I know you said *large,* but I would never have guessed that *anything* like this existed."

Lorcan smiles, happy at so much enthusiasm. He crosses the cobbled square in front of the stables and enters without knocking. Fergus follows him hurriedly, trying to take in his surroundings at the same time.

"Hello, anyone here? Tormey?" Lorcan calls.

"Who wants to know?" a voice calls back. A man, sinewy, his face lined and tanned from a life outdoors in all weathers, comes around the corner.

"Lorcan! Well bless me soul. And who's this?" he asks, approaching them. He slaps Lorcan's shoulder. "Surprise, surprise, what brings me the honour?"

"Are you alone?" Lorcan asks.

"Aye, as a matter o' fact, I am. What's all the secrecy 'bout then?"

"This is Fergus, Prince of Dalriada. We need to hide him for a bit. I told Old Mac down at the port, that he's my orphaned nephew looking to work for you."

"So, so." Tormey scratches his chin, covered in bristle. He's medium height, his black hair falls on his shoulders, he seems to consider the suggestion. "Do you know owt about horses?"

"A little sir, but I'm very keen to learn from you."

"Hmmn, well there's enough work to be done. The mares have already foaled as you see, but we'll need to mate them in a few weeks, an' another three months an' the horse fair is due. Plenty to be done. You'll have to ask the Laird mind; I can't take anyone on without his permission."

"Is it all right with you if I tell him he's my nephew?" Lorcan asks. "No need to hang his true identity out into the open."

"No harm in that," Tormey says. "Come back later then, I don't think Douglas 'll be bothered."

Fergus and Lorcan walk briskly along the dirt track, leading up to Castle Brodick. Fergus notices that Lorcan doesn't stumble over his long limbs even once. *I must remember to tell my brothers that when I write,* he thinks smiling. They pass through a stone archway and enter a courtyard. The Laird is standing in front of them, holding the reins of a bay horse, and talking to his bailiff. They turn to look at the newcomers. Lorcan makes a small bow.

"Laird Douglas, I have a letter for you from Donald Laird of Islay, I believe you know him." Lorcan withdraws the letter from his shoulder bag and gives it to him. Douglas looks at it, then tucks it, unopened, under his green léine.

"Donald? Of course! How goes he?"

"He was very well when we left him three days ago. We request your permission, for my orphaned nephew here," Lorcan pushes Fergus forward, "to help my cousin, Tormey in the stables."

"Orphaned nephew, huh? Have you asked Tormey, is he willing?"

"Yes, Sire, with your consent."

"Very well then, plenty of work to be done."

With his last words Douglas turns back to his bailiff and picks up his conversation, thus dismissing Fergus and Lorcan. They turn around and go back down the hill to the stable complex. Tormey shows them the tack room. It is large with at least thirty saddles of various shapes and sizes, bridles, bits, reins, and all sorts of other equipment. At one end there is a wooden ladder, leading up to an open loft.

"You can sleep there, with the other lads," Tormey tells Fergus. "Grab one of those blankets and pick out a straw mattress for yourself. Meals twice a day. I'd better introduce you to Hamish, our head lad, you'll be getting your orders from him. Now what about you Lorcan? Will you be staying at me wife's an' me croft?"

"If it's no trouble, I'd like to help too."

Truth was that Tormey's stud is specialised in and famous for its destriers, the war horses. Lorcan would give his right arm to help.

"Aye, we've got a couple of horses here, I'd like yer advice on. One's got a crumbly hoof we can't get right. Shame, he's a handsome brute otherwise."

"Right on, then. Now what about Hamish? Is that the lad you had here two years ago?"

"Aye, he's coming on promising. He'll be in the upper schooling field. I expect he'll have Thunderbolt on the lunge."

"Let's go then, you can tell me about Thunderbolt on the way and this horse with the crumbly hoof. Come on Fergus!"

***

Fergus soon has a routine that leaves him little time to feel homesick. He misses Loarn and Angus, but he learns so many new things every day, that he is too occupied to feel lonely. The day begins at six with feeding the horses and leading them out into the fields; then he mucks out the stables and fills the boxes with fresh hay. After breakfast, training sessions begin. He brings whichever horse is required to the appropriate ring, and if required, also the necessary equipment. In the evening, the horses are brought back to their boxes, groomed, fed, and given plenty of hay and fresh water. Then the tack would be cleaned. He gets on well with his fellow comrades and Hamish is fair. When the day's work is finished, Lorcan practises sword training with him. Fergus' shoulders broaden, and his muscles become toned and supple.

One day Lorcan calls Fergus to come and look at Lockwood, the horse with a crumbly hoof. He explains how healthy hooves have a nice sheen, almost like varnish. An unhealthy hoof looks dull and crumbly. Lockwood's front left hoof is clearly not in order. Lorcan gives Fergus a recipe for Lockwood's feed. It includes corn and other grain, an old druid's secret, he tells Fergus. From then on Fergus is responsible for Lockwood. Also, for Starlight, a promising three-year-old filly, as white as a swan; at least when she is groomed and hasn't just rolled over in the mud. Further horses, either young, or not star quality, complete his assignment. It's clever of Tormey to entrust each lad with their own special protégés, that way they all do their utmost to make sure their own charges shine. When the time comes for selective breeding or choosing which horse is suitable for what use, thus influencing the subsequent training or price at sale, the lads would take the decisions almost personally. There was always good-natured competition involved.

Fergus accepts the fact that none of his protégés are of age or attributes to win any trophies. He is the newest of the lads with the least experience. That doesn't stop him growing fond of his charges however, and he does his best to make the most of their positive traits.

About a month after his arrival Fergus is in an exercise area with Starlight, trying to get her used to a saddle. He rubs her nose and speaks soothingly to her, gaining her trust and letting her smell the lightweight leather saddle on his arm. She isn't keen when he places it carefully on her back, but this isn't the first time he's tried, and now she just snorts and no longer bucks to throw it off.

"Good girl," he whispers, secretly thrilled. "Good girl."

He clips a lunging rein on her halter and moves her around the field in circles. Tormey approaches and watches a while, then he nods his head and leaves again.

Fergus becomes aware of another spectator. About fifty yards away, a scruffy urchin crouches, half hidden, behind a boulder. Had the boy not been so secretive, he may not even have noticed him, but as it is, Fergus observes him keenly out of the corner of his eye. However, the boy is no bother. He stays where he is, just watching. He has long, brown hair, tangled, and wears a brown linen tunic. He seems to frown, either cross-patched or squinting against the sun. When he finally moves away, Fergus sees that he is barefoot.

After the first time, Fergus often notices the *scallywag*, as he tends to refer to him in his mind. He's always in the same place. Fergus vaguely wonders why the lad has no work to do, but dismisses the thought and forgets about it. It's none of his business after all. After a couple of encounters Fergus waves, calls hello, and invites the boy to come closer. But as soon as his presence is acknowledged, the urchin runs off, as if scared of some punishment.

***

The farrier comes rumbling up the hill with his horse and cart. He will stay a week before continuing his way, to return again six weeks later. The frequent visitor is keenly awaited and Tormey slaps him on his back.

"Not a day too soon, chap! Lockwood has lost his shoe again."

“Oh no, not again! I was hopeful it’d hold this time.”

“Well, we’ve been feeding him some secret druid recipe, have a look and see what you think.”

Fergus goes to fetch his charge and holds him while the farrier examines his hooves. Lockwood stands a proud fourteen point two hands at the withers and has massive, solid quarters. His coat shines glossy white, his mane and tail are long and wavy. He has been trained to be a war horse. He remains calm in the loudest hullabaloo and isn’t bothered in the slightest by the smell of blood, or of smoke or fire. If it weren’t for his hoof, he could be sold for five hundred gold pieces. And now Tormey, Lorcan and Fergus hold their breath, waiting for the farrier’s verdict.

“Well, I don’t know what you’ve been giving him, but here, you can see,” the farrier holds Lockwood’s hoof up to show them, “the horn has begun to grow well.” The men could see maybe half an inch of healthy horn. “But that is the good news, I’m ’fraid. I can trim his feet every six weeks and take the flare off, but look at them cracks!” He shows them long cracks in the hoof. “If you turn him out to pasture barefoot for the next few months and keep on giving him his nutrients, then you’ll see a much healthier hoof. But you’ll never get rid of the problem completely, and he’ll lose his shoe again and again.”

Tormey’s face drops. “He’s worthless then! We can’t sell him at the fair, and we can’t even use him for breeding. The Laird won’t be happy.”

The men all look dejected as the farrier continues, “No, you can’t use him for breeding, a hoof like that is hereditary. I tell you what, I’ll take his other shoes off and you turn him out to pasture. When I come back before the fair, I’ll try to get the nails in at the heel and toe. That way you can sell him.”

“Not for much though,” Tormey complains. “The buyers can examine the horses before the auction and only an idiot would offer a decent price for him.”

“Aye, it’s a damn shame! Now show me Thunderbolt, how’s he coming on?”

“Ah, yes. Now he *is* our star!”

***

Spring turns to early summer and the horses continue to be schooled. The three-year-olds are sorted, some will be kept for further training and others sold to make room for this year's yearlings to take their place. Fergus waits to hear about Starlight's fate.

"She'll be sold, I'm afraid," Tormey tells Fergus. "You've done a good job with her, an' she'll fetch a good price, but she's a lightweight mare and is best suited for hunting."

Fergus is a little sad, but he was expecting this outcome, so it is no surprise. He goes to Lockwood's pasture. His hoof is looking better, but he is a terrible baby. Without any shoes on, he steps on a sharp stone and hobbles about as if he's been shot in the leg. Hamish is watching him in the field too. He bursts out laughing

"What a play-actor!" he says.

"Well, we can tell the auctioneer to say he's got character," Fergus replies.

They go to the training ring where Lorcan is teaching Thunderbolt to step sideways. He hardly touches the reins; Thunderbolt responds to Lorcan's legs and use of body weight.

"I wish I could ride as well as him," Hamish swoons. Lorcan hears him, dismounts, and tells Hamish to mount. Then he explains what Hamish must do. Fergus listens intently as Thunderbolt starts to walk backwards under Hamish's command.

"He's tossing his head about too much," Lorcan complains. "Fergus, go and fetch a holding strap to fix to his girth. That should help."

Fergus sprints towards the tack room, enters, grabs a leather strap and is about to leave again, when he catches a flash of movement out of the corner of his eye. He glances down the row of boxes and sees the scallywag about to give Starlight something.

"Hey, you! What are you doing?" Dropping the harness, he races towards the boy who, startled, bolts out of the door, and charges up the hill towards the forest behind the castle.

Fergus runs hell for leather after him. The scamp is fast and surefooted. He jumps over the ledge of a low wall, Fergus vaults after him. The boy hotfoots it. Fergus is fit but his lungs press together, squeezing all breath out of him. The boy wants to jump the next fence, but he misjudges the height and falls head first over it. He tries frantically to pick himself up quickly, but Fergus is upon him, straddling his back and pinning his arms roughly to the ground. The boy squirms beserkly trying to escape, Fergus is raging and turns him over viciously onto his back. The boy blushes and Fergus's jaw drops between his knees.

"You're a girl!" he says, stating the obvious. He lets go of her, and the girl sits up angrily and yanks her léine back over her shoulder.

"What were you doing in the stables?"

"I just wanted to give Starlight an apple," she says, pulling an apple out of her pocket to justify herself.

"It's forbidden to enter the stables."

"I know, I just wanted to stroke her."

"Who are you?"

"Rhianna."

"Where do you live?"

"Up there," she says pointing vaguely to an obscure point in the distance.

"Next time you want to bring an apple, tell me first, then you can give her one. But only when you tell me first, agreed?"

Fergus can't forget that Cartan poisoned Niamh; the horses are much too valuable to take any chances. The girl nods solemnly and Fergus returns to the tack room to retrieve the holding strap.

"You took your time!" Lorcan says when Fergus finally gives him the leather strap.

"There was someone there, everything's in order though."

"Well go and saddle up the bay stallion then. I might as well give you both a lesson at the same time. Hamish, come here, we'll attach the holding strap."

Fergus rushes off, thrilled at the prospect of a lesson. When he returns, Lorcan demonstrates halting Thunderbolt mid canter and makes him turn on the stop.

"Now you both try," he says, dismounting and handing Thunderbolt to Hamish. "Fergus, you first. Careful! A *controlled* canter, don't let him run away with you, good. Try again. Yes, that's much better. Right, now you, Hamish. Keep your knees in tight."

That night Fergus lies awake on his straw mattress, trying to remember everything that Lorcan has taught him. But his thoughts are constantly distracted by much more disturbing matters. He can't stop thinking of Rhianna. Of her startling blue eyes and of her accidently revealed breast. Her skin was so pale under her léine. He keeps wondering who she is, and why she is always watching the horses.

The next afternoon, Tormey and Lorcan call all the lads together to discuss the horse fair. There is only one month left until it takes place, and there is a lot of organising to be arranged. They debate over which horses will be auctioned in which order, and who will ride which horse for various demonstrations.

A war horse must be strong, fast, and agile. A lot of training is required to overcome a horse's natural instinct to flee from noise, the smell of blood, and the confusion of combat. It must also learn to accept smoke and fire and any sudden movements.

Laird Douglas' horse stud, under the expert hands of Tormey, is particularly famous for its destriers, the most valuable horses of all, the war horses. Tormey uses selective breeding, choosing not only height and weight but also calm disposition. Unperturbed by noise but taught to kick, strike and bite in combat, the war horses become weapons themselves for the warriors they carry.

Hundreds of visitors are expected at the yearly horse fair; it attracts people from far afield. Many nobles have already announced their intention to come, and more importantly, to purchase an animal. They travel considerable distances, and all accommodation is full, weeks in advance. Laird Donald has also sent a letter to Lorcan, disclosing his intention to come, and asking for his advice about attaining a destrier. Fergus is caught up in the excitement and writes letters to his brothers and parents to give to Donald for safe delivery. He keeps his eyes open for Rhianna, but she seems determined to avoid him.

The farrier arrives a week before the fair and shoes Lockwood. The horses are all brought to their boxes and their coats brushed until they shine like conkers. Tormey orders four lads to guard the stables to make sure no unauthorised persons enter.

Laird Douglas inspects the stables on the eve of the fair. He has a visitor with him. He is smaller than Fergus, old, over sixty. His head is shaved, and he sports a tattoo of a horse's head on his left underarm. His right hand has heavy rings on all four fingers. The majority of his fifteen stones weight is concentrated around his belly, making him look a bit like an overgrown toad standing upright. They approach Starlight's box. Light falls in thin shafts between the rafters, her coat twinkles like ice crystals on snow. Laird Douglas stops, and Fergus can hear him appraising her. He calls Fergus to them.

"Ceredig, King of Strathclyde, would like to see Starlight in action. Saddle her up and take her round the exercise area a few times."

Fergus does as bid and then brings Starlight to a halt. Douglas and the king progress from their vantage point outside the fence, and enter the sanded circuit. Ceredig looks Starlight in her mouth and examines her hooves. His expression is haughty. He looks almost disappointed that he can find no fault with her. He feels her legs and then straightens himself up again and smiles crookedly, his eyebrows arched. Only now does Fergus realise that his head sits lopsided on his shoulders.

"Well, you'll give me a good price, I hope," he says to Douglas.

"Sire, I'm *desolate*. She's already entered for the auction, and you know the rules, I can't withdraw her now. I had no idea you were interested."

"She will make a good wedding present for my bride."

"Oh, my daughter is such a child still. Can you not wait another year?"

"No!" The king turns red with anger. "You've made me wait long enough. If I don't marry her within the next month, then the deal is off, and I shall march all over this island with my army. I'm sure my warriors will be pleased to have their way with her."

Fergus steps back quickly to avoid being hit by Ceredig's spit. Douglas' hands begin to shake. His face competes with Starlight's coat for whiteness.

"Very well then," he concedes, almost whispering. "I'll start the preparations straight after the fair."

Fergus leads Starlight back to the stables, glad to distance himself from the atmosphere charged with aggression. He wonders who Laird Douglas' poor daughter is. He can't remember seeing her about.

The night is short, the lads are up well before dawn putting the last touches to their wards. The auction begins with the yearlings. Fergus stands at the ring with Lorcan and Donald watching. They exchange letters to and from Fergus' siblings. Fergus puts his letters in his pocket, to savour at length after the fair. The three-year-olds are next, so he leaves to fetch Starlight and walk her around the ring. He sees Laird Douglas with King Ceredig and a young woman dressed in a long green gown. Her hair is shiny, chestnut coloured, and piled in intricate curls on top of her head. She looks very pale and fragile. She seems vaguely familiar, but he can't place her. *She must be Douglas' daughter,* he thinks.

The bidding begins and Fergus glows at the brisk offers toppling over each other. Ceredig finally crunches the deal, at a price well over that expected.

Fergus returns Starlight to the stables and Hamish slaps him on his shoulder, "Well done, that should bring you a nice bonus."

"Thanks. Do you know Douglas' daughter? Apparently, Starlight is a wedding present for her."

"Rhianna? Of course, you must've seen her around!"

Fergus feels his knees buckling beneath him and just manages to grab a box door to stop himself from falling.

"*Rhianna*?"

"Yes, I must hurry now, see you later."

Fergus takes a deep breath. *Are there two Rhiannas?* he asks himself. *Surely not, the name isn't that common.* He thinks back to the young woman in the long green gown. *Was she the scruffy urchin? There had been something familiar about her*. He shakes his head in disbelief. *It couldn't be. But if it was. What on earth was she up to?*

He hurries back outdoors to watch the coursers being auctioned. Coursers were generally preferred for hard battle amongst the cavalries. They are light, fast, and strong. They were valuable, but not as costly as the destrier, thus more affordable for the less wealthy. They were also used frequently for hunting. He is so absorbed watching a demonstration, that he nearly misses seeing Cartan approaching the ring. His heart skips a beat as he turns around swiftly. Pulling the hood of his tunic over his head, he starts to walk quickly uphill towards the castle. He forces himself not to run. Turning a corner, he reaches the castle's kitchen garden. He realises he's been holding his breath and takes a few gulps of air greedily. He is out of sight from the fairground now but his heart is still pounding. He decides to walk further, up the slopes of Goat Fell. *I will be missed but Lorcan will make excuses for me,* he thinks. He takes long brisk strides, attempting to work off his pent-up emotions.

Chapter eleven
455 A.D. Brodick, Aran

Donald sees Cartan approaching the ring.

He nudges Lorcan and says, “Keep him occupied, I’ll make sure Fergus disappears.”

He runs towards the stables but can’t find him anywhere.

Cartan sees Lorcan’s unmistakeable long, lanky figure and strides purposefully towards him.

“You here Lorcan, what are you doing here?”

“I could ask you the same. Why shouldn’t I be here? If you must know, I’ve been looking at the horses. Laird Donald wants a destrier, he asked for my advice.”

“Ah, any particular horse in mind? I’m looking for one myself.”

Lorcan tips the end of his nose. “Now that would be telling, wouldn’t it?” An idea forms in his mind. “Must go, I’ve business to attend to.”

He leaves Cartan standing at the ringside and ambles leisurely towards the stables.

Donald is amongst a mass of people, “I can’t find him. He must’ve seen Cartan and disappeared himself,” he tells Lorcan.

“Good. Now listen, I’ve got a plan. When the destriers are auctioned, bid for Lockwood until I rub my nose.”

“Lockwood? I thought we’d agreed on Thunderbolt.”

“Aye, I’ve no time to explain, trust me.” Lorcan finds Tormey and tells him to speak to the auctioneer. “Get him to auction Lockwood in third place, and Thunderbolt right at the end, I’ll explain later. Oh, and ask Hamish to do a demonstration on Lockwood before the bidding.”

Tormey looks a little surprised as Lorcan rushes off again, but he knows him well enough to do as bid without asking questions. Next, Lorcan goes around the ring until he finds Old Mac from the village.

“You and your friends bid for Lockwood till I pull my left earlobe. The drinks are on me tonight.”

“Oh, right you are, leave it up to me.”

Satisfied that his plan could succeed, Lorcan takes place at the ringside and watches the sales. The auctioneer calls for attention and announces that the highlight of the fair was imminent, the auction of this year’s destriers. Eight horses are trotted around the ring whilst the auctioneer praises their compact and well-muscled build, their skill, and their swiftness, before they file out again. The first two horses achieve prices over four hundred gold pieces. Lorcan notices with satisfaction that Cartan doesn’t bid, but turns his head constantly between himself and Donald like a ball game. Hamish enters the ring riding Lockwood. Tall and majestic the powerful animal strides out with confidence. He has an elegant gait, a refined head, and an arched neck. His white coat is glossy, and his mane and tail plaited. Loud, “Oohs and aahs” accompany his movements.

Lockwood doesn’t bat an eyelid at the noise. Hamish lets him jump over two smouldering sheaves of hay. The spectators applaud. Then Hamish steers Lockwood to the middle of the ring. He demonstrates a leg yield with Lockwood moving forwards and sidewards; lifesaving on a battle field. Finally, he canters the full length of the ring, pulls Lockwood up briskly and lets him turn a pirouette to face the opposite direction. Then he trots again to the centre and rears up on his hind feet. The applause makes Hamish’s ears ring. As he exits, the bidding begins.

The auctioneer has his instructions and begins at four hundred. Donald raises his hand, followed quickly by Cartan and Old Mac and his mates. In a matter of minutes, the bidding has reached eight hundred and fifty. Lorcan pulls his left ear lobe and Old Mac, and his friends drop out of the bidding, shaking their heads sadly.

“Eight hundred and eighty, who’ll give me eight hundred eighty?” the auctioneer bellows.

An awed silence falls over the ring. A collective holding of breath and eager expectation. The price is ridiculous, even for such a grand animal. Donald looks at Lorcan anxiously, but failing to see him rub his nose, nods to the auctioneer. The spectators let out their breath simultaneously. Lorcan grins at Cartan triumphally.

“One thousand!” Cartan shouts. A shocked silence, then enthusiastic applause.

Lorcan rubs his nose and Cartan sneers arrogantly as no one else raises his bid.

Lorcan turns on his heels quickly, and stumbling twice over stones that hadn't been there before, rushes into the tack room. He shuts the door behind him and collapsing on a bale of straw, thrusts his fist into the air. It was a small victory but a gratifying one. Donald enters, followed by Tormey and Hamish.

"By me God, I nearly wet my truis there!" Donald exclaims. Tormey laughs and slaps Lorcan on his shoulders.

"Well done," he says to Hamish. "You did us proud."

"Aye, that was magnificent lad," Donald says and Lorcan nods in agreement.

"What's he doing now?" he asks.

There is no need to call him by name, everyone knows who he's talking about.

"Paying the bailiff, emptying his purse," Tormey grins wickedly. "By God, I hope that shoe holds till he's back in Ireland. Mind you, I'd love to see his face when it falls off and he sees what's below it."

"Or rather the horn that's not below it," Lorcan grins wickedly. "Well come on, no time for dithering, we've got a horse to buy."

"Oh yes, Thunderbolt, I nearly forgot!" Donald says.

Outside, the spectators are in a festive mood. When Cartan leaves with Lockwood to return to the port, a huge cheer goes up. The sale of Thunderbolt, a handsome dappled grey stallion with an unusual black mane and tail, is almost an anti-climax in comparison. Donald gets him for a fair five hundred and twenty gold pieces.

The fair is over, and everyone goes to the tavern to celebrate. Laird Douglas pays for food and drink; the evening is long. Just one person is missing, Fergus.

***

Fergus walks along the track, through moors full of blossoming heather, towards the summit of Goat Fell. He reaches the mountain top and gazes over the Firth of Clyde, abundant with numerous islets. It seems as if he is on top of the world and he feels very small and insignificant in comparison. It is a clear day and turning around, Fergus can see as far as the north-eastern coast of Ireland, his home, Dalriadan territory. His heart lurches. He remembers the letters in his pocket and sits down on the heather, leaning his back against a boulder just below the craggy peak. He stretches his legs out comfortably, and opens the first.

Loarn writes happily of his experiences at Dunstaffnage, the waterside castle of the Laird of the Mac Dougall clan. Flora and her husband have no children of their own, and treat Loarn as if he were their son. He enthuses about the warriors who tone his fighting skills, and says that he will soon be allowed to accompany them to battle. Not to fight, but to observe and gain experience. The Mac Dougall clan battle constantly against the Picts in the east. Sometimes they assist the Britons to beat back the Saxons. His letter finishes with an invitation from the Laird, for Fergus to visit or stay with them, whenever he likes.

The second letter is from Angus. He tells Fergus that Grainne has given birth to a healthy girl, whom they call Megan. He misses Fergus and Loarn but is kept busy with his studies, and Fionn often takes him and Slevin out hunting. Fionn has a new falcon that he is training. He attaches raw meat to a fringed leather tassel, which looks like a bird to the falcon. He has shown Angus how to swing the lure on a string in a backward motion at his side, to attract the falcon out of a tree. Then when the bird approaches, he whips it around at the last minute out of the way. He repeats this procedure several times, to give the falcon exercise, with a reward attached, when it successfully grabs the lure.

Fergus is disappointed not to have received a letter from his parents. *Have they forgotten me already?* he wonders. The warm sun makes him drowsy, and he falls asleep. He awakes to something tickling his nose. He brushes it away, eyes still closed, and is annoyed when the tickling continues. He slaps his hand on his face, hoping to nab the insect. A startled 'yelp' makes him sit up quickly, his pulse racing.

"Rhianna! What are you doing here?" He looks at her, horrified. She has fallen back on her buttocks, a stalk of cocksfoot in one hand. She pouts.

"Hello to you too, just swallowed a wasp, have you?"

"Er no, sorry, I'm just surprised, I didn't expect to see anyone up here."

"Well, I didn't either, but I didn't bite your head off!"

"No, you just woke me out of my sleep. Look, I already apologised, just leave me."

"Why aren't you at the horse fair?" Rhianna persists.

"Why aren't you with your husband-to-be?" Fergus retorts.

Rhianna bursts into tears. Her whole body shakes uncontrollably and Fergus feels guilty.

"I'm sorry, I shouldn't have said that, it must be awful for you."

"*Awful*? Have you *any* idea at all? He is the most obnoxious, stinking, revolting individual, I've ever set my eyes on! And I must wed him and let him touch me. *Naked*!" Rhianna bursts out crying again.

Fergus stays silent. *What can I possibly say?* he wonders. He tries to think of something comforting.

"He's very old, maybe he'll die soon," he says.

Rhianna turns on her stomach and cries even louder.

"Well at least you got Starlight," Fergus tries again.

Rhianna whips around onto her back and sits upright. She points a finger at him accusingly. "Would you marry a fat, old, wrinkly woman just for a *horse*?"

Fergus pretends to consider the matter, "Well it depends on the horse—I might for Thunderbolt!"

Rhianna picks up a clod of earth and throws it at him forcefully. He ducks out of the way and grins.

"No of course I wouldn't. But then I'm not a princess and don't have to. Can't your mother help you?"

"She died giving birth to my little brother."

"Oh, I'm sorry, I didn't know. Your brother then?"

"Oh, you don't understand anything! My mother died fourteen years ago; my brother didn't survive the birth either. Anyway, my father doesn't *want* to force me to marry Ceredig, but he has no choice."

"Yes, I heard Ceredig threatening him. Is Ceredig very powerful? Can't your father find allies to help him protect his lands?"

"Ceredig is king over the whole of Strathclyde. He has thousands of soldiers. He attacked this island two years ago and the Epidii helped my father. But they didn't stand a chance against Ceredig's army and suffered huge losses. The elders told my father to give Ceredig what he wanted, and so I was promised to him."

"Why does Ceredig want to marry *you*?"

"What do you mean *me*?" Rhianna asks indignantly. "What's wrong with *me*?"

Fergus kicks himself inwardly. "I mean—" He stutters, embarrassed. "If Ceredig is so powerful, there must be plenty of er—older women willing to marry him."

"Yes, you are right and he's already been married four times but he has no heir. My maid, Beth, has a cousin in his household, who told her that Ceredig is desperate for an heir."

"You could always run away. After all, you're good at disguising yourself. Why did you do that anyway? As Douglas' daughter you can always enter the stables."

Rhianna sighs deeply. "You really don't understand at all. My father is terribly strict. He may not want to force me to marry Ceredig, but he doesn't want me wandering about meeting other men either. He is happiest when I'm locked up in the castle. When he is away on business or hunting, Beth sometimes takes pity on me and helps me to get out, past the other servants. The disguise is so that no one recognises me and tells my father that they have seen me."

"You're not disguised today," Fergus says, his eyes wandering over her long neck and pale throat.

She has a dark brown mole just above her collarbone and her décolleté reveals interesting round shapes. They look soft. He gazes into her blue eyes.

"Today is my last day of freedom," Rhianna declares dramatically, snapping him out of his reverie. "My father is with Ceredig at the fair and when they return, I have persuaded Beth to tell them that I have already gone to bed with a headache. But Beth says that this is the last time that she'll help me." Rhianna pouts and continues, "It is too dangerous for her if we're found out. I didn't think I'd meet anyone up here."

"I'm hiding from someone too," Fergus confides. "My half-brother wants to kill me, and he suddenly turned up at the fair, unexpectedly."

"Oh, what did you do that he hates you that much?"

"Nothing! He's evil and jealous somehow. He wants to become king and thinks I'll be chosen instead. So he schemes to get rid of me."

"Why should a stable boy become king?"

"My—our father is King of the Dalriada."

"So we are both oppressed. Life isn't fair."

"No, but when I'm older, I shall fight him and revenge my family. What about you? You didn't answer my question about running away."

"No one will help me off this island and there's nowhere I can go anyway."

The sun has reached its zenith and starts to descend.

"The horse fair will be over soon, time to return," Fergus says.

Rhianna leans back on her elbows and stretches her face towards the sun. "I intend staying here all night," she says. "I'm determined to savour every last minute of my freedom."

"All night, alone? Isn't that dangerous? Anyone might come and—and—"

"What? Mishandle me? They wouldn't dare! And anyway, nobody could be worse than Ceredig!"

Fergus doesn't want Rhianna to start crying again. He sighs. "I'll stay with you," he says. "Nobody at the stables will worry about me." He sprawls down on the heather and closes his eyes, pretending to sleep.

The sun disappears behind the horizon, leaving the sky streaked with grey, lavender and azure.

Rhianna stirs from her position and shivers. "It's cold now the sun's gone down," she grumbles.

Fergus stands up and goes to lie down next to her.

"Turn your back to me and I'll warm you," he offers. Rhianna turns on her side, with her back to Fergus. She squiggles backwards and nestles in close to him.

He wraps his arms around her. "Is that better?" he asks.

"Mmmn yes, thank you," she says, snuggling in tighter to him. Her proximity sends shivers throughout his body. Her neck feels soft and smells good, he wants to cover it with kisses but admonishes himself. She is betrothed.

Rhianna feels snug in Fergus' arms. He is warm and she feels protected. She would like to take his hands in hers and kiss them, *but he would probably snatch them away horrified*, she thinks. She bends into an embryo position to get even closer into his embrace.

Fergus feels her backside pushing against his crotch, and he gets an erection. His heart beats quickly and he wiggles backwards to create space between them. They stay frozen in position, scarcely breathing, neither one of them daring to move, both of their bodies taut with tension. Neither one of them speaks.

Dusk is slow in the northern hemisphere. When the moon begins to rise and the first stars start to glow, Rhianna breaks the silence. "Do you know the names of the stars?" she asks.

"A few," Fergus answers, pulling an arm out from her embrace, and pointing to a bright star in the inky sky. "That one is Andromeda and look, there is Cassiopeia!" He takes her hand in his and points it to the sky. "You can recognise her easily because of the 'W' shape." He traces a 'W' with her finger in the air, following the five bright stars of the constellation.

Rhianna is electrified by his touch. She doesn't really listen to his answer. She turns around to face him and opens her lips slightly. Fergus is overcome with desire and kisses her. Encouraged by her breathless response, he pushes his tongue into her mouth. They kiss, hungry for each other. Suddenly, feeling guilty, Fergus stops. He pulls himself away roughly and stands up.

"I'm sorry," he says. "I wasn't thinking, it's better we go now."

Rhianna wonders what she has done wrong. "But it's still dark," she protests.

"The moon and the stars will light our way. Come on now, before someone discovers us." He stretches his hand out to pull her up and they walk back towards the castle in silence.

They are nearly there when Rhianna pulls away from him without a tone, and runs towards the scullery door. Fergus waits until she enters, then a little longer. All is silent, not a sound can be heard. He takes a deep sigh, then returns to the stables.

***

The next day, Lorcan and Donald are glad to find Fergus back in the stables unscathed.

"You saw Cartan on time then, thank God for that," Donald declares.

"Yes, sorry for vanishing so suddenly, but I knew you'd understand as soon as you saw him."

"Yes. Now we've got a surprise for you. We've already spoken to Tormey and today you don't have to work. I want you to accompany me and Lorcan to the port, we are expecting visitors from Dunseverick."

"Dunseverick! Are my parents coming?"

"Yes, they cannot wait to see you! And on the way Lorcan can tell you what he did with Cartan yesterday."

The trio set off with a spring in their steps down towards the port. Lorcan grossly exaggerates his story, and Fergus is laughing happily when a horse pulling a carriage, canters much too speedily past them, nearly knocking them over. Fergus reacts as quickly as the crack of a branch, pushing Lorcan out of the way and simultaneously jumping off the road himself. Rolling out of the ditch, he looks for Donald. He is sitting on the road rubbing his hip and cursing.

"Did you see who that was?" Donald asks Fergus and Lorcan, who are still sitting fazed on their backsides. "Laird Ceredig!" he answers himself without awaiting their answer. "With that young bride of his. Who on earth does he think he is? I'll give him my mind when I see him!"

"Are you all right?" Fergus asks. He stands up and goes to help Donald to his feet.

"Aye, just about. He gave my hip a nasty knock though, and he didn't even stop to make sure we were unharmed!" Donald still shakes a little from shock.

Lorcan rises and brushes the dirt from his woollen ionar, "What a pea brained halfwit!" he exclaims vexed. "He'll injure the horse at that speed, and kill his bride before they're wed too!"

Fergus frowns thinking of Rhianna. "Let's get on," he says. "Hopefully we won't come across their dead bodies on the way, I don't want them to spoil our reunion."

They enter the port. The ship from Dalriada has not yet arrived, so they sit down outside the tavern, and drink a jug of ale. They calm down, and as soon as they see the ship entering the harbour, Fergus jumps up excitedly and goes to help them dock safely. Mista hugs him fiercely and then holds him at arm's length.

"Just look at you!" she says. "You're already taller than your father and just look at your shoulders!"

"Mother, please—" Fergus interrupts her.

Erc slaps his son's shoulder, hesitates, and then hugs him too.

"Forgive us son," he says. "We've missed you so much."

Erc and Mista greet Lorcan and Donald and thank them profusely.

"We cannot thank you enough," Erc says. "Anything, absolutely anything we can do for you, please let us know, anytime."

"We're family," Donald states matter-of-factly. "Mhairi and I are here for you, for all of you."

"What?" Lorcan asks as he sees them all looking at him, "I'm family too, am I not?"

Erc smiles at him gratefully and Fergus grins. "I always wondered where I got my elegant gait from," he says, nudging Lorcan's elbow.

Lorcan trips over his feet immediately, and just manages to retain his standing position. They all laugh and begin to walk back towards Brodick castle.

On the way, Erc takes Fergus aside. "Son, under normal circumstances you would go to Tara next spring in service of High King Laeghaire. But you cannot possibly go there now, Cartan is his second in command."

"But Father I've *got* to become a warrior. I'm determined to revenge our family against Cartan. Is there no one else whom I can serve?"

"Yes, yes wait, let me continue! But first let me warn you. *I* shall deal with Cartan; it is *my* prerogative. I shall find the right moment; of that I am certain. Now then, I've spoken to Laird Mac Dougall. In March you shall join Loarn at Dunstaffnage, Mac Dougall will introduce you both to the art of battle. You both have much to learn yet, bravery alone is not enough. But at least you'll be together again."

"Oh Father, thank you, thank you so much!"

"Wait, I have another surprise for you. Donald bought Thunderbolt on my behalf—for you!"

"What? Oh!" Fergus hugs his father and looks him steadily in the eye. "Thank you, this means a lot to me, truly. Now I must tell the others! Does Loarn know that I'm coming?"

"Not yet. I'm afraid we cannot stay here long, Fergus. Tomorrow we shall depart with Donald to Finlaggan, to see Angus and Fionn. Then we shall continue our journey to Dunstaffnage to visit Loarn and Mac Dougall."

As they reach the stud farm, they see Laird Douglas talking to Tormey. They greet each other and Donald introduces Erc and Mista.

"King of the Dalriada? We have a few of your fellow countrymen here on Aran. Good, honest, hard-working folk. I'm pleased to meet you. You must all be my guests at Brodick tonight, King Ceredig and my daughter will also be present."

They accept the invitation and then follow Fergus into the stables to appraise Thunderbolt.

Out of Douglas' earshot Mista complains, "Oh why did that have to happen. I would much prefer to spend the little time we have, here with our son!"

"I couldn't really refuse a ghrá, it would've been rude. And anyway, he doesn't *know* that Fergus is our son. But I could go with Donald and say you're unwell, if you like," Erc offers.

"Mother, may I speak to you first?" Fergus asks. "Privately."

"Oh, yes, of course!" Mista exits the stables with Fergus, and they walk towards some fields, where black cattle are lying down in the shade of a large sycamore tree.

"It's about tonight," Fergus begins. "You see, I have got to know Rhianna, the Laird's daughter—a little. She confided to me that she's scared of Ceredig. And well, I know he's old and not very um—attractive, but could you go tonight and maybe— well see what you think, if you think there's *more* to the matter. Whether it's possible, that he could actually *harm* her."

"Ah," Mista answers understanding. "Well, if her father has promised her in marriage to the king, I cannot do anything about that. You do realise that, don't you?" she asks kindly.

"Yes, I know the marriage cannot be stopped. But well, you see, his first four wives all died, quite young."

"Well, that does happen quite often, for example at childbirth. It's a tragedy, but not all together unusual. But four? Agreed! I shall go tonight and try to get an impression of the man. I can't promise anything, mind you."

"No, of course not, Mother. I hope you find him agreeable; it would comfort me."

***

The guests sit around a large wooden table, in front of a roaring fire. They drink wine and the table is full of platters heaped with game, vegetables, and fruit. Rhianna sits next to Ceredig, opposite Mista and Erc. She eats nothing but swallows her glass of wine quickly and refills it. As she lifts her glass to drink again, Ceredig puts his hand on hers, and returns it to the table.

"Steady my dear, eat a little first."

"I'm not hungry!" Rhianna speaks quietly but her eyes flash, reflecting in the flames like hot angry fireballs.

Donald addresses Ceredig, "I believe you passed us on your way to the village this morning."

"Ah, that was you, I apologise. I thought my betrothed—" Ceredig places an arm around Rhianna's shoulders and Mista sees her shudder and pull away. "Could drive a carriage, but she lost control and the horse panicked."

"That's not true!" Rhianna protests. "I was managing perfectly well until you—until you tried to kiss me!"

Ceredig chuckles. "But my dear, we are to be married a week tomorrow!"

"Unless one of us *dies* first!" Rhianna retorts dramatically. "Father, tell him I refuse to be touched before the ceremony!"

Ceredig bursts out laughing heartily. Mista cannot fail to notice that bits of food stick between his teeth.

"I like a woman with spirit!" Ceredig declares, planting a loud kiss on Rhianna's cheek.

A tiny piece of kale from his mouth remains sticking to her chin. Rhianna jumps up and brushes it angrily from her face. Ceredig is quick to rise too. He pushes her forcefully down onto her seat again.

"My dear, you must learn some manners. No matter, when we arrive at my stronghold, Alt Clut, you will learn, I'll see to that."

"Rhianna," Mista interrupts the embarrassed silence. "Do you have friends or relations in Alt Clut?"

"No, nobody." Rhianna sulks.

"Forgive me for interfering, Laird Douglas, but your daughter is still very young, and maybe—a little—immature. Strathclyde is far distant. Do you think that maybe she would feel happier and—settle down in Alt Clut more easily, if she were to take someone she trusts with her? A sister maybe, or a maid?"

"Oh yes, Father, may Beth come with me? Please." Rhianna's eyes brighten with hope.

"Well, it sounds like a reasonable idea, but it is not my decision to make. You must ask King Ceredig if he is willing, and Beth, if she would leave her family."

Rhianna plucks up all her courage and turns towards Ceredig. "My Lord, may I ask Beth if she will accompany us?" she asks demurely.

Ceredig hesitates, wondering how he can refuse before the guests.

"I promise I'll do my best to—to please you," Rhianna adds.

Ceredig sees no way out. "Very well then, you may ask her."

Walking back to Tormey's croft, Erc says, "What an unpleasant man! I understand the necessity of arranged marriages but that poor girl, he could be her grandfather!"

"There's talk in the village of coercion," Donald says. "I don't think Douglas is happy about it, but he has no choice, apparently."

Mista is quiet. "Promise me our sons may marry whom they wish," she says.

Chapter twelve
455 – 456 A.D. Alt Clut and Argyll

A fire blazes in the hearth in her chamber in Alt Clut, Ceredig's royal castle in Strathclyde. But in spite of the material warmth coming from the burning logs, Rhianna stands in front of the matrimonial bed in her night clothes and shivers. Beth has given her mulled wine to drink.

"It will help," she had said, before leaving the chamber.

Ceredig enters, gazes wordlessly at Rhianna's trembling figure, strides over to her and slaps her violently across her face. She screams out in shock and pain and stumbles backwards onto the floor. Ceredig leaps upon her, twists her round swiftly onto her stomach, and pushing her nightdress up, penetrates her from behind. Rhianna screams and he hits her again. He holds her head down forcefully with one hand and rams himself back and forth until Rhianna feels a sticky substance trickling down her thighs. Ceredig stands up and without a word, leaves the room.

Rhianna stays on the floor, tears of humiliation spill down her cheeks. She sobs. She hadn't known what to expect, but certainly not what she had just experienced. Beth enters the room quietly and kneels down next to her.

"Come now," she says helping Rhianna to stand up. She brings her to a chair next to the fire and wraps a rug around her shoulders. "It's over now. Stay here while I fetch some warm water."

"I feel dirty!" Rhianna cries out, "Defiled! Did you know?"

"No! It's—it's not usually like that!" Beth wipes Rhianna's face with a damp cloth and holds a glass of wine to her lips. "My mother said it's something nice."

"I want a bath!" Rhianna shouts hysterically.

"But Miss! It's night, the servants are all sleeping!"

"I don't care! Wake them up and tell them to bring the tub up here in my room. I'm the Mistress of this household now, they must obey me!

And I need buckets full of hot water and soap. I think I will never fell clean again."

Beth goes downstairs to the kitchen and relights the fire. She fills a cauldron with water and hangs it over the hearth. She is not sure what to do next. She knows she can't wake the household on her first day here, nor can she enter the men's quarters to look for her cousin and ask for help. She waits for the water to heat and pours it into a large jug. She tries to carry it upstairs quietly, but the wooden stairs creak with every step and echo across the cold stone walls. She is frightened and shivers. She is upset and shocked. Bad enough that Ceredig is old and vulgar, but not in her worst imagination had she thought he might abuse her mistress so viciously. She enters Rhianna's room on tiptoes and is relieved to find her slumbering in front of the fire. Placing the jug on the table, Beth adds another log to the embers and then curls up on the floor beside her mistress.

***

When the first snowdrops push their heads through the frosty soil announcing the end of winter, Fergus is happy and excited. Finally, the time is approaching to leave Brodick. He had enjoyed his year here. He was grateful for the months spent with the horses and the new friendships that had been sealed; he had learnt much. But from the moment his father had told him that he was to join Loarn at Dunstaffnage, he had been filled with restlessness.

The departure of Rhianna after the wedding hadn't helped. Of course he understood the inevitability of it, and he was indebted to his mother for contriving Beth's company for Rhianna. Yet he couldn't banish her from his thoughts. The notion of Ceredig touching her made him angry and jealous; were he older he would contest him. The state of Laird Douglas was more severe. He was a broken man since Rhianna's leave-taking. He neglected his duties and spent long periods alone, shut away in his castle.

Lorcan and Fergus pack the few belongings they have in a saddlebag, and sling it over Thunderbolt's back. Tormey and Hamish are present to wish them luck, and threaten them with all kinds of evil if they don't visit again soon.

"And bring Mahon with you next time!" Tormey shouts after them as they are already heading towards the port.

Once again, they sail to Campbeltown and from there to Islay. The coastal areas are full of boats, peaceful traders, and fishermen. They stop often and Fergus explores each settlement full of interest. Advancing towards Islay he realises his heart is thumping, and he curbs himself lest he behave anything less than like an adult. But when they dock and he sees Angus securing the line to the dock cleat, nothing can stop him. He jumps from board and sweeps his brother up in an embrace, before putting him down again and looking at him at arm's length. Just in time he stops himself from commenting upon how he'd grown. *I don't want to sound like mother,* he thinks.

Mahon has accompanied Angus. The reunion with Lorcan, his twin, is equally exuberant, despite them being thirty-years-older than the boys. Once the ship is secure, Lorcan and Fergus place a wooden ramp from the quay across to the boat and Fergus leads Thunderbolt proudly ashore. A small gaggle of town folk stop their work to shoot admiring glances towards the destrier, as Fergus and Angus lead him to the blacksmith.

"Don't you want to ride him to Ballygrant?" Angus asks.

Fergus strokes Thunderbolt's neck lovingly. "No," he says. "He was as sick as a beached whale on the boat, he needs a day or two to recover, poor boy."

"Well let's row up the river then, it's quicker anyway."

"That's fine with me. Come on then, let's find Lorcan and Mahon, and you can tell me all your news on the way."

***

Fergus spends a whole week on Islay. Angus shows him the shipbuilder's yard in Port Askaig, where he will soon be starting an apprenticeship.

"It's the biggest and the best shipyard on Islay," Angus tells him proudly. "Master Mac Arthur has so many commissions that he can afford to build solely ships! Most joiners have to take on other work too. They mend roofs or build houses, just to make ends meet. But Mac

Arthur here," he says, making a sweeping movement with his arm to embrace the whole shipyard and bay. "Is so well known that he gets orders from all over Brittania."

"Have you shown him your designs?"

"Yes. I didn't really think I should, but Brother Aedan encouraged me to. I showed him a model of a longship I constructed. He was very friendly and seemed quite interested."

"That sounds good!"

"Yes, I can't wait to start working here. I've so much to learn yet about the different types of wood, the art of planking and the types of tar he uses."

"You've got plenty of time to do just that. Don't forget, the first real ship you build is for me!"

"For the three of us," Angus answers. "Then we shall roam the seas and make our fortune."

***

Once again Fergus boards a ship with Lorcan and Thunderbolt. Apart from themselves, there is just the owner of the boat on board, the captain, a man called Logan. He is about fifty-years-old and looks unkempt, as if he doesn't give a damn about his appearance or what other people might think. He has a full beard speckled with dandruff and a ruddy complexion. His belly hangs in a loose flap over his belt, and every few minutes he gulps some strong-smelling liquor down his throat from a dirty leather pitcher.

"Those red cheeks don't come alone from a life at sea," Lorcan whispers to Fergus. "Better stay alert lest he steer us on the rocks."

They set sail from Port Askaig along a narrow straight between Islay and the Isle of Jura. Once they hit the open sea the captain heads for Colonsay, a small island directly in front of them.

"I'm slopping in port fer a couple o' hours," the captain slurs. He burps loudly and continues, "I've some goods to deliver, and t'others t' pick up. No worry though, it's just a couple of hours from here to Dunstaffnage. We'll arrive well before t' sun goes down."

Wanting to dock, Captain Logan misjudges the proximity of the harbour wall and knocks the boat forcefully against it.

"Bit fresh to-to-day," he stammers, as his ship rams the dock again. Fergus jumps on land, manages to catch the badly-thrown line by a whisker and secures it hastily. He throws a worried glance to Lorcan who has fallen against Thunderbolt. The sea is as calm as a seal basking in the sun, and once the boat is fast, Lorcan entangles himself from Thunderbolt and stands upright again. Logan starts to unload kegs of whisky from Finlaggan onto the dock. Within seconds his face takes on the colour of an overripe plum and sweat cascades freely down his face.

"Where do you want the kegs taking?" Fergus asks. "Let me help you."

"To 'The Cockerel's Roost', it's over there," Logan says, pointing to a tavern across the cobbled market place. "The landlord's expecting me." Fergus shoulders a keg and brings it to the tavern. He delivers the other kegs quickly, whilst Logan unloads crates of venison from Glengedale. When Fergus returns, Logan is out of breath, panting.

"Will you bring him these crates too?"

Fergus is happy to do anything that hastens their departure, and accelerates their safe arrival in Dunstaffnage. Logan accompanies him to the landlord and pockets a fair amount of silver. They return to the harbour and Logan buys twenty lobsters and two crates of oysters.

"For your uncle," he tells Fergus. "He ordered them when he knew you were coming."

"My uncle?"

"The Laird of Dunstaffnage!"

"Oh, yes, of course."

"I just need to pick up twenty pots of honey from Mistress Peigi. She lives along the lane down yonder, then we can leave."

"Right, I'll join you then, shall I?"

Fergus strides off towards Mistress Peigi's dwelling without awaiting an answer. It is obvious that Logan has trouble enough moving himself, let alone carrying anything.

They set sail again within the hour. Half an hour out to sea, Logan suddenly freezes in his movements and grasps his left arm. He cries out and plummets head down onto deck. He is motionless.

"Grab the rudder!" Lorcan shouts to Fergus. He goes to Logan and turns him over. He puts his ear to Logan's chest. "I think he's gone!" he says. "His heart maybe—"

"What shall we do?" Fergus asks.

"Sail on to Dunstaffnage, I suppose. The Laird's bailiff will deal with him."

They continue to sail in a north-easterly direction past Scarba, Mull and the Black Isles until they reach Kerrera. Passing this last milestone, they pull down the two rectangular sails and row east towards Dunstaffnage. The stronghold is clearly visible on a promontory above the entrance to Loch Etive. It is surrounded on three sides by water, guarding access to Loch Etive and the Pass of Brander beyond. Ahead of them, on land, each side of the narrow sea passageway, are two round towers. The walls are of coursed rubble, with sandstone dressings, and stand forty feet high. Arrow slits are the only openings. Just before the towers, starboard, is a harbour surrounded by massive stone walls. Unchallenged, they row into the harbour and secure their boat.

Fergus is knotting the last line as Loarn jogtrots up to them.

"At last, Fergus, I've been waiting hours for you!" Loarn is about to embrace his brother as he notices Fergus' sombre expression. "What? Aren't you happy to see me?"

Fergus breaks out of his cheerless trance guiltily. "Loarn! Of course! I'm sorry, but look what we've brought with us! The captain just dropped dead, from one second to the next."

Loarn looks inside the boat. "It's Logan! He's often here. He trades in these parts. He drinks a lot, too much. Wait! I'll fetch the guards and Mac Dougall's bailiff."

Loarn runs off and soon returns with guards, the bailiff and Laird Mac Dougall in his wake. The bailiff glances at the corpse and recognises his identity.

"Death by natural causes, no foul play." He determines. "Remove the body!" he orders the guards.

"What will happen to him?" Fergus asks of no one in particular.

"He will be buried at sea. The next outgoing boat will take his body with them," the bailiff answers. "My Laird, I presume the goods were meant for you. You can take them, no point in wasting good food. The ship and any valuables will be confiscated for the time being, until we know whether he had any family or not."

Fergus is a little surprised but also impressed by the bailiff's unsentimental, pragmatic, approach.

"Are you often confronted by dead captains aboard their ships?" he asks the bailiff.

"No, not so often." The bailiff smiles. "But we all know, Logan, it was just a matter of time. What's your name?"

"Fergus, sir."

"Well, Fergus, if you seek me out three months from now, I expect I can hand Logan's ship and silver over to you and your companion. He never spoke of any family; I doubt he has any."

***

Ceredig enters Rhianna's chamber night after night. Her body is covered in deep purple bruises. She becomes a recluse, refusing to leave her room, ashamed of being seen and recognised for what she was: a useless, ugly being; capable of nothing. She refuses to eat, trembles violently when approached, and barely speaks.

"Mistress, you must keep up your strength," Beth pleads with Rhianna, holding a spoon of soup to her lips. "Try it at least, the cook made it especially for you."

Rhianna presses her lips together and turns her head sideways. Beth gives up trying to feed her, and putting the bowl of soup down, picks up a pot of rose-scented cream.

"Then let me at least soothe your skin with this cream."

Rhianna folds her arms together and turns her body around on the chair away from Beth. Beth sighs and leaves the room quietly. Rhianna moves to her bed and curls up on her side. Silent tears pour from her eyes and cover her pillow until it is soddened.

Beth sits at the kitchen table, her head in her arms and weeps.

"Is there nothing we can do?" she asks the cook. "Was it the same with all his wives?"

"Aye. He won't leave her alone until she's with child."

"No sign of that yet. I fear she will die first."

"Poor wee lass." The cook bends in closer to Beth and whispers as if afraid the walls have ears, "Meet me in the woods behind the castle after breakfast, I'll find you."

A maid enters the kitchen, the cook turns away from Beth and busies herself chopping vegetables. "The king is expecting guests tonight," the maid says. "He wants venison."

"Right, venison it is. How many are coming?"

"He says ten."

***

Beth ties her cloak securely round her neck, picks up a basket and exits the fortress. Immediately, a gale force wind engulfs her, ripping at her garments with an icy grip. Beneath her the sea froths and waves crash against the rocks shooting spray across her path. She turns to walk around to the back of the stronghold and starts climbing the steps, hewn out of the rock, which lead between the twin peaks the fort is built below. They rise, almost vertically, each side of her, soaring into the sky. She hurries towards the narrow gateway, guarded by two bored-looking soldiers. Seeing her approach, the one nudges the other and grins. He stands astride the path, legs wide apart, a spear in one hand and blocks her passage.

"What's your business, fair maid?" he asks. He is glad of some distraction and finds it amusing to intimidate her.

"Get out of the way, you stupid gowl! The mistress wants some mushrooms, and I wouldn't like to be in your boots, if she tells the master you hindered me."

The soldier steps quickly aside, scowling. "All right, no need to get nasty. Got hair on yer teeth, 'ave you?"

"Something you'll never find out," she retorts, pushing past him. She presses on, breathing more freely now that she had got past the gatehouse and more or less into freedom. She feels like a prisoner in the castle, only able to come and go with a valid reason. *Those soldiers are a right pain in the neck*, she thinks, not for the first time. *One worse than the other, more bored than was good for them.* Not many guests came and went, regardless of Ceredig's status as king of the Brythonic

Kingdom of Strathclyde. She walks quickly towards the forest, glad to enter the leafy shelter from wind and rain. She starts to search for and pick mushrooms, to validate her absence. Briefly she wonders if she should mix some poisonous fungi amid the cep, chicken of the woods and chanterelles she finds, but dismisses the thought immediately. The cook would notice and anyway, the king didn't eat alone.

After half an hour, she hears a whistle and looking up, sees the cook on the path below her. She scrambles down through the trees, eager to find out what the cook has to tell her.

"Right," the cook greets her. "Let's get this straight right from the start, I haven't met you here and I've told you nothing."

"Don't worry, I'm discreet," Beth tells her, intrigued.

"Aye an' I'm sorry for your mistress but it's dangerous in the castle, don't trust anyone! There's a woman, lives here in the forest. She's knowledgeable 'bout all women's troubles. I don't say she can help, but you can ask."

"Thank you. Where can I find her? And what's her name?"

"You must carry along this path for half a mile, then take a right turn, go another two hundred yards and then a left turn. You'll see a wooden house of sorts, it's hers. She has a tame fox; it'll growl when it sees you. Stay still an' she'll come out. Her name is Wulfhild but everyone calls her 'the Wolf'."

"The Wolf?"

"Aye, you'll see why. I'm off then, good luck!"

"Thank you then and goodbye."

Beth walks on as told and finds a wooden shack leaning against a beech tree, half-hidden by bushes and more trees. A fox lies across the entrance. As Beth approaches, it stands up and growls in a deep, guttural gurgle. It sounds menacing and Beth is glad that she has been pre-warned. She stands still, not budging an inch. Eventually, a small woman appears from indoors. Her face is covered with dark hair; she has more facial hair than a man. When Beth glances down, she sees that the back of the woman's hands are almost furry. The Wolf is also inspecting Beth.

"There are no signs yet," she says. "I may be able to help you."

"What? Oh no!" Beth answers realising. "I've come for my mistress."

"They all say that."

"No, no. You don't understand, it's the other way round. My mistress *wants* a baby!" When The Wolf remains silent, Beth adds, "Her name is Rhianna, she is wife to Ceredig, the king."

"It's true then, he's taken another. I'm afraid I can't help you, the problem lies with him, not with your mistress."

Beth wonders how she can know this, but looking at her, realises she does. She sits down defeated on the forest floor.

"I fear for her life!" She tells The Wolf. He beats her violently. She refuses to eat, won't leave her room, and barely speaks. Her eyes have lost their lustre. He won't leave her alone until she's with child."

The Wolf remains silent, considering what Beth has told her. She disappears into her hut and returns minutes later, her hands full.

"Give your mistress five drops, three times daily," she says, giving Beth a flacon of tonic. "It will decrease her monthly bleeding. Tell her to rub this jelly into her vagina, the act will hurt less. This paste is for her bruises. Put this borage into hot water with honey. Make her drink it. It will help her appetite and drive away her sorrow."

Beth looks at the remedies in front of her. "You mean she should *pretend* that she's with child?"

"Yes."

"But what when he finds out?"

"For the present it is important that your mistress becomes well again. Return to me in three months."

It wasn't the solution she'd been hoping for, but as Beth starts walking back to Alt Clut, the medicines hidden in her basket under the mushrooms, she begins to see the possibilities. A miscarriage maybe or better still, Ceredig's death in battle. *All in all, it's not been a waste of time,* she thinks.

Back at the castle she goes straight to Ceredig's personal guard and says she wishes to speak to the king. She is ushered into a large room where he sits at a table, poring over a map. Beth curtsies.

"Yes?" he asks.

"My Lord, it is very early yet, and I am not sure, but my mistress is unwell. She has morning sickness and spells of dizziness. I think she may be with child!"

"What? But that is good news, yes!" Ceredig thrusts his fist in the air. "And what does she say, will it be a boy?"

"My Lord! As yet we are not sure that she is with child. But her monthly bloods are late. I would not have said anything, but due to her—condition, forgive me, Lord, but maybe it would be prudent not to visit her tonight." Beth blushes.

"Yes, of course. Tell my wife not to expect me for a while. Let me know of any change." With a wave of the hand, Beth is dismissed.

Beth is jubilant. It had been easier than she had thought, and she hadn't exactly lied. She goes to the kitchen and boils water for the special herbs. She also makes porridge and adds honey and cream skimmed from the top of the milk jug. She enters Rhianna's chamber and sees her sitting in her chair next to the fire. She puts the food and drink on a side table next to her. Rhianna turns her head away. Beth kneels down by Rhianna's feet and takes her bony hands in hers.

"Mistress, listen! The master won't bother you tonight."

Rhianna looks up with a flicker of interest.

"Nor any day soon," Beth adds.

"How?"

"That's a long story, including the adventure I had with a 'wolf' this afternoon. Now drink and eat and I will tell you."

Rhianna picks up her beaker and begins to drink. When she stops drinking, Beth refuses to continue her story. Finally, the tale is finished, the porridge also. Rhianna begins to come alive.

"Tell the maids to bring water for my bath!" she tells Beth.

Beth helps her into the bathtub. Rhianna winces with pain as she sits down in the warm water. Beth adds some rose oil and helps to wash her. Rhianna's shoulders, collar bone, hips and knee joints stick out, tautening her skin. Beth is distressed *she's almost skeletal,* she thinks. Rhianna allows Beth to rub The Wolf's paste onto her bruises.

Rather than retiring to bed, she asks, "Are you sure he won't come?"

"Positive, Miss."

"Then ask the cook to prepare some food for me. I must regain strength and then escape."

The jelly is not necessary, neither the tonic, Rhianna's monthly bleeds had stopped since her drastic weight loss. Beth puts them aside for later. Hopefully Rhianna would gain weight soon.

***

Fergus and Loarn are patrolling the parapet walk on top of the walls surrounding Dunstaffnage. The fortress is an irregular quadrangular structure, the walls are ten feet thick and provide a strong defence to the highly strategic location. Despite the splendid views they are both gloomy and bored sick.

"I thought being a warrior would involve more action," Fergus complains.

"I suspect that Laird Mac Dougall wants to keep us safe. It's all very well practising sword fighting with the warriors but I'm getting fed up too. We should speak to him, he's reasonable enough if we bring the right arguments."

While they discuss which arguments might have weight, they see a small army of warriors galloping on horseback towards the castle. Recognising their own men, Fergus and Loarn hastily turn the wheel which releases the chain supporting the drawbridge, the sole entrance into the complex. The warriors pull their horses up to a steady trot and clatter over the heavy, solid oak bridge, under the gateway and into the courtyard.

As the soldiers dismount, Laird Mac Dougall exits the main building and comes to meet them.

"My Laird, another thirty calves have been taken from Griogal's farm near Apainn. We scouted around in a ten-mile circle but didn't find anything, they could be anywhere." Murdoch, the commander, speaks.

"Another thirty! That makes nearly four hundred this summer! The audacity of it! And still no trace of them! And you're sure it's the Picts?"

"Well I doubt that outlaws could sell the cattle anywhere. Not in those numbers."

"And were the calves already brand-marked?"

"Some of them, Sire. A dozen were yet too young."

"Well, they must be somewhere; they can't just have vanished!"

"I expect most of the cattle are already in Fortrui, Sire. But nobody has seen or heard anything. There's plenty of open space, but it's still strange because you can't move that many cattle without somebody spotting something."

"I want every single man to join the hunt. We shall leave immediately and take the dogs, this time they won't get away. Hurry we have no time to lose!"

***

Fergus and Loarn are thrilled to finally take part in some action. Fergus rides Thunderbolt and Loarn rides Mushroom, a roan courser with black mane and tail. Mushroom is not as large or solid as Thunderbolt but is agile and fast. They are riding together with thirty soldiers, Laird Mac Dougall at the head, and two dogs, along the banks of Loch Linnhe. Twenty more groups of thirty soldiers are searching in other areas of the Laird's extensive properties. The dogs race on ahead, sniffing. Occasionally they dart off, following a trail, but then lose it again. They pass several of the Laird's tenanted farms. Each time they stop and Mac Dougall speaks to the farmer. Fergus sees the farmers shaking their heads.

They ride, the steep face of Bidean nam Bian clearly visible to the east. When they reach Loch Leven, they turn east, along Mac Dougall's northern boundary, and past a slate quarry at Ballachulish on the River Laroch. Mac Dougall speaks to the quarry master and then signals to his men to follow him eastwards. Eventually they come to the River Coe which forms the boundary, the end of Laird Mac Dougall's land. They haven't discovered a single sign of the cattle and the Laird and his men are all feeling frustrated.

"If it's really the Picts who have stolen my cattle, this would be the natural way for them to return, on their way back to their own territories," Mac Dougall speaks. "I was certain we'd find *something*."

The army turns south-east following the River Coe to Loch Achtriochtan. From here the Laird wants to turn south towards Loch Etive and back to Dunstaffnage.

"What's beyond the waterfalls, Sire?" Fergus asks.

"Oh, there is a deserted glen, but they won't be there, it can only be approached by a steep, narrow gorge. Much too dangerous for the calves, and it has no exit."

"But once inside, they would be well hidden, Sire. They could fatten the calves and move them again in autumn, when nobody is searching for them."

"No, surely not—" Mac Dougall hesitates. "What do you say, Stuart?" he asks, addressing his second in command.

"Well, that would explain why nobody's seen them, but it would still be very risky. I suppose we could look, Sire."

"Very well then, we should split up. If they are there, we don't want them to send the cattle stampeding towards us. Five men should stay here to guard the entrance, and the rest of us can ride through the woods. Half the men on the right side and the other half left. Any more thoughts?"

"The dogs should stay here, Sire. If they bark, they might give us away, and the soldiers should move stealthily," Stuart says.

"Right. If we see them, we'll sound the horn and descend on them from both sides."

"Do you think a few men should guard the Devil's Staircase, Sire? If we corner them, they may leave the cattle and try to escape themselves that way."

"I could do that with a few men, Laird," Fergus immediately volunteers. "Thunderbolt won't let them past us."

"Oh, very well. It's highly unlikely that they'll be there anyway, let alone try to escape up that steep pass."

The small army of men split up, each with their own task. Fergus and Loarn set off with Laird Mac Dougall, they will separate at the end of the glen. They traverse the gorge and enter a long wide valley. The south side is marked by a succession of soaring, dramatic peaks: Buachaille Etive Beag at the eastern end, followed by the Three Sisters. The river Coe continues east through the glen to the base of Buachaille Etive Beag. The western end terminates with the conical Sgùrr na Cìche, at the point where the glen opens out to Loch Leven. By contrast the north side of the glen is a stark wall of mountain, the Aonach Eagach ridge. The ridge is crossed at the eastern end by the Devil's Staircase. Below, the mountain peaks the lower sides of the glen are lightly wooded. Laird Mac Dougall leads the way through the trees; his men follow in single file. They urge their horses on quietly, keeping a sharp lookout for any signs of cattle below in the fertile valley. They see nor hear anything, and are approaching the end. Mac Dougall pulls his horse to a halt.

"Well, it would've been good, but I'm afraid there's nothing here," he says. As he speaks, a quiet but distinct mooing can be heard far below them. "What! Did you hear that?"

The men dismount and lead their horses down through the forest to the end of the tree line. Peering through the foliage they see a herd of young bullocks, grazing peacefully on the lush grass beside the river. Fergus counts five Pictish men and one woman. They are scantily dressed in loin cloths, made of hide. They have some kind of leather boots on their feet but are otherwise naked. The woman too is bare-breasted. Fergus can't help but notice her voluptuous breasts. He hears Loarn swallow beside him. The Picts have shaved their hair below their ears, leaving a circle of long hair atop their heads. This is tied either in a ponytail or a plait. One man is bald. Their bodies are tattooed with dark blue ink patterns. As they watch, some calves are being led to a corral. A fire is burning, and Fergus is fairly sure that the bald Pict is holding a running iron in the embers.

He nudges Mac Dougall, but he has already seen it. He doesn't speak, but his fury is visibly bubbling under his skin. With forceful signs, he indicates that Fergus, Loarn and three further men proceed to the Devil's Staircase. He beckons the other men to stand ready in a horizontal row, just behind the tree line. Then counting one, two, three with his fingers, blasts loudly on his horn and the men gallop down the valley slopes. Their comrades from the other side of the valley gallop towards them, the Picts are attacked from both sides. Arrows fly, immediately killing two Picts. Before they can retaliate, a spear kills the bald Pict. One Pict and the woman make a dash for the Devil's Staircase. Laird Mac Dougall jumps from his horse and personally kills the last Pict remaining, with his sword.

The men ride after the two absconders. At the base of the Devil's Staircase they have to dismount. They cannot catch up with the two fugitives jumping and springing up the rocks like seasoned mountain goats, but they continue anyway to block the passage back. Fergus already atop the pass, sees the two Picts scrambling up the loose rubble stone with astonishing velocity. He poises his spear and thrusts it with all his might towards the male Pict, leading at the front. It pierces the man's heart, and he stumbles backwards. Fergus jumps off Thunderbolt and pelts forward to attack the man again, should he not be dead. Behind him he feels a shot of air besides his ear and hears the whistle of an arrow, as it whizzes past him and hits the women in the middle of her breast. Fergus kneels beside the male, he is dead. Loarn rushes to the woman. The arrow has pierced her lung, but she still lives. Their comrades join them from below.

"Well done!" They congratulate the lads and start robbing the Picts of their weapons, jewellery and even their boots. Two vultures start circling above them. The female Pict groans.

"What shall we do with her?" Loarn asks.

"Just leave her, the vultures will finish her off," Stuart answers. "These thieving savages don't deserve a quick death."

"Kill me! Please!" The woman groans and turns her head between Fergus and Loarn. Her eyes plead with them. "Kill me!" Fergus takes his spear and thrusts it quickly through her throat.

"What did you do that for?" Stuart asks.

"Death is punishment enough," Fergus answers. Several men nod silently in agreement. Stuart turns around to descend the pass and return to their horses. "Come on!" he tells his men. "Back to the Laird!"

Fergus, Loarn and their three comrades go back to their horses to return the way they came. A little later all the men are in the Pict's camp. Mac Dougall is standing there, a running iron in his hand. He shows it to the men.

"Look! The crafty buggers have made the same brand-mark as mine, just the other way round!" The Laird's brand-mark is a capital 'D'.

The Picts had used the same centre stroke and burned the 'D' onto the Laird's mark mirrored, so that the mark looked like a broad oval shape with a line through the centre.

"Another couple of months and nobody would see the forgery!" Mac Dougall bursts into a fit of rage. "They could've sold the cattle in Castle Rock or anywhere!"

"What will happen to the cattle now, Sire?" Fergus asks.

Mac Dougall looks at the sky. "Dusk is falling," he answers. "We'll stay here tonight. Tomorrow I'll return with a couple of men to Dunstaffnage, to let the rest of the army know we have them. The remainder of this division will return the cattle to their rightful owners. Would you both like to go with them? It would be a good opportunity to get to know my lands, the nobles, and the farmers."

"Gladly, Sire."

"Right, that's settled then. Now come with me to join the men. The spoils will be divided and as you both killed a Pict; you'll get first choice."

The spoils are set out in a tidy row for everyone to look at. There are various weapons, some jewellery, pots, drinking vessels and sheepskins. Fergus picks up a silver pendant, crafted finely with an intricate pattern. *It will please Rhianna*, he thinks, before suddenly realising that he was in no position to make her any gifts. *Nor will I ever be*, he chides himself silently.

Fergus and Loarn spend the next couple of weeks driving the cattle to the various farms they belong to. The farmers are grateful, joyful, and welcoming and the young men make connections for the future. They also knit friendships with their fellow soldiers, most of whom regard this pleasant duty as a sort of holiday.

When they arrive back at Dunstaffnage, Mac Dougall has news for Fergus.

"Ah, there you are," he says. "The bailiff tells me that Logan's ship and silver now officially belong to you and Lorcan."

"Oh, thank you."

"What will you do?"

Fergus considers. Lorcan and Gair had long since left Fergus and Loarn in Dunstaffnage and returned to King Erc in Dalriada.

"Well, of course half belongs to Lorcan. I should sail to Dalriada and ask him what he wants to do. I think I would like to use my half of the silver as an investment to buy goods to trade. Do you need Loarn and myself here? I'm thinking maybe we could sail along the coastline buying and selling and visit Angus on Islay before crossing the western sea to Dalriada."

"Fergus, you and Loarn are your own masters, you may come and go as you please. My wife and I have become fond of you, you will both always be welcome here. However, please don't underestimate Cartan. Will you let me delegate three men to accompany you?"

"If you can spare them, yes. Actually, we get on well with Alistair, Sean and Bram, it could be that they would like to come with us."

"Very well. One more thing, Stuart spoke to me."

"Ah, the Pictish woman."

"Yes. Stuart is angry. He said you undermined his authority."

"Yes, I would do the same again."

"Stuart is on our side. You must learn not to make unnecessary enemies in our own ranks. There are enough real enemies out there."

"I have a conscience."

"As I. Next time wait until Stuart leaves, then kill the woman."

"You are right. I understand, thank you."

Mac Dougall looks at Fergus' glum face and slaps his shoulder. "Don't worry, as a lad you do well. Now then, I would like to order some lobster and honey from Colonsay. Do you think you can arrange that for me?"

"Oh, of course. My first order!" Fergus smiles.

Chapter thirteen
456 A.D. Strathclyde, Argyll and Dunseverick

Rhianna's outer wounds begin to heal. Her bruises fade and she no longer winces with every movement. She eats and drinks and starts brushing her long, chestnut-coloured hair again until it shines. But she feels weak and tired.

"You must go out, for long walks, you need fresh air," Beth pleads.

The mere thought sets Rhianna trembling again. "Someone might see me."

Beth sighs. "How often must I tell you that none of this is your fault."

"But they all know."

"Maybe, maybe not. You haven't left your chamber in months. But look, you've got this all wrong. Ceredig is a wretched, pitiable soul!"

"What! I've been wronged, not he!"

"Exactly, finally you see sense! But still he is pitiable, that he needs to beat women to become aroused. Come on now, put your brat on!"

Rhianna slumps back in her chair. "I can't, I might see him."

"And if you do, what is the worst thing that could happen? Remember, I will be with you and we shall be outdoors."

"He—he might try to—touch me!"

Beth picks up a cushion and slips it down the front of her léine to imitate Ceredic's pot belly. Then she tilts her head askew, takes up his stance and licks her lips so they are wet. Rhianna giggles.

"Now close your eyes Mistress, and pretend I'm the king."

Rhianna sniggers, but does as told. Beth approaches her chair.

"Good morning my fair lady," she says, mimicking Ceredig's voice. She takes Rhianna's hand and licks it.

"Ahh!" Rhianna gives a little scream, snatches her hand away and opening her eyes accuses Beth. "You *licked* me!"

"Well, you always complain that his kisses are *soppy*," Beth retorts. The two women glare at each other, then collapse in pleats of laughter. "Now then," Beth reprimands her mistress sternly. "That wasn't good enough. You can't snatch your hand away, he's your husband." Rhianna starts to protest, but Beth is having none of it. "Just think, Mistress. If you play your cards right, you'll have him wound right round your little finger. He thinks you are with child; he will fulfil any wish you have."

Rhianna considers this. "All right then. In that case you'd better lick my cheek too!" The women laugh so much it hurts. When they finish laughing, they practise Rhianna's worst dread. Eventually she manages to keep calm at Beth's touch.

***

Rhianna and Beth exit the castle and walk up and down the cobbled terrace facing the sea. It is a fine day but still the waves crash against the stone wall, sending spray across their path.

"There's no possibility to escape here," Rhianna says. "Even if we had a boat, who would sail it?"

"Yes Mistress. And the only way to get behind the castle and away from here is up those steps and through the gatehouse."

"And it is always guarded, day and night?"

"Yes, and the guards always ask questions, where I'm going and how long I'll be, and what I have with me and such like!"

Rhianna sighs, and as she begins to realise the impossibility of escape, her mood drops. But she is not quite ready to give up.

"I might be able to stop the guards asking so much," she says. "If they get used to seeing us regularly, they will drop caution. But what then? How on earth can I get away, without them riding after me and dragging me back?"

"Us," Beth says. "Us. I'm going with you and my cousin will help too, but you are right, at the moment I can see no solution."

"Oh yes, your cousin, I forgot about him. Rodric, right?"

"Yes Mistress, he works in the stables."

"So he could get Starlight for me and horses for you both. Are you certain he wants to come with us?"

"Well, he can hardly stay here, not after taking the horses, everyone will know he helped. But where could we go Mistress?"

"I don't know," Rhianna answers sadly.

***

Rhianna puts on a dark green, warm woollen léine with long sleeves.

"What do I look like?" she asks Beth.

"You look beautiful, Miss."

"Well, wish me luck then, I'm ready to face the 'pitiable man'. You know, it really does help to think of him like that."

"Don't forget, if it's too much, just hold onto your stomach and run from the room. He'll take it for sickness."

"Yes, but first I need to extract some promises from him."

Rhianna goes down the wooden staircase, cursing under her breath that they creak so much. She is feeling motivated and brave. She enters the hall where dinner is served at a long table. She sees Ceredig in front of the fire, freezes on the spot and nearly turns on her heels and flees. Biting her bottom lip, she continues towards him.

"*Rhianna*, my fair lady, this is a wonderful surprise!" Ceredig rises from his chair and comes towards her.

He takes her hand and ushers her to the table. Rhianna concentrates on biting her tongue painfully, she doesn't flinch at his touch. When he sits down opposite her, she congratulates herself and takes a sip of wine to spill down the bile that has risen to her throat.

"How are you feeling, my dear? Your maid said you had been unwell."

"I feel a little better, thank you. But—but in the mornings I am sick." Rhianna blushes at her lie but is determined.

"Is it true? Are you with child? Oh, my angel, I hardly dare hope."

"My monthly bleeding has stopped." Rhianna blushes again although this part is true. She hasn't had a monthly bleed for months, but she puts this down to her skeletal weight. "It is not far gone, many women lose a child in the first trimester, but I thought you should know."

"My angel, I cannot thank you enough. Can I do anything for you? Do you need anything?"

"I must regain my strength. The terrace in front of the castle is somewhat restricted and a fierce wind blows in from the sea. Beth tells me you have fine orchards behind the castle and kitchen gardens. I would like to walk there."

"But of course, I shall tell two guards to accompany you."

"That is not necessary, Beth shall be with me."

"But what if you feel sick? And anyway, two women out alone? No, it could be dangerous."

"What could possibly happen to us in the castle grounds? I'm afraid that two armed guards following us would make me feel anxious, and that would not be advantageous for my—condition. However, if you insist, Beth's cousin, Rodric could accompany us. I've known him since I was a child in Brodick."

"Rodric?"

"I believe he works in the stables."

"Oh, very well then, I'll speak to his taskmaster and tell him to excuse him from his other duties."

"There is one other thing—" Rhianna hesitates.

"Yes, my dear, anything!"

"Well, I have heard—in the first trimester—maybe it would be better if—"

"Oh, my dear, don't worry about that! So long as you are with child, there is no *need* for me to visit you."

***

When Rhianna retires to her room Ceredig thrusts his fist in the air. "Yes!" he cries out. *That will stop all those sniggers behind my back,* he thinks. He has waited forty years for this moment.

As a child he had suffered an illness. His cheeks were swollen and he had had a fever that lasted many weeks. When the cheeks looked better, then his knees had hurt and for a while he hadn't been able to walk. He remembered a healer coming, a woman. His mother had been frightened, she thought he would die. His room was darkened, daylight hurt his eyes. He couldn't remember much, just that the healer had had *very* hairy hands. He had felt scared. He had overheard her telling his mother that he would never have any offspring. But that had hardly worried him then. He had only started remembering it, after none of his four wives had produced an heir for him.

His first wife had laughed at him, and mocked him. He felt his blood boiling, just thinking about it. He had hit her then. She had screamed and it had aroused him, more than ever before. Since then, he had always beaten his women, before they had a chance to ridicule him. He knew that there were rumours in his household. That it was his fault that he had no heir. Well, finally he could hold his head up high. Hopefully, it would be a boy. *And hopefully Rhianna won't lose the child,* he thinks. *She is very thin, nothing must upset her.* Oh, he wanted this child *so* badly!

***

As Fergus and Loarn get ready to set sail in Logan's boat with Alistair, Sean and Bram, Laird Mac Dougall comes to wish them farewell. He has a small bundle of something writhing in his arms. He puts it down into the boat and it races back and forth excitedly.

"What's that?" Bram asks.

"Can't you see? It's a dog. It will guard the boat and chase the rats away; every boat needs one. It's my parting present for you." The men all look sceptically at the small white animal with brown patches, running around the boat sniffing.

It is Bram who speaks again.

"But what's happened to its legs, did someone cut them off?"

Mac Dougall smiles benevolently, everyone knows that Bram's assets aren't to be found in his upper storey.

"No, they're supposed to be like that. A small dog can get into places where large ones can't. He'll sniff the rats out."

"Thank you," Fergus says. "He can be our lucky mascot."

"He'll be wanting a name then," Loarn adds.

"He looks like one of them haggises my gran makes," Bram says. "'Cept they don't run about like that."

"He'll calm down soon enough." Mac Dougall reassures Bram.

Fergus and Loarn grin at each other. "Haggis it is then," Fergus says.

They row out of the estuary but as soon as they hit the sea, Loarn hisses the rectangular sails and Fergus takes the rudder. The sea is calm, and the sky is fair. There is a brisk wind chasing the clouds across the sky, and the boat cuts through the waves together with the dolphins leaping alongside them.

"They think we're a fisher boat." Sean smiles. Fergus feels the wind blowing through his hair and holds his face up to catch the spray.

Bram, a huge hunk of a man, taller than any man on board with shoulders as broad as an ox's backside, sits on deck leaning his back against the mast. Not yet twenty, he has a full beard and shaggy eyebrows. His black hair hangs in long curls down his back. He holds Haggis on his lap and strokes him behind his ears lovingly.

They arrive in Colonsay after just a few hours. Fergus goes to the landlord at the Cockerel's Roost.

"Can you remember me?" he asks. "I came with Logan at the beginning of the year and brought you whisky and venison from Islay."

"Aye, I remember. Haven't seen him since then, matter o' fact."

"He died. I have salted beef and whisky from Dunstaffnage if you're interested."

"Aye, we don't get much meat here, just fish. How much do you have with you?"

Fergus strikes a deal with the landlord and promises to deliver the goods. "We've got fine wool with us too. You don't happen to know anyone who might be interested, do you?"

"Well, as a matter o' fact I do. The widow mistress Peigi who sells the honey. She'll buy your wool and dye it with the colours from the meadow flowers."

"I know her, thank you."

By the end of the day, Fergus has exchanged the wool for honey and made a profit on the salted beef and whisky. He feels pleased and goes back to Logan's boat. He gives Alistair the honey to store away carefully, as Haggis drops a dead rat at his feet.

"Good boy," he praises, giving the dog a titbit of meat from his pocket. He picks the rat up by its tail and flings it into the sea. "We've made a small profit," he tells the men. "Tomorrow we can buy oysters here and sell them at Port Askaig, the trip shouldn't take long."

"How about celebrating at the Cockerel's Roost?" Sean suggests.

"Yes, you go, I'll stay here and guard the ship with Haggis. Who will stay with me? Mac Dougall is right, we must guard our silver and merchandise."

"I'll stay," Bram offers. "I'm growing quite fond of this little chap here," he says, picking up Haggis and stroking him.

"Thank you, we'll take it in turns, so that there's always at least two of us on board. And those who go to the alehouse should keep their eyes and ears open. There are plenty of traders about, we need to make some connections and offer wares that others don't."

Early the next morning, Alistair buys oysters straight from the oyster banks. He has a keen head for numbers and reckons they will make a good profit on Islay. They set sail immediately and arrive in Port Askaig by evening. Fergus and Loarn trust their companions as if they were family.

"Sell the oysters," Fergus says, "and keep your eyes open for new merchandise, but don't invest in anything perishable. Loarn and I want to visit our brother, I'm not sure how long we'll be."

Fergus and Loarn hire two horses and ride to Finlaggan. Angus, Donald, and Mhairi are overjoyed at the surprise visit. Fergus and Loarn must recount the story of the cattle rustlers twice and Angus tells them all about Mac Arthur's shipyard.

"He's very generous," he tells them. "He lets me use leftover planks in my spare time and I've started building *our* boat."

"He praises you," Donald says. "He told me you did the work of three men and had the mind of half a dozen."

"Tomorrow, I'll show you the yard and the skeleton of our boat," Angus says. "You'll get a rough idea of the size. I'll ask Mac Arthur if he can spare me a couple of days, I want to accompany you to Mother and Father. What's *your* boat like?"

"Middle-sized and a little sluggish, depending on the wind. It has storage chests though, it's ideal for trading up and down the coastline."

"But you say it was stuck in the harbour for three months. Isn't the hull full of barnacles?"

"I didn't look!" Fergus exclaims, realising his mistake. Angus claps his hand against his head. "No wonder it's sluggish! You'll need a brisk wind to get it moving."

"Well up till now, we had good wind. But you're right. Can we leave the boat here over the winter? You could overhaul it, I'll pay you."

"It won't be seaworthy in winter storms. Yes, leave it here and I'll look it over."

Fergus and Loarn ask to speak to Donald privately. They have discussed the matter together and are of one mind.

"Donald, we don't like to keep our silver on our persons, nor on board. Can we leave it here with you? It's not much, but we hope to save more, and then when a farm or land comes up for sale, we wish to buy it."

"You can leave any valuables with me; I have a heavy iron chest that can be locked. It will be safe here. The farms are usually tenanted, and when the tenant dies, a son normally takes it over. But yes, occasionally a farm becomes vacant. I can keep my eyes open for you. But what is this, you are warriors, you're not ready to settle down and farm yet, are you?"

"No, we would like to let the farm out, maybe to younger brothers, who inherit nothing and must make their own living. They would pay us rent and we could buy more land. Cartan is too rich and powerful for us to hurt him; he has an enormous army. We want to start gaining some power too."

Donald shakes his head. "Don't waste your lives seeking revenge," he says. "I understand, I really do, but he's not worth it, listen to an old man."

"Yes sir," they say, but they leave their few valuables with him anyway.

Two days later they return to Port Askaig. Angus, Fionn and Slevin accompany them. They also have twenty kegs of whisky from Finlaggan. Angus immediately begins to inspect Logan's boat, tutting occasionally. Slevin makes a fuss of Haggis. The weather is still fair and as dawn breaks, they set sail for Dunseverick. The journey goes smoothly and Erc and Mista shed tears of joy.

"Father's hair's going grey," Loarn whispers to Fergus, "and look at Mother! She's aged."

"You've come at a good time," Erc tells them. "I told you that Laeghaire died, didn't I? His son, Lugaid has succeeded him as high king and he strives for peace, but it's not simple. Britons have attacked our south coast again. They had scores of currachs! Anyway, Cartan is away fighting, so he won't bother us here."

"There's his name again!" Fergus complains later to Loarn. "Will we ever be rid of him?"

"Not only that, but he's making a name for himself in the army. He has a huge number of followers, Lorcan told me."

"Ah Lorcan, he accepted his share of the silver, but he's more or less given us the boat. He just wants to sail with us occasionally."

"He's very generous!"

The men invest their profit from the whisky in silver jewellery from the gold and silversmiths who live in crannogs on Lough Neagh. The brooches and pendants are finely crafted in delicate intricate patterns. They also purchase leather belts with magnificent buckles. Then they sail to Campbeltown on Cantyre and from there to Brodick.

Despite his exciting and prosperous ventures with family and trusted friends, Fergus cannot dismiss Rhianna from his thoughts. Against his will he realises that he has fallen hopelessly in love with an unobtainable woman. He is apprehensive as they arrive in Brodick, and wonders how he'll find Laird Douglas.

They secure the ropes to the docking cleats, and Lorcan and Mahon set off immediately to the stud farm. The rest of the men need to sell their merchandise first; they decide to go to the castle, and offer Douglas first choice. Fergus is completely surprised. The desperate, broken man he had left behind, has awakened with new vigour.

"Rhianna is with child," he tells the men. "I'm going to be grandfather. Everything is well after all." Fergus feels as if a mill wheel has just dropped in his gut, his knees almost give way below him. He's glad that the other men are busy congratulating the Laird, so he has time to recuperate from the blow and utter his good wishes too.

"Ah Fergus! Rhianna spoke of you in her letter, you must visit Alt Clut," Douglas says. "She is worried about Starlight. I will write a letter and give you presents for Rhianna."

From that moment onwards Fergus can think of nothing else. He has no valid reason to refuse Laird Douglas, nor is it his decision alone. *Loarn or one of the others can visit her,* he thinks, only for his thought to be immediately overthrown by his burning desire to see her again, no matter how painful the encounter is sure to be for him. *And Starlight? What could possibly be wrong with her that the men in Alt Clut couldn't deal with. Was it an excuse to see him?* He is torn one way and another. He cannot sleep nor find rest.

Chapter fourteen
456 A.D. Alt Clut

Rhianna and Beth, followed by Rodric, go for long daily walks around the kitchen gardens and through the orchards behind the castle. The guards get used to seeing them wandering about and Rhianna's cheeks regain a rosy glow. One day the cook pushes two empty baskets in their hands as they are about to leave.

"Can you pick some beans, I'm running late," she asks.

"Yes, of course," Rhianna replies.

They go to the kitchen gardens and start picking the beans. A while later the cook appears.

"You must be careful around the maid, Cilla. I heard her whispering with the Laird's counsellor. He wants her to spy on you. He doesn't believe you are with child."

"Oh, but I am!" Rhianna lies blatantly.

"You have my best wishes, Mistress. I just wanted to warn you. Don't trust Cilla."

"Thank you Cook. I appreciate your concern. In that case, please keep an eye on my meals, I wouldn't like to be poisoned or suffer a miscarriage."

"Yes Mistress." The cook makes a little curtsey and taking the baskets of beans from Beth, returns to the kitchen.

"She means well," Beth says when she's gone. "We must visit Mistress Wulfhild soon and prepare the ground for your miscarriage."

"No!" Rhianna raises her voice.

"What do you mean, Mistress?"

"Ceredig has said quite clearly that as long as I'm with child, he'll leave me alone. I *can't* have a miscarriage."

"But Mistress! If we leave it too long, then one would expect to see—some remains—of an infant."

"You are right, tomorrow we'll visit Mistress Wulfhild. But I'm not going to lose this child!"

Beth worries a little about Rhianna's state of mind, but she remains silent. *The Wolf will make it clear to Mistress tomorrow,* she thinks.

***

They set off early the next morning, two baskets in their hands. The guards greet them cheerfully as they pass and proceed towards the stables to pick Rodric up. They hurry towards the woods and once under cover of the trees give their baskets to Rodric.

"We need mushrooms in case anyone questions us," Beth tells him. "We'll be back soon." Then they run quickly along the path to the Wolf's house.

Her fox sees them first and stands up growling.

"Stay still," Beth tells Rhianna. "She'll come soon." Sure enough, a woman exits the hut. Rhianna looks at her openly and curtseys.

"Mistress Hilda, may I call you that? I cannot thank you enough, you have saved my life!"

"Nobody has ever called me Hilda since my mother died. Yes, you may call me that. Have you come about 'losing the baby'?"

"Yes!" Beth answers.

"No!" Rhianna contradicts.

"Tell her!" Beth pleads with Hilda.

"Let her speak herself!" Wulfhild looks at Rhianna appraisingly.

"I cannot *possibly—ever*—be subjected to that man's raving violence again. He's demented, *insane*!" Rhianna's eyes are wide open with terror. Beth hugs her, whilst Hilda looks on silently.

"No child has stayed in its mother's womb for ever," Wulfhild finally speaks solemnly. "It must come out sometime."

"I've worked it out," Rhianna speaks quickly. "This baby," she says one hand over her stomach, "is due sometime after Easter. It will be the fighting season and Ceredig will be fighting somewhere. He'll be absent from Alt Clut. All I need is an unwanted baby from someone to substitute mine."

Beth draws her breath in.

"And then?" Wulfhild asks. "Even if you find such an infant, Ceredig will want a second child, especially if it's a girl."

"He'll leave me in peace for a month or two, and then I can escape."

"Then you can escape now," Beth says.

"No. It is already the end of October. Ceredig is often at home and there are winter storms at sea, the weather will get colder. I need time to arrange things. In summer it will be easier."

"And how do you wish to escape? Even if you get past the guards, he'll send an army of soldiers after you."

"No, I can't get past the gatehouse, it is guarded day and night. The only way to escape is by sea. I've worked it out. I shall sneak out of the castle by night, and leave my shoes and cloak on the steps down to the shore. Everyone will think I've drowned myself."

"And then?"

"I need someone in a small boat to row around the headland, pick me up and row me to the harbour, then I'll board a ship and hide somewhere far away."

Beth covers her face with her hands and sighs.

Wulfhild looks on thoughtfully.

"Do you know Lady Mac Farlane?" she asks Rhianna.

"No."

"I have helped her, more than once, in the past. She will help us now. In three weeks, there is a large market in town. Tell Ceredig the first trimester has passed and all is well. Persuade Ceredig to accompany you to the market. Lady Mac Farlane and Ceredig know each other, as all the gentry in these parts. You will tell her you're with child, and she will recommend me warmly as midwife."

"But you can't let her go on with this!" Beth pleads.

"Ceredig's first wife became depressed and refused all food and drink. She died painfully. His second wife supposedly had an accident, she hit her head on the hearth, and died. The third jumped from the castle tower to the courtyard and the fourth drowned. Your mistress is right. It is risky but she has nothing to lose."

"And where do we find a baby, born just after Easter?"

"I have heard of women who leave babies on a nunnery's doorstep," Rhianna says eagerly.

Beth looks at her and at Hilda sceptically. "We'll need more than luck for that to happen."

"Let's solve one problem at a time," Wulfhild suggests. "First, I need to be able to come and go to Alt Clut without a problem. Beth you should start bandaging your mistress's stomach. Don't overdo it, a small bump is sufficient. Rhianna, you should write to your father and tell him you're with child. Do you know of anyone from your home who would be willing to help? If possible, a boatsman."

"Not a boatsman no, but possibly someone else, I must think about it."

"Very well. Then hurry home now before someone wonders where you've got to!"

Rhianna and Beth hurry back to Rodric, who has filled both baskets full of mushrooms.

At the gatehouse a guard says, "Your master was looking for you, Lady Rhianna, you weren't in the orchard."

"We went to the forest to pick mushrooms," Rhianna says. "Where is the Laird now? I shall go to him."

"In the hall, Mistress, he's waiting for your return." Rhianna and Beth enter the hall with the baskets.

Ceredig stands up and demands angrily, "Where were you? I was worried."

"I'm sorry Dear, look we have picked fresh mushrooms." She shows the baskets to Ceredig, then gives hers to Beth.

"Beth, bring them to the cook please, and return with some warm wine." Rhianna sits down on a chair by the fire. "Come Dear, sit down next to me, I have some good news." Ceredig sits back down in his chair warily. Rhianna takes his hands in hers. "My Dear, the first trimester is over and—all is well!"

"Is it true? Oh, my Angel, you make me so happy!"

"So you forgive my little walk to the forest? I'm sorry, I should have told you before we went. I just felt like eating mushrooms tonight, that is all, I didn't realise you would worry."

"My Angel, of course you are forgiven, it is no matter."

"Good. Now I shall drink a little wine and then go upstairs to rest before dinner."

***

“Water, soap, and a towel, quickly!” Rhianna slams the door behind her “I must wash my hands. Ugh, I had to touch him to soften his anger!”

“It was Cilla, I bet it was! Cook was right,” Beth says forcefully. She is indignant. “She must have seen us slip off and reported straight back to Ceredig’s seneschal.”

“Yes, we must try to get rid of her.” Rhianna scrubs her hands to get rid of Ceredig’s touch, and then picks up her feather pen and begins to write to her father. She tells him the good news, and asks ‘Is that stable lad who looked after Starlight still with Tormey? I’m a little concerned about her, she’s rather excitable. I wonder if you could send him here to have a look at her. He seemed to be very good with her in Brodick’. Then Rhianna continues to write about the orchard and Beth and life in Alt Clut. She finishes the letter, seals it, and lies down to rest. *I should’ve run away whilst I had the chance on Aran*, she thinks, *Fergus was right*. She remembers his kiss on Goat Fell. It had been soft and tender. She would like to kiss him again.

***

“My dear, there is a market in town. I would like to go and buy some things for our baby. Will you accompany me?”

“When is it?”

“Soon, next week I think.”

“Very well then, remind me and I’ll ask the guard to prepare the carriage.” The market day arrives and Ceredig accompanies Rhianna, as promised.

They wander along the stalls and Rhianna buys cloth, wool, and ribbons. Now and again, they are greeted by nobles and thanes, well known acquaintances of Ceredig. He introduces Rhianna and relates proudly of her condition. The flood of congratulations boosts his ego, and he is generous to Rhianna. They stop at one stall selling mulled wine and drink a little. A lady wearing a dark-green brat lined with fur approaches them. She is tall, well-groomed and has brown hair plaited on top of her head. She is accompanied by a man, also tall with jet-black hair, now peppered with grey.

"Laird Ceredig!" The lady calls, waving and hurrying towards them. "How nice to see you here."

"Lady Mac Farlane, Laird." Ceredig nods politely "May I introduce my wife, Rhianna?" Rhianna lowers her glance and curtseys. "You have travelled far to our humble market," Ceredig continues.

"Not voluntarily!" Laird Mac Farlane grumbles, "But my lady here, refused to leave me in peace until I consented."

Lady Mac Farlane smiles. "It is true, I was desperate to get out and about and meet some people again. And now I've met *you*, so the journey was worthwhile."

"Then I must tell you my good news," Ceredig offers. "Rhianna is with child."

"An heir, that is wonderful news. When is it due?"

"Sometime in April, after Easter."

"And do you have a midwife yet?"

"A midwife? No. That won't be necessary until the birth, and then someone from town will come, I suppose. I haven't thought about it yet."

"But *no*, you will want the best care for your lady, surely! I had an excellent midwife and she cared for me throughout the whole time. I was so grateful. You know sometimes we women feel a little sick or tired or dizzy. She had a remedy for everything. She is so knowledgeable. And we already have three strong sons, don't we dear?" she asks her husband rhetorically.

"Aye, the woman was invaluable, I'll give you that."

"Oh, Ceredig dear! I would love to have someone like that. And you know how tired I get. Please let me ask her name."

"She is called Mistress Wulfhild," Lady Mac Farlane says. "If you like, I could ask her to visit you?"

"Oh yes please!" Rhianna pleads. She looks at Ceredig with her large blue eyes. He cannot refuse.

***

Fergus, along with his brothers and friends, sails past the Isle of Bute along the Firth of Clyde, around the mull, and into the estuary of the river Clyde. They see Alt Clut at the base of twin rocky pinnacles, domineering the right side of the promontory where the river Leven joins the Clyde. It is a formidable stone fortress, fronted by a wall of rock boulders to protect it from the rage of winter storms. A flight of steps leads up to a gatehouse, set in the crevice between the twin peaks. They row up the river Leven, to the town behind the castle and enter the harbour.

Fergus picks up the letter and packages for Rhianna.

"I won't be long," he tells his friends. "I'll meet you in the alehouse later."

He starts walking up the sloping hill towards Alt Clut. On his left he passes animal enclosures, to his right there are various barns, shelters, and quarters for Ceredig's soldiers, guards, and other labour force. The buildings are nestled under the dramatic rocks, soaring more than two hundred feet into the sky. In front of him Fergus sees extensive orchards, now bare of fruit and with scarcely any leaves. A November mist lies low over the ground. He feels the chill and hurries on towards the gatehouse. Before he gets there, he sees a large kitchen garden, and recognises figures walking along rows of vegetables. Getting closer he sees that there are two women walking together, followed by a man. His heart begins to thump heftily. Sure enough, it is Rhianna with Beth. He sprints up to them quickly.

"Rhianna!" he says panting, out of breath.

Rhianna turns around and her jaw drops. "Fergus!" She looks around hastily and is glad to see no one. "Come," she says. "We'll go to the stables; we'll be undisturbed there. Beth, Rodric, follow us and warn us if anyone approaches!"

The group almost runs to the cover of the stables. Rhianna looks at Fergus all the time, it feels as if her heart will explode it hurts so much. She enters the stables with Fergus and goes to Starlight's box. Beth and Rodric wait outside. Fergus is disappointed. *Does she really just want me to look at her horse*? he thinks. His face falls.

Once there Rhianna opens Starlight's box and pulls Fergus inside.

"Fergus!" she says once more, savouring the sound of his name. "Thank you for coming!"

"I must congratulate you on the coming birth."

Rhianna looks horrified. "Oh Fergus, it's not what you think! I love *you*," she whispers.

Fergus thinks he's misheard. "What? What did you just say?"

At that moment there is a commotion at the door, and Ceredig rushes in.

"Come again in six months!" Rhianna whispers hurriedly, then continues in a loud voice. "Are you satisfied with Starlight?"

"Ah, there you are!" Ceredig booms in a deep bass. "I was searching for you. Who is this and what are you doing here?"

Beth turns to face her husband. "Ceredig! Do you remember the stable lad who broke in Starlight? He comes from my father, with a letter and gifts from him. He asked how Starlight was, so I was just showing him."

Fergus makes a small bow, and addresses Ceredig politely. "Sire!"

"Well, come with me now Rhianna, I wish to take a walk with you. Young man, you can bring the packages to the servants' entrance, a maid will take them from you!"

Ceredig leaves the stables holding tightly onto Rhianna's hand. As they exit Fergus hears him admonish her.

"Really dear, you can't just disappear into the stables with a man like a common whore, you're married now." He doesn't hear her answer.

Slowly he picks up the parcels and goes to the gatehouse. The guards let him through, and show him the side entrance of the castle, for deliveries and servants. He knocks at the door. Beth opens it immediately, as if she's been waiting for him.

She takes the packages, and putting them aside on a table, calls to cook, "I won't be long."

Then she grabs Fergus' hand, and pulling him across the terrace, descends some stone steps down to the beach. Huddling against the back of the stone wall protecting the fortress from winter storms, they cannot be seen from the castle.

"What is all this about?" Fergus shouts against the wind.

"Sssh!" Beth says. "We are not safe, spies are everywhere, don't trust anyone! The mistress is in great danger; she must escape from here."

"But she is with child."

"No, it's not as you think. Look, we need help. Do you have a boat?"

"Yes, but why?"

"How big is it?"

"Middle-sized. I don't understand."

"I don't have time to explain now, someone could come anytime. Come again in May, please. And bring a smaller boat, a currach. One that you can row around this headland, and beach here without being seen from the castle."

"Beth! Beth where are you?" Cilla appears at the top of the steps; she sees Beth with Fergus. Beth grabs hold of him and begins to kiss him. "Beth!" Cilla cries.

Beth breaks away from Fergus and turns towards Cilla, as if surprised. She blushes.

"Oh Cilla! I didn't see you. Please don't tell anyone!" she pleads. She runs up the steps and hurries back to the kitchens.

Fergus is flabbergasted *What in on earth is going on?* he asks himself. He walks back to town, greets his friends at the alehouse, and orders a jug of beer.

***

"What's the plan then?" Loarn asks his brother.

"Tomorrow we'll return to Islay. We'll leave the boat over the winter months at Mac Arthur's shipyard so that Angus can overhaul it, and then we must say our farewells to our brother and friends here." Fergus makes a large circular sweeping movement with his arm to include the band of merry men drinking ale. "Just you and I, Sean, Bram and Alistair, will buy some horses in order to return to Dunstaffnage."

"It will take longer riding."

"Yes, but we'll get to know the lay of the land."

"What about Rhianna?"

"She wants me to return in six months to help her escape. I'll need some assistance."

"Well count me in," Loarn says.

"Yes, me too!" It echoes from around the alehouse. Fergus hadn't noticed they had been listening. He is moved.

"Really? It could be dangerous."

"All the better!" The men cry.

"Then the next round is on me!"

Chapter fifteen
456 – 457 A.D. Strathclyde, Dunstaffnage and Castle Rock

Wulfhild places a dense woollen veil over her head, and secures it with a braided ribbon. She wears mittens over her furry hands and pulls the hood of her sheepskin brat over her head. Thus disguised, she is confident that no one will recognise her disfigurement. It is winter and her apparel is not so much different than that of other women, just the veil is less transparent. She fills her basket with various remedies and sets off to Alt Clut.

On this, her first trip, she doesn't speak much to the guards. They are expecting her though, and let her pass without an inquisition. She comes and goes often. One day she hands a guard a flacon of syrup.

"For your cough," she tells the surprised man. Gradually they become accustomed to the visitor, and Wulfhild gets to know the guards. She knows when their duty rota changes.

"The guards have got used to me; they no longer give me so much as a second glance," Wulfhild tells Rhianna and Beth.

"How often do they change duty?" Beth asks.

"Three times daily: at dawn, midday and then a couple of hours after dusk."

"So they'll be tired a couple of hours before dawn."

"Aye, but they'll still be there. Late morning would be the best time to slip past, they're busiest then. Deliveries arrive, messengers come and go, Ceredig's bailiff runs back and forth. If we're lucky Ceredig will go out hunting."

"I would prefer him to be far away fighting," Rhianna says. "How are we going to get an infant past the guards? What if it cries?"

"We still have to find an infant," Beth sighs. "It's never going to work."

"I sent a messenger to Whithorn," Wulfhild says. "I know the prior at the monastery there, at the Candida Casa. He is absolutely trustworthy. He has promised to let me know if an infant is brought to the monks by some poor woman. It happens sometimes, he says, it is just a matter of timing. I've also spoken to Lady Mac Farlane; she too will be on the lookout for us."

"There are so many problems, my head feels quite dizzy with worry. I don't want anybody to suffer because of me. I think we should call it off. It was a stupid plan anyway, Ceredig won't be easily fooled." Rhianna begins to have doubts.

"Don't give up yet Mistress," Beth pleads. "We've already convinced him you're with child."

"Ah yes," Wulfhild says. "Now you should be able to feel the baby moving soon. I'm going to place my hand on your stomach, and I want you to hold your breath in, then push your stomach out quickly. Then breath out again slowly, unnoticeably. That's it! good! Now you put your hand on her stomach Beth, what do you think?"

"Oh, oh yes, it feels like a kick! It could work, especially with Ceredig. He won't know any different."

"Good. Then I want you to put a little padding under Rhianna's bandages, it's time she put on some more weight."

***

Flora and her husband, Laird Mac Dougall, are overjoyed to welcome Loarn and Fergus back to Dunstaffnage. Flora hugs them both, holding onto Loarn a little longer than necessary.

"I'm so happy to see you both!" she says.

"I'm leaving here tomorrow," Laird Mac Dougall tells them. "my men and I have over a thousand cattle to drive to Castle Rock. Why don't you join us?" he offers. "See a bit of the countryside *and* a large town."

"They've only just arrived!" Flora protests.

"I'd love to come with you." Loarn beams at the Laird.

"Me too!" Fergus says.

“Well, that’s settled then. We’re thirty men already, so strictly speaking we don’t need you, but we’re always glad of a few extra hands in case we’re waylaid by outlaws, or the going gets rough.”

***

Fergus and Loarn love the bustle and adventure of driving so many cattle over the mountain passes to the west. The hubbub of the excited cattle is deafening. Again, and again, a couple of obstinate beasts tear away from the herd, and shoot off looking for greener pastures. Then one of the men would gallop off, hollering at the top of his voice, to round them up again.

Reaching higher ground, the going gets tough. Icy snowflakes swirl around them, obscuring their vision. The mountains are covered with deep snow, and a bitterly cold wind whips round their faces, penetrating their thick woollen clothes. The cattle find no food and are discontent. They camp at night besides huge log fires, and sleep to the sound of wolves howling in the distance. The livestock shifts around mooing.

Descending to lower ground the snow turns to persistent rain. The cattle move more quickly, and they arrive before the walls of Castle Rock within two weeks. Landowners, bailiffs, and butchers arrive early the next morning, appraise the cattle, and haggle with the Laird over the price. By midday, the cattle have all been sold and led away.

The Laird pays the men. “Enjoy a night in town,” he tells them. “I’ll return tomorrow with those fit enough to join me!”

This is met with a few guffaws of laughter as the men pocket their wages, and drift off in small groups towards town. Fergus and Loarn group with their friends Alistair, Sean, and Bram. Alistair is the only one of them who has ever been to Castle Rock before.

“Shall we visit a brothel?” he asks them. “I know one with girls so saucy, that you’ll get an erection within *half a minute*! And they’re cheap too!”

Loarn and Sean are keen. Bram can’t wait.

Fergus isn’t particularly eager on visiting a brothel, but he doesn’t want to spoil his friends’ fun either, so he goes along with them. They enter the town gates, and walk along narrow streets lined with wooden houses. The smell of foul rubbish and stale urine hits them immediately.

They screw their noses up, and pull their brats over the bottom half of their faces. The air is so fetid with the stench of ammonia, that it makes their eyes sting. They continue along a jumble of twisting and turning lanes, until Alistair realises he doesn't know where they are. Now and again, they encounter people along the alleyways; they ask their way to the next brothel and finally come upon a mud track between two rows of wooden buildings. One house is dimly lit up and signposted as a tavern. The racket, babble and yelling emerging from indoors, suggests that they have found their target.

Alistair pushes the door of the establishment open. A wave of heat, body odours and alcoholic haze rolls over them like a tsunami. He takes a step backwards in surprise, knocking into Bram, who's peering over his shoulders in awe. They all enter, buy some ale, and look for somewhere to sit. Scarcely have they sat down at a table, the first 'lady' comes up to them and drapes a leg over Fergus' knee. She bends towards him, showing off a pair of admirable breasts, and asks if he'll buy her a drink. Bram's eyes spring out of their sockets. He hastily pushes his chair back, stands up, and asks what he can get her. Changing her attention to him, they go to the bar, and then disappear out of sight.

"Damnú air!" Sean exclaims, eyes wide open. "Did you see that? She had an 'erse like a bag o' washing!"

"I was na lookin' a tha!" Alistair retorts. The men burst out laughing and slap their thighs.

Two more females approach them, and one by one, Fergus' companions vanish. He finishes his ale, and leaves the tavern. He doesn't know why, but he doesn't feel comfortable about that kind of sex, however commonplace it is.

Fergus starts walking along a warren of alleys, below the stone fortress that towers above the town on a granite rock. He hopes that he'll arrive at the town's outer wall, and thus find his way to the gates. He passes houses, all built next to each other, and all looking identical. He hasn't a clue where he is. He sees two men walking towards him, and is just thinking that he'll ask them the way, when he realises that they are swinging heavy wooden clubs in their hands. He turns around on the spot and see two more men approaching him from behind. He takes his knife from his belt and positions himself against a house wall, ready to attack whichever one of them comes first.

The four men form a semicircle around him, barring any hope of a misunderstanding. The first one is mid-thirty, has a burly figure and a dark beard. He wears dark, dirty rags and has a hood over his head, casting his face in shadow. He sticks his chest out like a randy cock, and sneers at Fergus, clutching onto his knife.

"Come on then! Want ter fight? What yer waiting for?" The other three men laugh contemptuously.

Fergus knows that he is hopelessly outnumbered, but he is not willing to give up without a fight. He darts forward to the first man, holding his knife in front of himself and hoping to plunge it into the man's heart. The man grabs hold of Fergus' wrist and twists it painfully around, until the knife clatters to the ground. He gives Fergus a withering look.

"Is that the best you can do?" he asks scornfully. Then he raises his club and swings it towards Fergus' head.

In a split-second Fergus ducks evading the club, at the same time grabbing the man's arm, and yanks him head over heel forwards with his own momentum. Packing all his strength into one consolidated blow, he kicks the man in his stomach. Then he falls upon him and boxes his head with his fists.

The other men wake from their momentary stupor, and drag Fergus off their comrade. With combined effort they turn him onto his back and kick him in the ribs so that the air leaves his lungs. Fergus beats wildly with his fists and legs, but the men punch his face, and then continue to kick and beat him until he loses consciousness.

He awakes shivering with cold, and tries to open his eyes. He can half-open one eye and attempts to take in his surroundings. He sees buildings shrouded in blackness and a patch of inky sky. He struggles to sit up, and cries out in pain. He can hardly breathe. He waits a while until the cold becomes unbearable and tries again. He makes it onto all fours and realises that he's entirely naked. He groans. *I shouldn't have put up a fight,* he thinks, *too late.* He crawls from the middle of the alley to the nearest house and knocks at the door. He hears a dog barking inside and a male voice cursing.

Then a female voice. “I’ll go.” The door opens and he catches her indrawn breath. “What in the Lord’s name? Cennet, come here and help me! There’s a lad, more dead than alive. Help me carry him indoors.”

They sit him down in a chair and drape a rug over his shoulders. Whilst Cennet makes a fire, his wife fetches a bowl of water and clean cloths. She begins to wipe the blood away. Fergus cannot stop shivering.

“Give him a gram of whisky!” the woman tells her husband.

Cennet holds a beaker to Fergus’ lips. It burns down his throat and warms him. He nods gratefully and drinks more. The woman dabs around his left eye carefully.

“You’ll have a second scar to join your old one,” she scolds. “You should stop fighting an’ get a decent man’s work!”

“Leave him alone, Muira, can ya na see that the lad’s been mugged? You don’t know what happened.”

“Don’t want to cause trouble—” Fergus manages to say.

He licks his tongue around his mouth and realises that he’s lost two teeth. He opens his left eye; the right eyelid refuses to budge. He touches his nose carefully; he has difficulty breathing.

“Aye, your nose is broken, and your right eye will need more than a day or two to heal. We’d better look at the rest of you now,” Muira tells him.

Fergus tries not to wince with pain, but he fools neither Muira nor Cennet. They move him nearer to the fire, now burning, and spoon a little porridge into his mouth. He falls asleep, exhausted.

***

He looks around the room, confused, then he remembers. A dog lies at his feet before the fire. He tries to shift his position and groans out loudly. Muira enters the room.

“Just you stay sitting there. You’re in no fit state to move!”

“Is it day yet? My friends will be looking for me.”

“Where are they lodging?”

“Before the town gates. We’re drovers.”

“Ah. Don’t worry, Cennet will find them for you and bring them back here.”

"Ask for Loarn or the Laird Mac Dougal."

"Right, I'll tell him. Stay there now."

***

Cennet enters his house, quickly followed by the Laird and Stuart. Fergus, upon seeing them, tries to rise. Muira, standing behind his chair, pushes him down again.

"You're not going anywhere," she says, looking at the two strangers defiantly.

"What on earth happened?" the Laird asks. "The men are all around town, searching for you!"

"I was stupid," Fergus admits. "I left the others at the tavern and walked the streets alone."

"How brainless is that!" Stuart digs.

Fergus swallows down the bitter bile that rises in his throat. *I'm not going to rise to the bait,* he thinks.

"Well, the good lady," the Laird says, "is right. You're not going anywhere in a hurry." He opens his purse and gives Muira silver. "You and your husband are good people. Will you look after my boy until he's fit to travel?"

Moira curtseys, "Gladly, Laird. His young bones will heal quickly. Cennet will return him to you personally in a few days."

***

The ground is white with frost and crunches under her feet, as Wulfhild makes her way to the gatehouse. *February already,* she thinks. She is a little uneasy that she has not, as yet, heard anything from the prior, nor from Lady Mac Farlane. She knows she mustn't let her anxiety show, Rhianna is already too fragile, without worrying more. As always, she covers her basket with a woollen cloth. Today is time to prepare the ground further.

"Good morning," she greets the guards.

"Morning Mistress Wulfhild, bit nippy today."

"Aye." As Wulfhild speaks, the woollen cloth begins to move a little, a mewing can be heard. She clamps her hand down on the cloth.

"That's not tonics in there!" the guard protests. "Let me see!"

Wulfhild is reluctant. "Please! Your mistress is lonely, stuck all day indoors." She pulls the cloth back a little, and reveals a kitten. "I thought it might amuse her. Please don't mention it to the Laird, you know what he's like about all the animals running around. It won't do any harm, I promise, and I'll take it home again tonight."

The guards grin. "Right you are, Mistress, we haven't seen anything," one of them says.

"Thank you. Oh, your hands look chapped. I'll bring you some more of that salve tomorrow, shall I?"

"You're very kind Mistress Wulfhild."

Wulfhild hurries down the steps. She'll show them the kitten again in a couple of hours, when she leaves. From now on she'll bring it often, until they no longer ask to look. Another problem dealt with, a newborn baby won't sound much different. *So now we just need an infant, a war to distract Ceredig, and preferably some way to get rid of Cilla for a few days,* she thinks.

They had decided not to try and get Cilla dismissed. 'If you know your enemy, the war's half won', Beth had quoted her mother. Cilla was a real troublemaker though. A month ago she had told Ceredig that she had seen Beth washing out bloody rags, and that she didn't believe Rhianna was with child. He hadn't believed her, thank the heavens. Especially as Rhianna had let him put his hand on her belly just a week before. She had emphasized how strong the baby was.

Still Ceredig had called for Beth and confronted her. She had looked confused and blushed as deep red as a burning fire. Then she had told him, that she herself, had had her monthly bleed. He had apologised then and told Cilla off. *She wasn't to bother him again!*

Well one problem at a time, Wulfhild decides.

***

It is the middle of March when Lady Mac Farlane is shopping at the local market in Grianáig, her home town. She has almost everything she needs;

she just wants some of the delicious, sweet buns that the baker makes. As she reaches his stall, she sees a bedraggled woman in front of her. Her clothes are torn, her bare feet filthy and her hair hangs in dirty streaks around her face. Most noticeable however, is her belly. She is clearly with child. Lady Mac Farlane watches as the woman sneaks her hand behind the lady being served, and takes a loaf of bread.

The woman obviously wants to disappear quietly without paying, but the baker witnesses the theft and calls out, "Hey!" The woman makes a run for it and the baker shouts, "Stop the thief!"

A scene of uproar and confusion breaks out as men race after the thief, and drag her back screaming.

"Take her to the stocks!" someone cries.

"Fetch the guards!"

"She'll get her hand cut off for that!" The baker shouts indignantly. "Serve her right too. Stealing off hard-working folk!"

"No, no stop!" Lady Mac Farlane calls out. "It's a misunderstanding, she's with me! Let go of her. I'm sorry," she says to the baker giving him six pennies. The baker looks at her not believing a word, but six pennies for a loaf of bread was three times too much.

"For your trouble," Lady Mac Farlane says. She takes the woman by her elbow and leads her away from the market, along the lane to her magnificent home.

"What's your name?" she asks.

"Anna."

"Well Anna, I would like to help you, and I think you can help me too." She gives Anna the bread, and watches as Anna, holding it in both hands, tears into it with her teeth like a starving wild animal.

"Come with me now!" Lady Mac Farlane bids her. "Let's get you cleaned up and fed properly."

She takes Anna to her home, and orders her servants to fill the iron bath tub in her chamber with warm water. She insists on helping Anna to bathe, herself. She throws Anna's dirty rags away, and gives her a warm woollen léine and soft sheepskin brogs to wear. Then they go to the kitchen together, and the cook prepares a hearty meal of venison in rich gravy and vegetables. Lady Mac Farlane gives Anna a jug of warm ale to drink. She eats and drinks hastily without pause. It is as if she is afraid someone might take the food away from her any second. She finishes with a loud burp and wipes her mouth clean with a cloth.

"Come child, you must be exhausted. I'll show you where you can sleep, and tomorrow we'll talk."

The next morning, Lady Mac Farlane tells her servants, that she wishes to have breakfast with Anna alone and undisturbed, in the hall. A fire is blazing in the hearth and the table is heaped full of ham, cheese, bread, and apples. Despite the cold stone walls and freezing temperatures outside, the atmosphere is warm and cheerful. Anna enters the room. She looks around herself and then at the table, unbelievingly.

"Good morning, Anna, did you sleep well?"

"Yes Mistress, thank you. Thank you for everything. I'm not normally—I mean, I'm not a thief!"

"Well sit down and tuck in, that baby of yours needs feeding."

Anna doesn't wait to be asked twice. When she finishes Lady Mac Farlane tells her. "Come and sit by the fire with me, we should talk." Anna does as bid.

"When is your bairn due, Anna?"

"Not long now Mistress, in about another month."

"Do you have family nearby, or anyone to help you?"

"No Mistress, I have been foolish." Anna folds her hands together on her lap and presses them so tightly that the knuckles turn white.

"Take your time, dear. I'm not here to judge. I will help you, if you would like me to, regardless of whatever decision you may make, after we've spoken."

Anna takes a deep breath and lets it out slowly. "I come from down south, from Britannia. I used to work at a big house in the countryside, just a couple of miles outside of the town of Corinium. I was my mistress' personal maid. One day my master and mistress invited guests to the house for a hunting party. A couple of men stayed longer and one man, a thane, stayed for over a month. He said he loved me and that he wanted to marry me—"

"And you believed him and let him make love to you."

"Yes. I know it sounds stupid, but he turned my head completely. He made such fine compliments and yes, it was my fault."

"And then?"

"One day he left. I found out afterwards that he lived just thirty miles away, with a wife and four children!"

"Oh, you poor girl!"

"When I realised, I was with child, I went to his home and waited nearby. He nearly fell off his horse when he saw me. He was very angry and told me to disappear quickly!"

"Did you say you are with child?"

"Yes," Anna lowers her glance. "He wasn't concerned. He asked me what I expected if I acted like a whore, and that it probably wasn't his anyway!" Anna wipes away a tear angrily. "I returned to my mother and father and confessed. My father was livid; he beat me with his leather belt."

"And your mother?"

"She just looked on and said nothing. My father beat me so fiercely, that I feared I would lose the child. He threw me out of the house. At first, I just wanted to get as far away as possible. I walked in a northerly direction for four days. I thought I could find work until my time came, but nobody wanted to give an outlander honest work. I began to look unkempt, and my situation got worse. Occasionally someone took pity on me and gave me a crust of bread. Yesterday—I was desperate—I hadn't eaten for seven days."

"You will starve no longer, whatever you say to my suggestion, whatever you decide. I promise you that. Now tell me, were you brought up in the Christian belief?"

"Yes Mistress."

Lady Mac Farlane stands up and takes the family bible from a shelf. "I bid you to swear on this Holy Bible that, you will as long as you live, never disclose what I am about to tell you to any living person, not even to your own child."

Anna takes the bible and places her hand on it. "I swear," she says.

"Very well. About twenty miles from here, on the other side of the Clyde, there, lives an old man with his young wife. She is his fifth wife, the other four— died. The man is rich and very powerful, but he cannot father children. However, he doesn't know this, or at least he doesn't *want* to believe it. He thinks it is his wives who are barren. He is desperate for an heir. He beat his present wife until she almost died. Then she told him she was with child, and the violence stopped. But she is not with child."

"Oh!"

"Exactly, she needs a child."

"Mine."

"If you are willing."

"I—I don't think I can just give it away. My baby is part of me."

"Of course, we have thought of that. The lady will not be able to feed the baby herself and will need a wet nurse. We would 'find' you, and say your own child had died."

"So I could stay with my baby?"

"At first yes, at least for a year. Afterwards you could either work in the house, or nearby, and see the child often. But you could never say that the child is yours, not even to the child itself. However, you will both have a roof over your heads and not go hungry. Your child would want for nothing."

"And if I say no?"

"I have promised you that you won't go hungry. When the baby is born, I will help you to find work. You will need to pay a woman to look after your child, whilst you work."

"So I wouldn't see my child much, but neither would I need to lie."

"That is true. But you could never give your child the upbringing and future it would have as the man's heir."

"Can I think about your proposal?"

"Yes, I will give you two days to consider. Then we must take action, if you agree. If not, you can stay here, as I promised."

***

The next morning Anna finds Lady Mac Farlane at the breakfast table.

"Yes," she says.

"Yes? Are you sure?"

"Yes, Mistress."

"Then we must leave today, before you are much noticed here. I will inform my maid, Roswith. She will pack a few things and we'll leave in an hour. Eat something—and Anna?"

"Yes, Mistress?"
"Thank you."
"No, thank *you* Mistress, for giving me and my child this chance."

Chapter sixteen
457 A.D. Strathclyde

Roswith packs a basket with foodstuffs and warm rugs. The three women dress warmly, and set off walking the three miles to the harbour on the River Clyde. Anna breathes heavily, and Lady Mac Farlane links her arm through Anna's to support her a little.

"Your bairn looks heavy," Lady Mac Farlane says.

"Yes, and it's boxing mightily. Oh! Just a minute, I must disappear behind some bushes."

The two women wait understandingly for Anna.

"It'll be pressing on her bladder," Roswith says. "It looks like her stomach's already sunk."

"I hope not! It's not due yet."

Anna reappears, relieved. "Sorry! Right I'm ready."

Reaching the harbour, they start looking for the ferryman who transports passengers and livestock back and forth across the Clyde. An old man with a crooked back sits on the mole, his legs dangling over the side, and gazes at the waves lapping lazily against the harbour wall. A currach swims on the water below him.

"Hello, good man. How much does it cost to row us to Alt Clut?" Lady Mac Farlane asks.

The man stands up with effort, and looks the three women up and down. "Neh, can't do that," he says. "My son's not here."

"When will he return?"

"Don't know. Could be an hour, or tonight or tomorrow."

"We can't wait that long."

"I can't row you alone, the tide's turning."

"And if we help you?" Lady Mac Farlane is not ready to give up.

The man appraises them again. "All right then, six pennies paid up front, and if we have to turn back, no returns."

Lady Mac Farlane pays the man. They all board the boat, and take up an oar each. Once out into the middle of the estuary, the women realise that the man wasn't exaggerating.

"Crivens," Roswith curses. "Oh, sorry Mistress! But heck, I feel as if my arm is about to drop off!"

"Save your breath!" Lady Mac Farlane pants.

They pull hard on the oars, feeling muscles in their backs and arms that they have never felt before. They have nearly reached the north bank of the firth of Clyde, but are still downstream from Alt Clut, when Anna lets out a loud gasp. A pool of liquid gathers between her feet.

"Holy Maria, my waters have broken!" she cries out in panic. "The bairn's coming, it's too early! Aaargh!" She grips her stomach and bends over double in pain, dropping her oar.

Roswith, sitting next to her, grabs the oar and rows with two. "Hang on Miss, we're nearly there!" She pulls with double strength towards the river bank. "We'll have to pull ashore now," she cries trembling with effort. "Or we'll all drown!"

"It's sanded up here," the old man rules. "I can't get nearer to the bank, or the boat'll get stuck. Water's not deep though, yer can get out and wade."

Lady Mac Farlane gets out first. She sinks into the silt mid-calf deep, the river swirls around her hips. Roswith joins her, and together they help Anna out of the boat. The old man gives them the basket, and Roswith ties it around her neck. The man rows back into midstream, and the current bears him quickly away. Lady Mac Farlane and Roswith stand each side of Anna wobbling, each with an arm under one of hers. They stand there, not moving, trying to get their balance.

"I think I'm sinking deeper," Roswith groans.

Anna screams in pain as a new contraction comes, and bends over double, nearly toppling head first into the water.

"Whoa," Lady Mac Farlane shouts, pulling Anna up with unknown strength. Concentrating, she heaves her right foot with enormous effort out of the silt, and places it a few inches further inwards towards the shore.

"Copy me!" she orders Anna and Roswith urgently. "Come on now, we can do this!"

The first steps feel as if she is pulling a two-hundred-pound weight behind each foot. Sweat runs down her forehead, and tears of frustration run down her cheeks. Roswith fights for her life.

"Sorry Mistress," she says, pulling the basket over her head and letting it sink into the river. "I canny carry it any longer."

Lady Mac Farlane is biting her teeth together, trying to help Anna. She is in no state to reply. Anna tries not to cry out in pain. She feels so much pressure in her groin that she fears her baby will be born mid-river.

They tackle the first six feet heroically and then feel pebbles, mixed with silt, under their feet. The going becomes a little easier. They drag themselves out of the river into the rushes at the water's edge. They rest a minute.

"Have we low tide or high tide?" Lady Mac Farlane asks.

"A dinnae ken!" Roswith answers.

"We'd better get up the bank then."

The women look at the six-foot high river bank in front of them, as if it were a massive, twenty-foot high, fortified stone castle. Lady Mac Farlane hitches her woollen dress up into her belt and rolls her sleeves up. Roswith follows her example. With combined effort they push, pull and half-drag Anna up the bank. She collapses on her knees and then lies down, bent together and clutching her stomach tightly. Lady Mac Farlane and Roswith sink down onto the ground next to her. For the first two minutes no one speaks, they are intent on catching their breath back.

"My bairn will be born in the rushes, like Moses!" Anna says.

Lady Mac Farlane smiles. "Yes, there is a similarity I suppose, although I think he was found, not born there."

"We're all lucky to be alive," Roswith says. "I really thought I was going to drown."

Anna groans as another contraction comes. When it passes, Lady Mac Farlane says she must look between her legs.

"The first child usually takes many hours, but I'd better look before we continue to Alt Clut. Oh! The cervix is already four inches open; we cannot possibly move you now! Roswith you must hurry to Alt Clut. Go to the stables and ask for Rodric, he will know how to find Mistress Wulfhild. Tell them it's an emergency, they must hurry. You too now, go!"

Lady Mac Farlane worries. It is at least five miles to Alt Clut and Roswith was already exhausted before she set off. And before she gets there, she must first cross the river Leven; hopefully, she will find a ferry boat quickly.

She holds Anna's hand and tells her, "Don't worry, everything will be fine." But Lady Macfarlane's heart is thumping wildly and she frets.

I don't even have a knife to cut the umbilical cord, she thinks. *Oh, Mother of God, please let this birth go well, please let the baby be healthy, and please let Mistress Wulfhild arrive soon,* she prays.

***

Roswith doesn't bother to pull her dress back down. With her legs free, she can run quicker. *Ridiculous,* she thinks, *that even a bit of woollen cloth could slow me down.* Her muscles ache, and she dreams of just collapsing and going to sleep. *No time for that!* she admonishes herself. She is under no illusion of the emergency. She grimaces, clenches her jaw tightly together, and battles on, taking long strides and ignoring the pain. When she sees the river Leven in front of her, she guesses that she's taken half an hour to get there. She pulls her skirt down, and clutching the silver penny that the lady had given her tightly in her hand, goes to the first boat she sees. "I'll give you a silver penny if you get me across the river in ten minutes," she says to the lad idling next to the boat. She shows him the penny to prove that she has it.

"Right Miss, jump in quickly then!" The lad pulls on the oars as if his life depends on it. They cross the river without giving the current the slightest chance of diverting them and land on the other side at a staggering speed. Handing the penny over, Roswith jumps out and hurries up the hill to the castle, clearly visible behind the town. She finds the stables and Rodric, and tells him what's happened. As Rodric hurries towards the gatehouse, she plumps down on a straw bale, and is happy to wait until he returns. He is gone just a few minutes before he returns with Mistress Wulfhild, carrying a large basket. He brings Wulfhild's pony to her, and asks Roswith if she'll ride on his own horse, together with him.

"I can't just take one of the Laird's horses from the stables," he apologises. "I can only come and go freely, as it's Lady Rhianna's wish."

"I don't mind," Roswith says. "As long as I don't have to walk another inch myself. Let me sit up front so that I can show you the way. First down to the river, we must cross it, and we'd better hurry!"

***

Anna's contractions come quicker. She wants to push.

"Try not to push yet dear, your cervix isn't quite fully open." Lady Mac Farlane can already see the baby's head.

She glances back in the direction Roswith disappeared, hoping against hope that help will come soon. Her common sense tells her that she will be on her own with Anna for a while yet, but her heart lends her hope against reasoning. She takes her linen léine off, and with her teeth and fingers, rips a strip of cloth from the fabric. Anna cries out. Lady Mac Farlane comprehends that nature must take its course. She tells Anna to turn onto her hands and knees.

"Now you can push," she says. The baby's head pushes through, and the shoulders and limbs follow. The baby cries.

"It's a boy!" Lady Mac Farlane tells her.

"Is he all right?" Anna asks breathlessly.

"Yes, he's perfect. He has a good weight; are you sure he's early?" She binds the umbilical cord tightly with the strip of cloth, and is just thinking that she must bite through it with her teeth, when she hears the sound of horses' hooves.

Rodric, Roswith and Mistress Wulfhild arrive.

Mistress Wulfhild hunkers down in the reeds and cuts the umbilical cord with her knife. She examines the baby.

"He's fine," she pronounces. "A good, strong, healthy lad. About seven pounds, I would say." She removes linen cloths from her basket and swaddles him, then gives him to Anna. He immediately begins to suckle, and everyone smiles with relief.

A few minutes later Anna groans, and has another contraction. The afterbirth comes. Wulfhild wraps it up. They sit and wait in silence a few minutes longer, happy just to watch the baby sucking Anna's breast. Finally, Mistress Wulfhild breaks the silence.

"We were all expecting more time to plan," she says. "But to all intents and purposes it doesn't change anything. Anna, are you willing to take part in this plan? I'm sorry, but I must ask you myself."

Anna looks at her baby, and then at the faces watching her intently. A tear rolls from her eye.

"Yes, Mistress Wulfhild," she replies. "I'll still see a lot of him, won't I?"

"You can watch him grow up but only from a distance. We'll do our best. Well then, first the practicalities. I need to get Anna and the bairn to my house. I can boil water and clean them up there, ready for Rhianna's 'birth' tomorrow. It would be better if nobody notices Anna tonight. I will go upriver with her, and cross the Leven at the ford. Lady Mac Farlane, will you go with Roswith to Alt Clut? Ceredig is away hunting for a few days, but you couldn't know that. Concoct some story about having wanted to visit Rhianna, and having a boat accident on the way. It's always better to stick as close to the truth as possible. Cilla is there, we must think of some way to get rid of her tomorrow."

"I'll do that, leave it to me!" Lady Mac Farlane offers.

"Good. Then tonight let Rhianna and Beth know that tomorrow is the day. They will prepare everything in Alt Clut. Now how will I know when I can bring the baby to the castle tomorrow? Late morning would be best."

"Bring the baby to the kitchen gardens. I'll send Cilla on an errand to town and then come to find you. Then I will engage the guards at the gatehouse in conversation, whilst you slip past." Lady Mac Farlane says.

Mistress Wulfhild considers the suggestion. "Good, it could work!"

"How can I help?" Rodric asks.

"Well, if Lady Mac Farlane and Roswith think that they could manage to walk to the castle alone, I was hoping that you could accompany Anna and myself to my house. Could she sit in front of you on your horse, side-saddle?"

"Yes, gladly."

"Lady Mac Farlane?"

"Of course we can walk!" she answers. "There's no need to rush now."

***

Late next morning, Lady Mac Farlane asks Cilla to take her ripped tunic to the seamstress in town. She had already told the whole household a hair-raising, dramatic story of her near drowning in the River Clyde. Roswith had added spicy details about the ferryman being drunk and lecherous. So Cilla had gone unsuspiciously to town, happy not to be scrubbing the floor for once. Ten minutes after her departure, Lady Mac Farlane climbs the steps to the gatehouse and pretends to be sorry that she has missed Cilla.

"Lady Rhianna wants fresh herrings," she tells the guards, whilst Wulfhild slips past them with her basket. "When Cilla returns, will you send her back to town?" she asks. "The Lady will be very disappointed if she has to make do with ham."

Back in Rhianna's chamber, Lady Mac Farlane finds Beth and Rhianna and even Cook, swooning over the baby boy.

"Oh, isn't he just bonny!" Cook gushes over the sleeping bairn in her arms. "You're lucky, he has dark hair like the Laird used to have!"

"And my blue eyes," Rhianna looks at the baby lovingly.

Mistress Wulfhild claps her hands. "Back to your places before Cilla returns. Cook start boiling water. Beth tells the guards that the baby is on its way, and they are to send a messenger to Ceredig. Rhianna, whenever the baby cries, groan or cry out or scream like blue murder! Main thing is that Cilla doesn't hear him before he's 'born'!"

The combined effort is a full success. Mistress Wulfhild has brought some pig's blood in a flagon with her. It smells bestial, but is excellent for keeping Cilla busy, washing out bloody rags and changing bowls of soiled water. The baby is 'born' whilst Cilla is busy in the kitchen. She hears lady Rhianna screaming out in pain and terror. When she returns to the chamber, Rhianna is holding the bairn in her arms. Wulfhild gives Cilla the afterbirth to dispose of. Ceredig comes galloping home and is greeted with congratulations.

"It's a boy!" his men tell him. Ceredig bounds up the steps, and bursts into Rhianna's chamber. "Is it true?" he asks.

Rhianna sits, propped up by pillows, in her bed. Her face is flushed from the steam of a bowl of boiling water, that Mistress Wulfhild has held under her chin, her hair is in disarray. She holds a tiny baby in her arms and smiles. "Yes dear, it's a boy!"

Ceredig drops to his knees besides her. "Oh, my fair lady! How can I thank you enough? Is he healthy? Did he arrive early? I wouldn't have gone hunting, had I known!"

"Mistress Wulfhild says he's strong and has a good weight. Maybe—" Rhianna lowers her glance and looks at her husband from under her eyelashes. "I got a little muddled with the dates. Look he has dark hair, just like yours! Do you want to hold him?"

"May I? Are you sure it's all right?"

"Of course."

Ceredig picks the baby boy up, and holds him in his arms. The baby grasps Ceredig's finger with his tiny fist.

"Oh, he's holding me!" Ceredig looks at the baby. His heart of ice melts and is filled with love.

"What shall we call him?" Rhianna asks.

"Tudwal, the ruler, my heir."

***

Ceredig leaves so Rhianna may rest. Rhianna dips the corner of a muslin cloth into a flacon of mother's milk, that Hilda has brought from Anna. She lets Tudwal suck on it. Then she rubs a salve onto her own nipples, so that they become red, sore, and swollen. They itch. *It's not for long,* she consoles herself. The next day Ceredig hears Tudwal crying. Mistress Wulfhild tells him that Rhianna has mastitis, and cannot breastfeed Tudwal herself. He agrees that they need a wet nurse.

"Leave it to me," Mistress Wulfhild tells Ceredig. "I know of a poor widow whose bairn was stillborn. She's a respectable lass."

Wulfhild goes home and finds Anna fretting.

"Don't worry, your bairn is doing just fine. Come on, I'll bring you to him now. I've told the Laird and his household that you're grieving, and that they're not to ask you questions. We'll practice your story later."

Chapter seventeen
457 A.D. Alt Clut, Strathclyde

It is the middle of April. The snow has melted from the mountain tops, filling the rivers and brooks with fresh, clear, icy water. Trees begin to bud, spring is approaching.

Saxon raiders harass the coasts of Northumbria. Scores of currachs land on the north-eastern shores releasing thousands of savages, who level the northern towns with their battering rams. Swords gleam, and flames crackle from all sides. The people, if not murdered or taken into slavery, flee to the hills.

The Britons send messengers to Alt Clut, asking for the help of Ceredig's army. It makes sense for Ceredig to form an allegiance. Should the Saxons proceed inland unhindered, then it would soon be his territory they were encroaching. Reluctant to leave Tudwal, but seeing no alternative, Ceredig sets forth with his warriors.

***

The mild weather continues and May dawns. Fergus and his companions sail up the River Leven, and dock at Alt Clut's harbour. Fergus goes to the castle with two crates of oysters for lady Rhianna. Beth meets him in the kitchen, and whispers quickly that they should meet at the stables, that very night. The walls are listening and take account of Beth coercing with, what they believe to be, her young man. Nobody thinks it's worth hindering her. She exits the castle and meeting Fergus, tells him what he should do.

***

Rhianna dons Mistress Wulfhild's heavyweight veil, mittens, and cloak. She pulls the hood over her head and leaves the castle with Beth. Her heart thumps madly as she follows her up the steps to the gatehouse.

"I'm going to market," Beth tells the guards, as Rhianna slips past. "Is there anything you'll be wanting?"

A little surprised at Beth's sudden friendliness they nonetheless decline, and turn their attention to a messenger wanting to enter the castle grounds.

Rhianna is walking down the hill towards town so quickly, that Beth has to run to catch her up.

"A piece of cake!" she says, smiling happily.

"I thought I'd have a heart attack!" Rhianna answers. "I can't believe how easy it was!"

Beth looks suddenly sad, "We'd better say farewell here, Miss, there'll be too many eyes around the harbour."

"Oh Beth, how can I ever thank you enough? Without you I'd be dead! I'll never forget you. Are you sure you'll be all right? You can still come with us, you know."

"I'll be fine, Miss. Tonight I'll tell the household, that you have a headache and will keep to your room. Then in the early hours, I'll sneak out of the castle, like we planned. I'll leave your brat and brogs by the shore. Tomorrow everyone, except Cook and Anna of course, will think you've taken your life."

"They might come looking for me."

"Aye, but you'll have had a head start. They won't even suspect Fergus' boat. It'll have left the harbour today, before you go missing tomorrow."

"Oh Beth, I'll miss you so much!"

"I hope we'll meet again, Miss."

"Me too, Beth."

The two women hug, then Beth turns right and walks quickly towards town without turning back.

***

Fergus and his companions have lain in the harbour since the previous day. As usual they had sold their wares and bought new goods. Everything should appear as normal. Now they were preparing to leave. Pretending to busy themselves with ropes, they keep a sharp lookout towards the road leading down from the fortress, at the same time scrutinizing the harbour for anyone paying them attention. But the harbour is bustling as usual, the people are hurrying about their own business.

"There she is!" Angus states quietly and does not point.

Sure enough, a veiled person in a hooded brat, walks towards the boat. Fergus gives her a hand to help her aboard, and leads her straight to a storage unit. He opens the hatch, Rhianna climbs inside, and Fergus closes the opening again.

"All clear!" Loarn says. He unties the mooring ropes, and the men start rowing down the River Leven.

They soon reach the point where the Leven flows into the Clyde. Alt Clut towers above them, two hundred and forty feet high, sitting atop a volcanic plug. Waters swirl around the base of the crag. The current gyrates in circles and the men pull strongly on their oars to steer clear of the jagged rocks just beneath the water's surface.

"Impossible to navigate by night!" Angus exclaims. "We wouldn't have been able to see those rocks. Thank goodness Mistress Wulhild came up with an alternative plan."

Fergus steers right into the firth of Clyde, and his men continue to row towards the estuary. At Grianáig the river is nearly three miles wide. Far enough from shore to release Rhianna from her hiding place, without fearing that she may be seen or recognised. Fergus gives the rudder to Angus, and tells his men to pull up the rectangular sail. As the wind catches the sail, they lay their oars to rest.

Fergus raises the hatch to the storage chest, and offering Rhianna a hand, helps her climb out. She stands up and pulls off first the mittens, then the brat and finally the veiled headdress. She stretches her arms out wide and takes deep breaths of the salty air.

"Freedom!" she speaks softly and gazes at the faces surrounding her. "Thank you," she says looking into each man's eyes. They come to rest on Fergus' face. "What happened to your nose?" she asks, surprised.

"Oh nothing, just battle wounds." He shrugs it off, fibbing a little.

Loarn and Alistair choke up. Rhianna looks at them not understanding.

"Actually, it makes you look quite dashing," she says. "Swashbuckling!"

"Yes, that's what all the girls say," Fergus retorts with a straight face.

Rhianna looks him in the eye, momentarily outraged. Then she sees the corners of his mouth curve upwards.

"Oh you—!" She rushes towards him and stretching her hands out to his chest, attempts to push him backwards.

Fergus catches hold of her hands and holding them down, sweeps her up into his arms. He lowers his lips to hers and kisses her long and lustfully. The men whistle and caterwaul, but Fergus and Rhianna ignore them. As the boat changes direction and they turn south towards Bute, Fergus breaks away.

"Time for your disguise," he says.

Rhianna takes hold of her ionar and pulls it off, over her head. Beneath it she wears a long-sleeved knee-length léine. A padded leather jerkin covers her chest. Around her waist she has a leather belt and knife. On her feet she still wears the sheepskin brogs.

Taking the knife from her belt she asks Fergus, "Will you do the honours or shall I?"

"I couldn't!" Fergus shies away.

Rhianna shrugs, and holding her hair in her hands, begins to cut it off with the knife. The men wince, but Rhianna is dispassionate about it.

"It will grow again," she says.

When she finishes, Fergus goes towards her again, and scruffs her hair up.

"My little scallywag," he says softly. Then in a loud voice he asks his men, "What do you think, will she pass as a boy?"

"No way!" Loarn says.

"From a distance, maybe," Alistair says.

"She's too clean and smells too nice," Bram says.

"Did you hear that, A stóirín? You are too clean," Fergus says, wiping his hands on the ship's deck.

"Oh no you don't!" Rhianna squeals.

"Oh yes, I will!" Fergus grabs hold of her, and rubs her cheeks with dirt whilst his men howl with laughter.

Pouting Rhianna sits down next to Bram and takes Haggis from his lap. She strokes the little dog and speaks to him.

"You're my friend, aren't you little one? Not like that wicked man over there!" Once again, the men chortle.

***

When peace is finally restored, Bram asks, "Why does Mistress Wulfhild need a veil, and how will *she* escape from the castle now? The guards already saw her leave today."

"Mistress Wulfhild was born with a rare defect that left her whole body covered in hair. She is sensitive to snide remarks from stupid, unthinking people. So when she goes out, she always wears a thick veil and covers her hands. She knows Ceredig from a long time ago, and didn't want to risk him recognising her, so she always left her veil on inside the castle. She has a second set of mittens, veil, and brat. It isn't a problem for her to leave the castle, because the guards change duty. She's always coming and going, so they don't really pay any attention to her. Anyway, she said she would stay a few days to give Beth moral support in the turmoil of me going missing. Everyone knows Beth's my friend, so they might suspect her. Apart from that, Ceredig may come home, or send men to my father, or even go there himself. Oh, I'm so worried about my father, he'll be heartbroken!"

"Don't worry Miss," Lorcan replies. "Mahon and I have already discussed this with Fergus. When we dock at Islay, we'll bid you all farewell, and then sail on further to Aran. We'll visit Tormey at Brodick, and he will let your father know you're safe."

"Oh, thank you, Lorcan! I was so worried. It seems that you men have thought of everything!" Rhianna beams at them all.

"But what about your baby, Miss, won't you miss him?" Bram asks.

Rhianna places her hand gently on top of his. "Oh Bram, of course I'll miss Tudwal, I grew very fond of him. But he's not *my* child, he belongs to Anna, and she will look after him."

"Oh," Bram replies uncertainly.

Rhianna is not sure whether he has understood, but thinks maybe it is for the better if he hasn't. He might otherwise betray them, without realising. Rhianna had wondered whether some of the precautions they were taking, were exaggerated. But Mistress Wulfhild had been adamant. She had warned her not to underestimate Ceredig. 'So long as no body is found', she had said, 'his pride will be dented and he won't give up searching for you'.

***

Not daring to stop at Brodick in case Rhianna be recognised, not even for a few minutes to let Lorcan and Mahon disembark, the crew sail onwards to Campeltown. By the time they arrive it is nearly dark, and they anchor. The next day they continue to Islay, and arrive at Mac Arthur's shipyard the same evening. Before they eat, drink or rest, Angus insists on showing them his new ship, that he has built himself. An ocean-worthy longship, with which they will sail the next morning. The vessel is built of oak and has no keel, but instead two broad keel planks.

"It's high bow and stern will protect us from heavy storms," Angus tells them. "The hull is made entirely from oak and extremely strong, we shall conquer the oceans!"

Fergus examines the cross-timbers, with beams a foot wide. They are secured with iron nails as thick as a man's thumb. The two sails are made of raw hide, so as to stand up to the violent Atlantic winds.

"It's awesome," he tells Angus.

"Have you seen the figurehead?" Angus asks. The three brothers walk fore to the hull. A larger-than-life head of a sea hawk, intricately carved from oak, adorns the bow. It looks fearsome. Its large eyes are painted realistically, and it seems to eyeball them. "Do you remember our last day together," Angus continues, "atop the cliffs at Dunseverick?"

"Aye," Fergus says. "The sea hawk."

"It's incredible," Loarn says. "I've never seen such a grand boat before."

"Really?" Angus asks.

"Really," his two elder brothers reply in unison.

"I knew you were talented," Fergus says, "but this is—well—just phenomenal."

Angus soaks up the praise. "I told you then, that I'd build you boats to conquer the islands. Well, I have done, and I will build many more. I will build hundreds of boats, currachs and longships. Together we will rule the islands, we shall be the sea hawks!"

Fergus looks at Angus, amazed. His younger brother had grown-up.

"Now what about the Minch?" he asks. "Do we have enough men to navigate it? Without Lorcan and Mahon, we're just seven men."

"No problem at all, but we're to pick up passengers on our way. Mother and Father don't want to miss out on this girl's maiden voyage," Angus says, patting his ship fondly. "Gair and Feradach will accompany them, we're to meet them on Tiree. From there we'll sail to Rum and Skye, and then cross the Minch. I want to avoid landing in the territory of the Creones, there is no point in wasting our energy fighting them, and it could be dangerous for the women. Oh yes, I forgot to say, Mhairi wishes to come with us too. She wants to visit her brother, Conan, again. She thought she could stay with him for a couple of months, to keep Rhianna company until she settles in. So the crew is plenty large enough. Come on now, let's hurry to Finlaggan, hopefully Mhairi has cooked for us, I'm starving!"

***

Early the next morning, the company wastes no time and sets sail on Angus' boat for Iona, a small island that lies south-west off the coast of the Isle of Mull. The distance to Tiree is too great to overcome in one day.

At the same time, Lorcan and Mahon sail in Logan's boat to Aran, to assure Laird Douglas that Rhianna is safe.

The day before, Beth has alerted Ceredig's household that Rhianna is missing. Shortly later her brogs and brat are found on the shore in front of the castle. The worst is presumed, and a messenger hurries to the front battle lines to inform Ceredig.

Chapter eighteen
457 A.D. The Hebrides; the Isle of Lewis

Angus' ship, named Sea Hawk One, cuts through the waves with exhilarating velocity. The men are thrilled, and Angus basks in compliments. They head for the south coastline of Tiree, and land between Hynish Bay and Gottbay, at a small settlement named Scarinish.

The Isle of Tiree is quite small, about twelve miles long and three miles wide, and as flat as a wooden plank. To the east the hills of Mull stand out amethyst, against a background of pale lemon sun-blessed sky. In the far north the isles of Uist, lie spread out like a string of blue pearls.

The crew disembarks, leaving their weapons on board, but bearing gifts. They are met by the local inhabitants of Scarinish.

"We come in peace," Fergus tells them. "We are on our way further north and ask for your hospitality for the night."

"Do you belong to the Dalriada?" an elder asks. "Sons and friends of Erc, King of Dalriada?"

"Yes, we do."

"Then you are welcome, we were expecting you, as Erc also. He sent a messenger seven days back, to let us know you would be coming soon. Follow me, we have a house for guests to rest and eat."

The men, together with Mhairi and Rhianna, follow the elder along a sandy path leading behind the dunes. The villagers walk besides them, and children run about excitedly. The children try to catch Haggis to stroke him. They laugh happily; he is running around in circles, leaping back and forth. They arrive at a settlement of twelve large round houses, with dry stone walls and thatched rooves. They follow the elder through the doorway of one such house. It is dark inside. The only light comes from the open doorway, a single deeply inset window, and in the centre of the floor, a down hearth: a circular kerb of flattish stones laid around the fireplace. It is the focus of the house. Two women are cooking a meal in a large, copper cauldron, hanging over charcoal embers. Smoke spirals upwards. The fire expels a warm, comfortable heat.

"Sit, eat and drink." The elder invites them, "and tonight you can sleep here." A villager runs up to the elder and tells him that a second ship has arrived. "Stay here," the elder tells them. "If it is Erc, I shall bring him to you."

Erc arrives with Mista, Feradach and Gair. Old friends greet each other, new acquaintances are introduced, and the three brothers hug their parents. They sit around the hearth eating, drinking, and recounting their stories. Sparks from the fire spit, and the constant cone of smoke makes Rhianna's eyes water. Fergus notices.

"Are you all right?"

"Yes, the smoke is just stinging my eyes."

"Let us go for a walk, it is still light outside."

The evening is warm and barmy. They walk, hand in hand across the rich machair plain, bursting forth with an abundance of radiant wild flowers, towards the west coastline. Miles upon miles of white sandy beaches stretch before them. Removing their brogs, they run to the waterline and let the incoming waves trickle over their toes. The sun begins to drop and the sky changes to tangerine, gold, and blushing pink. The clouds above the setting sun turn burgundy.

"It's an enchanted island!" Rhianna sighs.

Fergus takes hold of her face gently and looks into her blue eyes.

"You have bewitched it," he says. Then he places his lips on hers and they kiss.

They walk back to the dunes and lying down, make love. At first slowly and gently; then quicker with urgent desire. Finally, slower again, taking time to discover each other's bodies.

***

They awake to the sound of seabirds calling to each other. Dawn has broken. They dress hurriedly and run back to the harbour. The crew is already busying itself with daily chores aboard Sea Hawk One.

"Just in time," Angus calls out to them good humouredly.

They put to sail within minutes, and passing the Isle of Coll, head to Rhum. Docking in port, they stock up with provisions, and decide to stay overnight, aboard their ship in the harbour. The next day they will cross the sea of the Hebrides to the island of Skye. The harbour master warns them to stay close to the coastline.

"This time of year, we often see orcas passing through these waters," he tells them. "On their way to warmer climates. Watch out for them, it could be the death of you all, if you meet a pod."

"What about minke whales?" Angus asks.

"They're usually further up north in the Minch. But they're smaller, if you keep your distance, you shouldn't have any trouble from them. Where are you going?"

Angus doesn't want to disclose their exact destination, "The Outer Hebrides."

"So far! By God, you're a braver man than I! Are ye not afraid of the *blue men*?"

"The *blue men*? Ah—do you mean the *storm kelpies*?"

"Aye, some folk call them that."

"But they're not real, are they? I've heard stories about them, but I thought they were just like—well—*fairies*."

The harbour master beckons Angus closer to him with his forefinger.

"Look lad, I don't know if they *really* exist or not," he whispers, as if afraid someone might hear him. "But you're young yet, it'd be a pity to die. I tell you this: learn your answers, *just in case*."

"My answers?"

"Aye."

"I don't understand."

"The blue men are always on the lookout for sailors to drown, and boats to sink. If a group approaches your ship, their chief, they call him Shony, will rise up out of the sea and shout two lines of poetry to the captain, that's you, right?"

"Aye."

"Well then, he'll challenge you to complete the verse, and if you fail, then the blue men will capsize your ship." The harbour master makes the sign of a cross across his forehead and chest.

Angus looks at him sceptically. "I don't know—" He hesitates.

"Tell yer what. Have yer got a silver sixpence?"

"That's a lot of money."

"Not if it saves your ship and the lives of those on it, it isn't. Now then, give me your silver and I'll teach you the lines."

Angus gives the harbour master silver, which he immediately pockets. Angus waits. The harbour master clears his throat and begins:

"Shony: Man of the black cap what do you say
As your proud ship cleaves the brine?
Captain: My speedy ship takes the shortest way
And I'll follow you line by line.
Shony: My men are eager, my men are ready
To drag you below the waves.
Captain: My ship is speedy, my ship is steady
If it sank, it would wreck your caves." [1]

"That's it?" Angus asks.

"Aye, learn the answers off by heart, the quicker you reply, the better."

Angus returns to Sea Hawk One repeating the lines to himself, *just to be on the safe side,* he thinks.

That night he falls into a disturbed sleep. He tosses his head back and forth, dreaming of blue storm kelpies threatening to capsize his ship. Shapeshifting water spirits, now in the form of humans, now of powerful horses, blue in colour from the hue of the sea, swim around the Sea Hawk, with their torsos raised out of the ocean, twisting and diving like dolphins. Their faces are grey and long in shape, some have long arms and they wear blue headgear. They are able to speak, and a group approaches his ship. Its chief shouts two lines of poetry to Angus, challenging him to complete the verse.

"Who has built this boat so fine.
That races across my waters at ten to nine?"

"No, no! That's the wrong question!" Angus cries out panicking in his sleep. The blue men soak his vessel with water spray, roaring with

---

[1] Mackenzie, Donald A. (1917), Wonder tales from Scottish myth and legend, Blaickie P.82

laughter as they try to capsize it. Angus despairs and tries to answer quickly:

"Tis I, your humble servant, come aboard, be my guest.

To wine and dine, the very best."

No, no, that's not good enough! He thinks in his nightmare as Shony answers:

"Alas, it is not possible for we are creatures of the sea,

But for your kind offer, we will let you be."

Mista, awakened from Angus' cries, comes over to him and stroking his hair, wakes him.

"What is it, Mo Chroi? What's bothering you?"

Angus wakes up, disorientated, and covered in sweat.

"Mother? Oh, I was dreaming!" He grins sheepishly. "Don't tell the others, the harbour master told me tales of the blue men, and I listened!"

"Oh, that slibhin! Did he take money off you?"

Angus looks abashed, he doesn't answer.

"Oh Angus!" His mother ruffles his hair. "Go back to sleep now."

***

A messenger reaches Ceredig on the battle front.

"Her body hasn't been found; you say?"

"No Sire."

"But Tudwal is safe and unharmed?"

"Yes."

"Well, I cannot return to Alt Clut now; my men wouldn't understand that. Ask the harbour master where the tide would wash her body up, and send a search party out. And ask him also about any boats that left the harbour that day. Send messengers to Laird Douglas to let him know, and whilst they're there they should ask around discreetly if anyone has seen her." Satisfied that he has done all he can, Ceredig returns his attention to the matters at hand. *Main thing is that Tudwal is safe,* he thinks.

***

Sea Hawk One crosses the sea of the Hebrides to the Isle of Skye. A pod of nine orcas passes them two hundred yards away. They leap out of the sea, dive back under the water, and resurface spouting spray.

"They're magnificent creatures!" Rhianna enthuses; she has not seen orcas before.

The orcas and Sea Hawk One pass each other, respectfully at a distance, neither disturbing the other on their voyage.

Angus wants to sail in the long hours of daylight. "We could sail at night," he tells Fergus. "But this is my first voyage in these parts, and I want to study the coastlines and the water currents for the future. We will need a few days longer, but it will be safer, and I doubt anyone is following us."

And so, they continue their voyage, sailing during the day and anchoring at night. After spending the night at Uig, they leave Skye and sail towards Harris. Circuiting the Shiant Isles, they pass through tempestuous waters.

"Mac Arthur warned me that this area is subject to rapid tides in all weathers. He said it is known as the 'Current of Destruction' because so many ships wreck here," Angus tells Fergus. "The tide flows beside the caves inhabited by the storm kelpies."

Pillows of fog swirl around them, alternated by pockets of bright sunshine. None of the crew spot any kelpies, nor blue men, but the sea is very choppy and Loarn begins to feel sick. He turns white and green and hangs his head over the railings. He throws up and looks like a drowned cat. The Dalriada are excellent mariners. Born with the rhythm of the sea in their blood, they are happier at sea than on land. Loarn is an exception. Angus is unsympathetic and laughs.

"Just wait until we're on land again!" Loarn groans.

***

Angus and his crew reach Harris and turn north along the coastline. They pass numerous brochs, and are certain that they have been seen. But they are alone, on a sole ship, and the locals choose to let them pass in peace.

After seven days aboard Sea Hawk One, they sail into the sheltered natural harbour of Stornoway. It is raining heavily, obscuring their view of the flat island of Lewis afore them. Thatched stone houses are clustered around the harbour, and along the narrow lanes and alleys which branch off from the main square on the seafront. They disembark and Angus informs the harbour master who they are.

"We're here to visit Conan, our brother and cousin, he is expecting us."

"He lives five miles from here, on the road to Barabhas. You can hire horses at the tavern if yer wish."

"Aye, we'll go there now, good day to you."

"It feels as if the ground is swaying beneath my feet," Rhianna says as they cross the cobbled square to the tavern.

Fergus smiles and links his arm in hers. The innkeeper leads them to the back of the tavern, where stables surround a large courtyard. They choose their mounts and set off.

The island lies low. They pass farmed land on both sides of the road. Conan lives in a two-storey stone manor with a thatched roof. It is surrounded by at least forty further buildings. Houses for craftsmen but also stables, a butchery and a mill. Conan comes out of his home and hugs his sister, Mhairi, and cousins Mista and Fionn. He is a tall, strong man with the build of a solid oak wardrobe. His iron-grey hair falls straight to his shoulders, and he has a full beard, neatly trimmed. His eyes mirror the family trait, they are large and blue. They are now looking upon Fergus, Loarn and Angus benevolently. Conan hasn't met them before.

"It seems like yesterday you told me about the birth of these fine young men," he addresses Mista. "And which one of you is the shipbuilder?" he asks.

"That's me," Angus replies.

"I've heard a lot of your talent, I can't wait to see your ship with my own eyes, tomorrow maybe? And you are the horseman?" he asks, looking at Fergus.

"Yes Sir, how can you tell?"

"Well, it looks as if you've fallen off a few times." The group laughs, then Fergus corrects him.

"Those are battle wounds, Sir."

"Well in that case I must show you and your brothers a few tricks, so that the enemy is at the receiving end. We can't have your mother worrying. This is my son Uther," he says, introducing the tall dark-haired man beside him.

He is a little older than Fergus.

"So come now, let's go inside before the rain clouds burst again, you must be tired from your journey."

"Yes sir, and famished," Angus adds.

***

Conan leads them inside his house. They enter a large rectangular hall with a wooden table in the centre of the room, surrounded by narrow benches and chairs. The room is dominated by a huge log fire, burning cheerfully, set into the wall at one end. A wild boar's head is hung above the fire, and the guests mill around it in awe. Mounted on an oak shield, it is more than three feet long with powerful neck muscles. The eyes are small and deep-set, the ears long and broad. It is covered in dark-brown coarse bristles. The main attraction are the boar's tusks. The upper canine teeth, whetters, protrude from its jaw forward in a lateral direction out of their sockets and then curve upwards towards its snout. They are eight inches long. The lower tusks are the most magnificent.

"They're called cutters," Conan tells them, pointing to a lower tusk. "Just feel how sharp the tip is!"

The tusk is semi-circular in shape and eighteen inches long. The guests take turns in touching the lower tusks.

"Are all the boars here so big?" Angus asks.

"No, much bigger, this is just a toddler," Conan jokes.

"Seriously?"

"Neh, lad. I brought this chap here, back from a hunting expedition on the mainland." His eyes twinkle with amusement.

He leads the men into the kitchens where they can wash, and takes Erc and the women upstairs to the guest chambers. Erc and Mista are shown into one, and Mhairi and Rhianna into a second.

"I'll send a maid up with warm water," Conan says. "Come down when you're ready, and we'll eat."

***

The next morning, Bram is agitated. "I can't find Haggis anywhere," he tells his companions. "He was in my arms when I fell asleep last night, and now he's gone!" The men had slept together on the floor in the hall.

"He can't be gone far," Fergus says.

"He may have sniffed out some mice in our storerooms downstairs," Conan suggests.

"Downstairs? Aren't we downstairs now?" Fergus asks.

"We have cellars. Another floor souterrain, for storage mainly, but there are prison cells, passages, and more rooms too. I'll show you later. Let's have some breakfast first, then we'll search for Haggis, and I'll show you our underground world."

***

After breakfast Conan leads them down stone steps into a room with low eaves. It is four hundred square feet large. The walls are made from tight-knit stone slabs. Nailed into them are exquisitely smithied iron torch holders. Candles are burning in them and cast the room in warm light. Stone shelves are packed with food, preserved in clay vessels. Barrels of pickled herring and whisky are on the floor; cured hams hang from the ceiling. Conan leads them further down a passage into a second room, where there is a small, watertight stone tank with fishing bait. Even further they come to a granary filled with corn, and find Haggis sleeping there, four dead mice between his paws. He wakes up when they enter, and wags his tail. Then he rolls on his back hoping for, and getting, a tummy rub from Bram.

"How on earth did he get in here?" Conan wonders aloud. "There must be more secret passages, that even I don't know about!" His guests chuckle and Haggis looks very pleased with himself.

Bram picks him up. "You're coming with me now," he tells the dog. Holding onto him tightly, he follows the party further into a warren of small rooms and passageways. They twist and turn with passages forking off in several directions.

"I'm completely lost," Rhianna admits with a sigh. "I would never find my way out of here. How on earth do you know where to go?"

Conan points to small marks engraved on the stone slabs. "It's signposted," he tells her. "If we branched off right here, we could walk underground all the way to the coast."

"We have plenty of souterrains in Hibernia too, but they are just primitive tunnels compared to this." Erc points his hand all around himself. "I like the way you store your food; it is well protected from fire."

"We sometimes have violent storms here in winter, they can sweep right across the islands," Conan replies. "Our peoples take shelter underground. In winter it is warmer here, and in summer, cooler. The tunnels are used for escape too. If foes attack us, we can use the passageways to retreat, and then attack them from behind, or even from several sides."

The younger men listen keenly to Conan's tales. When they come back to ground level, Conan organises horses for those who wish to explore the island with him. Everyone does.

***

Seven days pass like seven hours; it is time to depart. As they prepare to take their leave, a messenger from Dunstaffnage gallops into the courtyard, dismounts and demands to speak to Conan urgently. He is shown into his study.

"Nechtan has gathered his army together in Moray, Sire. They are marching at this moment in a south-westerly direction. Mac Dougall begs for the help of your army."

"Nechtan, the king of the Picts marching Southwest? Along Glen Mór, what is he planning?"

"Well, it *is* fertile land, Sire."

"But it doesn't belong to him! Return immediately and let my brother-in-law know that I'm on my way. Hurry now, make sure you take the fastest scouts to carry the message on."

Conan stands up and goes outdoors. He blows long and loud on his hunting horn, three times. His captains and commanders drop everything and hasten to the courtyard.

"There's no time to waste," Conan tells them. "Nechtan has gathered his army and is marching along Glen Mór. We must stop them. Get all the men you can muster together. If the Picts establish themselves in the west, there'll be no stopping them. Next thing we know, they'll be invading our islands too!'"

"I'll come with you, Sir!" Fergus says. Loarn, Bram, Alistair, and Sean volunteer also.

"Well, I've no time to argue. Colin, take these men with you, and give them weapons!" he tells one of his commanders.

Fergus hugs Rhianna quickly. "Don't be sad a chroí, I'll return as soon as I can."

"Come back safely, my heart. Thank you for bringing me here."

Fergus hastens with his fellow warriors to the harbour. They make an imposing scene. More than a thousand men, armed with swords, spears, knives, axes and even farm tools, crowd into forty currachs that are already awaiting them. They row quickly out of the protected bay before hoisting their sails and disappearing.

***

Conan's army lands at Dunstaffnage. The scouts tell them that Laird Mac Dougall and his army are advancing towards Glencoe, about a day's march away. Conan's troops set off immediately to follow, close up on, and join them. Fergus and Loarn go to the fortress to saddle up Thunderbolt and Mushroom. Flora runs out to the stables and brings them helmets and bronze armour plates.

"From the Laird," she tells them breathlessly. "He said I was to insist you wear them, should you come with Conan."

The brothers ride off and quickly catch up with Conan's army. Fergus dismounts and holds Thunderbolt's reins out to Conan.

"No." Conan declines the offer. "Carry on riding to Mac Dougall and let him know we're not far away. He should wait if possible."

Laird Mac Dougall is relieved and happy to see Fergus and Loarn, and hear that help is on its way.

"King Nechtan has passed Loch Ness and is now marching towards Loch Lochy. Conan is not a moment too soon. Loch Lochy is lined on both sides by forested hills. The Picts will try to separate our army and lure us into the mountains. They prefer to strike swiftly from the shadows, ambushing their foes in small, outnumbered groups. We must stay together on all accounts, and meet them as one body. They don't like battle on an open field, this is where we must meet them."

The Laird points to a small area of flatland, open on all sides.

Conan and his army join Mac Dougall's troops as the last strip of grey light disappears in the sky, and black night engulfs them. The commanders gather together to discuss the proposed strategy. A map showing the lay of the land is before them.

"The Picts will know that we are here, but will try to reach Loch Lochy before we confront them," the Laird says. "We should leave here immediately, this night, so we can challenge them here," he says pointing on the map. "Before they reach the cover of the forest."

It is Fergus and Loarn's first large battle. Mac Dougall tells them to hang back at the rear. "The archers will go up front," he says. "I'd like you to stay back and fight any men who break through our lines."

The brothers do not argue with the Laird. The situation is too serious, and the Laird has worse worries on his mind, than two greenhorns. Their father, Erc, has told them often enough, tales of foolhardy men, disobeying orders.

So they watch from the back of the lines, as their archers shoot arrows into Nechtan's advancing army. Some men are hit and fall, but the rest surge forward, roaring and screaming. Men and women, scantily clad, ferocious savages, tattooed with blue ink, wield square-headed axes and force their way through Mac Dougall's men, cutting throats, stabbing, and slashing. They swing nail studded clubs against the heads of their enemies, and seemingly with sheer determination, begin to deplete the defending army.

Fergus sees a Pict oscillate an iron ball, studded with nails, on a chain. The Pict lets go of the chain, and the lethal weapon flies and meets Alistair's head with a startling crack. It splits open like an overripe pumpkin and Alistair's headless body plummets to the ground. In Fergus something goes 'click'. His brain switches off his emotions, and he turns into a battle machine. Spurting forward with his sword, he plunges it into angry bodies, just as resolved as he, pushing towards him. He notices a savage, about to thrust a halberd into Stuart's throat. He takes a knife from his belt and throws it forcefully into the enemy's face. Stuart scrambles up over the savage's body, the knife lodged in one eye. He gives Fergus a nod before continuing to battle on. A Pict knocks Fergus' sword from his hand. He uses his fists and legs for a second, until seeing a knobbed spearbutt on the ground. He picks it up in a flash, and beats it against the foes' heads. He senses that Mac Dougall's men around him, have awoken from their initial shock, and are now fighting back with frenzied energy. It is kill or be killed.

They fight all day. Climbing over dead bodies, slipping on blood, and scarcely able to stand on his own two feet, Fergus continues battling until the Picts turn on their heels and retreat. He doesn't have the strength to cheer. He sinks deflated to the ground, and thinks he'll never be able to get up again.

The losses are severe. Mac Dougall and Conan lose seven hundred men. More than a thousand Picts lie dead on the battlefield. Already vultures are circling in the sky above them, screeching and calling. King Nechtan is not amongst the fallen.

Chapter nineteen
458 – 462 A.D. Argyll

Fergus spends the summer months trading with fine wool and whisky, with pottery and shellfish, and with silver jewellery. He sails along the coastlines, back and forth between Argyll and Dalriada, and throughout the archipelago of islands that are located in the western sea and Atlantic Ocean. Loarn, Bram and Sean are at his side, and fellow comrades from Dalriada and Caledonia join them. Angus builds boats, currachs and ocean-going vessels. Mac Arthur's shipyard prospers, and provides work for scores of men.

The brothers begin to form small fleets of vessels. Enemies, Britons, and Saxons alike, attack settlements in Ireland, steal booty and slaves, and then attempt to sail back to their homeland. Angus' boats are fast-tracked whirlwinds. The brothers waylay the outlanders' boats on their journey back across the sea. Their maritime forces surround the adversaries, seize their boats, kill the antagonists, and repossess their plunder. The three brothers become well known at sea, and on both sides of the channel. Their fellow countrymen cheer because the enemies no longer escape unpunished. The enemies think twice before assaulting Ireland again; it's not just a pushover after all. Fergus and his band of sailor warriors become popular and more powerful. Fergus buys farms and land with his silver. He finds tenants for his properties; they pay him rent and provide him with additional income.

Fergus never sails an identical route, but there is one island that he always visits. The knowledge that Rhianna is on Lewis, entices him into the port of Stornoway like the incoming tide. He smells her fragrance wafting over the waves and feels her soft skin brushing against him like a silk shawl. The current is strong, resistance hopeless. Fergus lets himself be drawn in, and closes his eyes in happiness.

"We need more wool from Harris," he says. "Laird Douglas has given me a letter for Rhianna. Conan promised to give us venison for

Colonsay." Are other favourite excuses. Of course he doesn't need an excuse, nor are his friends deceived, but the combination of work and pleasure is pleasing. At the end of the summer Rhianna surprises him.

"I'm with child," she says.

Fergus feels a warmth diffuse his body. "Oh Rhianna!" He is lost for words.

***

Ceredig returns from war. The Saxons have retreated from the Northumbrian coastlines *at least for the present* he thinks, *no doubt they will come again when winter passes.* His pulse quickens as he approaches the gatehouse to Alt Clut. He runs down the steps and into his castle, then up the stairs to the second floor. Tudwal is sitting on the floor playing with a wooden horse, Anna sits on a chair next to him. As soon as Ceredig enters she stands up quickly, but he waves his hand to signalise she should sit down again. He has eyes only for Tudwal. He looks strong and healthy. He moves the horse up and down making clicking noises with his mouth. Ceredig kneels down next to him and smiles at him tenderly.

"Hello," he says. "I'm back now, your Papa."

Tudwal looks at him and then at his horse. "Gee, gee," he says.

Later Ceredig returns downstairs, and sends for his bailiff and tackesman. They discuss property business, and when they finish, the bailiff talks of Rhianna.

"We've heard nothing of her, despite asking all around," he says. "Maybe she did drown, despite her body not turning up. Are you sure you don't want to proclaim her dead? Or at least separate yourself from her, so you can marry again?"

"No, what for? I have an heir, and if I feel like sex there are enough slaves. It's more trouble than it's worth to take another wife. What about her maid? I hear she's gone."

"Beth? Yes. She waited a month, but when nothing was heard, she went back home to Brodick. Her sweetheart picked her up."

"Her sweetheart?"

"Yes, you remember that stable lad at Brodick? Well apparently, he gained possession of a trading boat somehow. He docked at the harbour and sailed back to Brodick with her. That's what I was told, at least. She didn't really have any reason to stay, she was the Lady's personal maid, after all."

"Mmmn, well I'll go to Aran myself in a couple of weeks. A surprise visit, see if I can catch Laird Douglas off guard. I wouldn't be surprised if he's hiding his daughter somewhere, that villain. I'm surprised she left Tudwal here though."

***

Cartan hears of his three half-brother's growing popularity. It irks him like a pickle up his backside.

"They don't have anywhere near the number of resources you do." Mairead attempts to console him. "They cannot harm you."

He looks at Caelan, sitting next to his mother with his arm around her neck. His head rests on her shoulder and he strokes her hair. *How can such an eejit possibly be of my blood?* he thinks with distaste. After Caelan, no more children had followed. He'd done his best, at least at first. It wasn't his fault he'd married such a barren bitch. The trouble was he couldn't just separate from her. Not with her father being the king of the Ui Neill. Now he was stuck with the cow.

***

Rhianna gives birth to a healthy baby boy. He has brown eyes and brown curly hair and is always hungry. They call him Domangart.

"I would like to show him to my father," Rhianna says.

"I'm so proud of him I would like to show him to the whole world!" Fergus agrees. "If only we didn't have to live in secrecy! I want to marry you and let Domangart be christened." They both sigh, but it is only a small cloud on their horizon.

A year later, Rhianna gives birth to a girl. She looks almost identical to Domangart, but she has Rhianna's blue eyes. They call her Lisanda.

***

Ceredig travels to Aran. He surprises Douglas, but soon realises that the Laird has nothing to hide. He also sees Beth on the island.

"Has the mistress' body been washed ashore?" she asks Ceredig. She sheds a tear at his negative answer. He notices that the stable lad, her sweetheart, isn't on the island. "He sails around the coast, trading," she tells him, blushing.

Ceredig goes to the port's only tavern. He takes account of a man playing dice and losing. The inhabitants of Brodick are loyal to their Laird, but this man is easy to bribe. He promises to let Ceredig know should Rhianna visit, or Douglas or Beth go away on a journey. Ceredig promises him silver for his trouble.

***

As soon as he hears the news, Stuart gallops on horseback to Dunstaffnage. He storms into Laird Mac Dougall's study.

"Ceredig is dead!" he pants, breathless.

"What! How? Where?"

"Nechtan—Ceredig was fighting the Saxons south of the wall when scouts warned him that Nechtan was approaching with his Pictish army from the north. He turned his back on the Saxons, to march north and challenge Nechtan. The Saxons followed him, and he got caught up between the Picts in front of him and the Saxons behind him."

"My God, there must've been a massacre!"

"Yes, at Fordel. His whole army was slaughtered!"

***

A fresh breeze chases billowing clouds across the blue sky. The sun shines brightly. Guests, dressed in finery, arrive in pairs and small groups. As many as possible crowd into the small chapel at Dunseverick, to witness the marriage ceremony of Rhianna and Fergus, and the christening of Domangart and Lisanda. The rest wait patiently outside the chapel doors. The atmosphere is festive and light-hearted. Everyone is happy to celebrate this joyful occasion. Nothing indicates the tragic line of dire events that follow.

Patricius performs the marriage ceremony. Brother Aedan christens the children as Patricius cannot. He is Domangart's godfather. Later, outside the chapel, he gives the child two rubies.

"These used to belong to an enchantress," he tells the fascinated boy. "The bearer shall be protected from all evil."

Brother Aedan is shocked. "Patricius, what are you telling the boy? You cannot believe in such heresy!"

Patricius smiles, "Not I, no. Therefore, I have no use for such jewels. But the folk here still believe in these tales, whether they are Christian or not. Once I was saved from sure death, merely by showing some Gaels the rubies. The old king of the Dalriada, Miliucc, had them inserted as eyes on a fox stole, which he never removed from his neck. When he died, I came across them in his ashes, and picked them up without thinking. I've had them ever since. They collect dust on my book shelf. This morning I saw them and thought it was time to pass them on."

"Well, I suppose they might have some material value for the child, later on in life."

"Come," Patricius says. "Let's join the other clerics, I can see Olcan with them, and I'm thirsty too, let us drink and be merry."

The party is in full swing. Fergus and Rhianna stand next to each other accepting congratulations from their family and friends. Douglas has come from Brodick, as Donald and Mairi from Finlaggan and Flora and Mac Dougall from Dunstaffnage. Loarn and Angus are present, both with young ladies at their sides; Lorcan and his twin Mahon, Feradach, Gair, Sean, Bram with Haggis, and many others. Domangart and Lisanda have been playing catch with other children, but now they run up to their parents.

"Mother," Domangart pleads, pulling at Rhianna's hand. "I'm *thirsty*, are you coming now?" Rhianna bends down and picks him up in her arms.

"In a minute, a stor, let your grandfather finish talking."

"*I'm* thirsty too," Lisanda complains. Fergus lifts her up over his head and onto his shoulders. She squeals with delight.

"Hold on tightly now," he says. "Let's race your mother and brother to the drinks table. What will you have now? A beer?" Lisanda grabs hold of Fergus' ears and giggles

"Father! You know—" She doesn't finish her sentence, as a dozen warriors on horses, armed in helmets and breast shields, and bearing swords and spears, canter straight through the guests, sending them scattering, and right up to Fergus. Cartan, at the front, pulls up Lockwood and stops just a foot away from the happy family. Fergus and the guests around him gasp in shock.

"You don't invite your own brother to your wedding?" Cartan accuses Fergus.

Before he can answer, Erc steps forward. "*I* sent the invitations," he says, "and *no,* you were not invited. What do you think you're doing, arriving here fully armed and scaring the children? Leave this minute!"

Cartan turns to look at Erc. "You speak to *me*, your son, like that?"

"You are no son of mine," Erc retorts spitefully. "Your mother was already with child, when I was forced to marry her!" Cartan sucks his breath in and turns white. Beads of sweat appear on his forehead, and he sways in his saddle. Erc immediately regrets his rash words, spoken in anger.

Cartan grips his saddle to steady himself. "Who is my father?" Cartan asks in a deceivingly soft voice.

Erc remains quiet.

"Tell me!" Cartan insists. Erc still doesn't speak. Cartan raises his spear and hurls it with all his force towards Domangart. In the split second before it reaches the child, Lorcan dives in-between. The spear pierces Lorcan's chest, and he falls to the ground. Then everything happens at once.

Rhianna screams, stumbles backwards two paces, and still hugging Domangart tightly to her breast, turns on her heels and runs towards the safety of the castle.

Fergus thrusts Lisanda into Loarn's arms and orders, "Follow her!" Cartan pulls his spear from Lorcan's chest, blood spurts out in a fountain. Fergus pulls his cloak off, kneels down beside Lorcan, and presses it against the wound. The monks run up to help, clearing the space around Lorcan.

Cartan looks with distaste at his own garments, soaked from the blood that squirted from Lorcan's wound. He pulls on Lockwood's reins to turn him around, and digging his spurs into the horse's belly, starts to canter away in the direction he had come from. Lorcan dying, but not yet dead, raises his head slightly and gives a short sharp whistle. Lockwood stops dead in his tracks, rears up on his hind legs, and throws Cartan off his back roughly to the ground. Lorcan sees Cartan fall, smiles, then drops his head back, and dies with a smile on his lips. Cartan gets up furiously brushing dirt from his clothes, remounts, jerks harshly on Lockwood's reins and rides off, surrounded by his warriors.

A monk closes Lorcan's eyes and gently folds his hands across his chest. Patricius says a special prayer, it is too late to give him the last rites. The spectators stand back respectfully as Mahon approaches. His face is pale and drawn, his steps are slow and deliberate. Tormey walks at his side, his hand supports Mahon's elbow. Mahon kneels down beside his twin's body and takes his hand in his.

"It is cold," he says. Tormey lays a hand on his shoulder. "I feel as if half of my own self is missing," Mahon continues, "we were always together. What shall I do now?"

Tormey answers, "He told me once that when his time came, he hoped it would be quick, he didn't want to be an invalid. He had a good life and a death he wished for."

The crowd murmurs in agreement. Servants arrive from the castle with a blanket and wooden board. Lorcan's body is moved carefully onto the makeshift stretcher and covered. They carry him to the castle hall. Monks begin to prepare his body.

***

Rhianna gets the children ready for bed. "Will Lorcan get better, Mother?" Domangart asks.

"I don't know, my treasure, Lupus will do his best. Let us include him in our bedtime prayers." The children kneel down to pray. Rhianna notices Domangart's hand screwed together tightly in a fist.

"What do you have in your hand, sweetheart?" Domangart opens his fist and reveals the two rubies.

Rhianna gasps, "Where did you get them from?"

"Patricius gave them to me, Mother. He said they were magic and would protect me from evil."

Rhianna swallows. "Let's put them on your shelf and pray now," she says. The children settled, she goes downstairs. She slips into the hall and taking hold of Fergus' hand silently, joins the night watch.

***

Erc travels with a delegation of family and witnesses to the king of the Ui Neill.

"He won't go unpunished this time," he says. "There were too many witnesses."

The king of the Ui Neill is in a dilemma. The punishment for murder is death, or under special circumstances, banishment from the tribe, casting the whole immediate family as outlaws, into poverty. He can do neither. Cartan is his son-in-law. He lets the wretch speak, interested as to what he would say this time to defend himself.

"I had an angry argument with my father," Cartan says. "The spear was meant for him, to wound, not kill. I can't help it if some fool jumps in-between!"

Erc's blood boils. "It is not true! He tried to kill my grandson, an innocent child, I stood in a completely different direction!"

"A case of one man's word against the other," the king says.

"No!" Erc cannot believe what he is hearing. "I have witnesses!"

"As Cartan also. Nevertheless, the death of your loyal warrior cannot go unpunished. Cartan, you will make a payment of two hundred cattle to Erc as reparation."

***

"Two hundred cattle? That is the price of my brother?" Mahon shakes his head in disbelief at the judgement. "Nothing will bring Lorcan back, nor can recompense his life. Give the cattle to the monks, I have no use for them."

***

The death of Lorcan leaves Fergus sorrowful. Cartan's 'punishment' was a scornful mockery of justice. He is more determined than ever to get revenge. His father is deluded to think that Cartan can be punished lawfully, the man is too powerful by far. Fergus will deal with him, but for the moment more pressing matters are at hand, Cartan must wait.

He sails with his family, Douglas, Beth, Mahon, Tormey and loyal friends to Aran. For the present they can live at Brodick castle. He allows Rhianna a week to settle, and then suggests they go for a walk, up Goat Fell. He must talk to her without any distractions. He takes her hand and they set off uphill through the heather. Rhianna feels a shiver of arousal go down her spine at his touch, but as she strides out powerfully beside him, the wind ripping through her auburn hair and the sun beating down on her face, she braces herself for what she knows must come. He will speak of Alt Clut. They must return. She doesn't want to.

***

The return to Strathclyde can be delayed no longer. Ceredig has been buried six weeks ago, and the seneschal has taken care of his estate; but the nobles and landowners need a new king, and Tudwal is but six years old. Rhianna is filled with foreboding and guilt. The nobles and landowners, justices, elders, and counsels meet in the great hall at Alt Clut and she must answer before them. Fergus is at her side. She looks around the faces surrounding her and recognises a few. Laird Mac Farlane is friendly and encourages her to speak.

"Lady Rhianna, we are all happy to see you here, healthy and well, we thought you had drowned."

Rhianna takes all her courage together. She clears her throat.

"Thank you, Laird Mac Farlane. I am guilty of deceiving you all," she says, looking openly into the mens' eyes, "and I apologise for that. By law I have no excuse and deserve to be punished. To my defence— I have witnesses who will lay testimony to the fact, that my husband, your king, Laird Ceredig, beat and injured me in the most brutal manner. I nearly died. Fearing for my life, I ran away."

"And left his heir here alone." Ceredig's seneschal is as compassionate as a block of ice.

"In the good care of Anna, his nurse. Ceredig loved Tudwal, he would never have harmed him."

"Is it not true, that you have remarried?"

Fergus steps forward. "I am Fergus, Prince of the Dalriada. I wed Lady Rhianna two weeks gone at Dunseverick."

"We all *know* who you are." The seneschal glares at him. "The question is—"

"No!" Laird Mac Farlane contradicts him. "We are here to listen to Laird Ceredig's last will and testament, and then decide what is to be done. This is not a trial. Colin, please open the document now, and read it to us."

Colin, a judiciary counsel who wrote down the wills of those happy enough to have anything to pass on, stands up. He breaks the wax seal of a parchment scroll, and begins to read: "*'In the name of God amen. This is the last will and testament of Ceredig Cambeul, king of Strathclyde. First, I commit my soul to God and my body to Christian burial. I bequeath to my lawful wife, Rhianna, the territory of Inverclyde and all the farms therein. Also, the right to live in Alt Clut so long that she lives. I beg her forgiveness for all the wrongs I did unto her. I bequeath unto my son, Tudwal, the whole of the rest of my estates and the monies therein. I leave and ordain my wife, Rhianna, my true and lawful executor of all ye rest of my goods movable and unmovable. This is affirmed to be ye last will and testament of Ceredig Cambeul'*. It is signed by witnesses and there is a list of inventories." Colin concludes.

"Tell me, when did Laird Ceredig write this will?" the seneschal asks.

"It is dated the eleventh day of November, 559."

"*After* Rhianna was presumed dead. So he didn't believe her drowned, but neither did he hold her actions against her," Laird Mac Farlane speaks. "Well, we should withdraw and discuss this matter together; but if Laird Ceredig wished that his wife be regent—" he trails off.

***

The nobles and landowners argue. “We cannot accept a *woman* as our ruler,” they say.

“She isn’t a warrior, and cannot lead us in battle nor defend our lands.” Laird Mac Farlane is of the same opinion.

“Tudwal is our king, but is yet a child. We could elect Fergus as our representative and regent king.”

“He is a tested warrior,” a second noble agrees. The men think it over and then take it to vote. The decision is unanimous.

“Now he just needs to agree,” Laird Mac Farlane says with a grave tone in his rich voice.

***

Rhianna stands by the burning fireside and shivers. “Can we go home soon, a chroi? I miss the children so much and every room here, every wall, every object holds terrible memories for me. I cannot sleep and feel anxious.”

Fergus steps over to Rhianna and holds her gently. “We should give Tudwal a couple of weeks to get used to us, and anyway I have so much to do.”

“You are right about Tudwal, this is his home; although Anna will come with us, of course.”

“Rodric asked my permission to marry her.”

“Really? Well, that’s some good news!”

“Aye, he’ll come with us when we leave here. He wants to build a croft and find work on Aran. I thought I’d ask your father if he could give him some land, we have a lot to thank him for.”

“I’ll ask him; he will find something, I’m sure.”

“Good. I sent a servant to Whithorn asking for five monks to come here. I need a good map of the whole of Strathclyde. I will ride to every single property with them, and they will draw the boundaries on the map, or several maps if need be. I need a new army to protect our land, and with over a thousand men dead, I shall probably be looking for new settlers too.”

“That will take months!”

"I'm afraid so, yes. I propose that we travel to the major settlements, and show ourselves and Tudwal to our folk. Then in a couple of weeks I can sail home with you both. I can't stay long at Brodick myself though, there is too much to be done here."

Chapter twenty
462 – 474 A.D. The Dalriada clan

Fergus rides with five warriors and five monks to the late Laird Ceredig's tenanted farms. Some he finds deserted. Widows of fallen soldiers, many with small children, cannot cultivate the land and tend to animals all by themselves. They have sold their pigs and whatever other animals they possess, to a neighbour, and sought out relations, or tried to find alternative work. With over a thousand men in prime age now dead, adolescents and old people struggle to scrape a living from the land.

They arrive at a farm, the fields not yet harvested. A woman with a young child crawling about in the mud beneath her feet, is digging up vegetables. A few scraggy hens are picking at the ground. She looks up when the company of monks and warriors arrive. Wiping the sweat from her forehead with a grimy hand, she eyes them suspiciously.

"If it's your rent you'll be wanting, there's nothing to be had."

"No, good woman, we won't be wanting any rent this year. Your husband was killed in battle?" Fergus asks.

"He was."

"And how do you propose to farm the land?"

"I've not had time to work that out yet, I'm too busy getting food on the table once a day."

"Do you have older children?"

"Two sons, ten and twelve. They're in the upper field trying to harvest the oats."

"We're here to see how we can help. I can find you a labourer if you wish. He'll be able-bodied and work hard, but you must give him food, somewhere to sleep, and ten shillings a year."

"Another mouth to fill! We're near starving as it is!"

"It's up to you."

The woman considers. "Aye, when my husband was here, we were doing all right. And we don't pay any rent this year, right?"

"No, and next year just half the rent."

"Fair enough, Sire, I thank thee."

"Very well, a monk will write down what else you need. Seeds perhaps? Now show him where the borders of your farm are, and give him your name and those of your children."

"There's nothing changed with the boundaries."

"No, I'm sure, we're just checking our papers and making an inventory."

***

Fergus visits every single one of Laird Ceredig's farms and his three quarries and one mine. The monks write everything down. He visits the nobles and the landowners. He is not responsible for their properties but he needs to speak to them, at first individually. Once he has an overview of Strathclyde, he calls the nobles and landowners together to speak to them all.

"The last battle was a decapitating blow to Strathclyde," he begins. "Your kingdom has been left vulnerable to attack, and with so many dead, there are not enough men to form a new army, to cultivate the land, nor to carry out workmanship."

"We all know that, but what can we do about it?" Black Malcolm is impatient with small talk, he wants answers.

"Well, I have some suggestions, but first I want to make two points. The first is that we need a new army. In the past, all able-bodied men between sixteen and forty were expected to fight, thus leaving the settlements naked of protection. We should make a law that every twenty houses should provide twelve men to fight. The twenty houses can decide themselves who to send, and who to leave at home. In addition, every twenty houses must provide for one seven-bench seagoing currach. If we don't just defend our borders, but also actively attack regions overseas, we can acquire slaves to work for us, and take possession of spoils, to buy building materials and tools. The second point is that we must build brochs along our borders. The monks have marked strategic positions on this map, here and here and here," Fergus says, pointing.

He pauses for breath. The men look stunned, Ceredig was a sleepy dog in comparison to this powerful, dynamic youngster.

"But how are we going to get started?" Black Malcolm wants to know. "We haven't got enough men."

"Neh at the moment, we haven't, but with your consent—" Fergus sweeps his arm in a circle to include all the nobles and landowners. "I shall sail to Dalriada and look for men willing to settle here."

The men let their breath out. "You mean, *immigrants*?" Laird Mac Farlane says the word as if it is somehow dirty.

"Aye, they'll have to work hard, and obey the same laws as we do."

The men are quiet as they consider this outrageous suggestion. Black Malcolm begins to chuckle and slaps his thigh.

"By me Gods, I like it!" he declares. The men look at him, at first astonished, then they join in his laughter.

"He's right!" they say. "Let's do it!"

***

The Dalriada are caught between the powerful Ui Neill on one side and the Dalfiatach on the other. With these two powerful and warlike neighbours, they have no avenue for expansion. Fergus, already well known and popular in his homeland, visits the natives, younger brothers who have to scrape a living together somehow, without their own property. He tells them of the rich and fertile lands in Strathclyde, of the wild game and coastal food resources. It is easy to attract the first settlers. They come with their families or alone, and they intermarry with the Caledonians. More natives, hearing only good, follow them.

***

Back at Brodick, Rhianna tells Fergus that she is with child again.

"I think I must have guessed," he smiles. "Brodick is too small for us. I have bought some land on the southern shore of East Loch Tarbert. If you like it, well I would like to build a castle there."

"A castle? For us? Oh yes, our first family home! Tell me what it is like."

"I'll do better than that, we can sail there together and look at the site."

"Can I help plan the building?"

"Well, some of it, yes. How many chambers do you think we'll need?"

Rhianna sees Fergus' eyes twinkling mischievously. She gives him a playful clap.

"That depends," she retorts, one hand protectively over her stomach. "On just how many children you intend having."

***

Loarn has fallen in love with a Caledonian princess. They want to marry. Laird Mac Dougall and Flora are happy and already hoping for 'grandchildren'. They give Loarn a large estate on the coast, to the south-west of Dunstaffnage, with thirty adjoining farms. Loarn knows the area well. Just north of a large settlement on the coast, called Little Bay, there is a hilltop bounded by steep, and in places vertical, slopes. The hill commands exceptional views along the sound of Kerrara and outlying Isles, of Little Bay and its harbour. To the south and west are sheer rock faces. Atop, around the north and east, there are the remains of stone walls, formerly a fort. Loarn decides to rebuild it.

First, he builds a road, a winding track ten feet wide, that climbs up the grassy slopes from Little Bay. Building materials are brought by ship to the harbour, then loaded onto carts and pulled by oxen up the hill. A pair of concentric defensive ditches and earth embankments are dug out to surround the whole of the sloping summit, compassing nearly eight acres. Inside this area Loarn erects a high square tower, a keep, to protect his family. It is adjoined by a stone castle with a grand hall and kitchens. A wall surrounds the courtyard. Outside this area, in the bailey, are at least thirty further buildings: stables, a smithy, a bakery, accommodation for soldiers and more. There is just one entrance, it faces the north, and is protected by a massive iron gate and rampart. It is an impressive stronghold. Loarn names it Dun Ollaigh.

***

Cartan writhes in anger at the success Fergus and his brothers are having. Fergus, the eldest, is in particular, a thorn in his eye. He curses every hair on his head, his eyes, his nose, his ears, and every tooth in his mouth. He damns every bone in his body. He begins to plot strategies on how to harm him. Fergus has a firm foot holding in Argyll. Protected by his followers, Cartan cannot reach Fergus there personally. He burns with desire to destruct him. He has no other thoughts than that of his ruination and obliteration. He visits Morag, Mista's former cook, whom he had bribed to poison Mista, and caused several miscarriages before the birth of Fergus.

"I heard that Fergus has built a stronghold near Tarbert. He's looking for immigrants. I want you to go there and apply for work in his household. As a cook, or better still, a nurse for the children," he tells her.

"There won't be much I can accomplish, all by myself out there."

"Don't worry, I'm bribing spies to be on the lookout, and ferret around for opportunities. I'll stay in close communication."

***

Molly is a slip of a girl, just eleven years old. She has seven younger siblings. Her mother and father, hard-working yet poverty-stricken, walk up the hill with her to Castle Tarbert. They knock at the servants' door. A maid answers and brings them to the seneschal. The impoverished parents push Molly forward.

"Have you got work for our daughter?" they ask. "She's hard-working and doesn't eat much."

The seneschal looks her up and down. "We need a scullery maid. Food and a sixpence at Michaelmas. One afternoon free, every two weeks."

"Thank you, Sir," her parents answer, and leave her there alone.

***

Rhianna gives birth to a healthy boy. They call him Eòghann, meaning 'God's gift'. Rhianna breastfeeds him. She has many other duties to perform, and looks for a woman to help her look after the infant, between feeds. The seneschal gives Morag the job.

Molly enters the kitchen, and sees Morag dipping the corner of a cloth into some cloudy liquid. She pushes it into the baby's mouth and lets him suck on it. Eòghann is violently sick. Frightened, Molly exits the kitchen quickly before she's discovered. The oldest of seven siblings, she has often helped her mother look after her younger brothers and sisters. She's troubled; she knows that she's witnessed something that she shouldn't have seen.

***

Eòghann loses weight and becomes pale and sickly. The monk in charge of the herbarium, cannot find anything wrong with him.

"I'm sorry," he says. "I cannot explain it."

More monks and healers are consulted. The boy eats well but continues to lose weight. He becomes weaker and weaker. He is christened in an emergency ceremony. Molly is alone in the kitchen; Morag has left a bowl of the cloudy liquid on the table. She dips the tip of her small finger into the milky substance, and tastes it carefully. It is salt water! Brought up to keep quiet and stay out of trouble, Molly says nothing. Eòghann dies and is buried. Rhianna and Fergus grieve; Rhianna is inconsolable.

"Why did God give us a wonderful child, and then take him away from us again?" she asks the priest. "Have we sinned?"

Father Brothaigh has trouble finding a suitable reply, there is so much he doesn't understand himself. Rhianna is kneeling before him. He puts a hand gently on her shoulder.

"I don't know," he admits. "God's ways are often incomprehensible to us, but this does not mean he has forgotten you. Let us pray together."

***

Molly doesn't really understand what she has seen, but she's suspicious. One day she sees Morag pull an expensive-looking, gold jewelled ring out of the pocket of her léine, and try it on. She holds it up in the light and admires it. Suddenly realising that Molly is watching, she pulls it off quickly and stuffs it back in her léine.

"What are you staring at? Got no work to do?" Tipping a bucket of kitchen waste onto the floor, she tells her, "The floor needs scouring, get a step on it!"

Molly quickly picks up the rubbish and puts it back into the bucket. She brings it outdoors before the seneschal comes. Then she fills a pail with water and starts scrubbing the floor.

***

On her half-day off, Molly goes home. She tells her mother and father what she has witnessed.

"Why, that Morag murdered the poor wee bairn! You must go to the lady and tell her!" her mother says.

"Neh!" Her father vetoes. "You'll do no such thing. You'll get us all into trouble, it's never the real culprits that get punished!"

"What?" Her mother is indignant. "We can't just let that woman get away with murder, she's got to tell someone!"

"Neh, Molly will lose her job, you'll see."

"She could speak to the seneschal, he seemed nice enough. Let him decide if the Laird and lady need to be told."

"Well, I'm against it. Mark my words."

"Och, ye old caitiff! I'll go back with her meself, and speak to the seneschal with her."

***

The seneschal is stern.

"This is a very serious accusation, Molly. It could have grave consequences; Morag will receive the death punishment. Are you ready to swear an oath at court, and say you saw her murder the babe?"

"Well, I didn't see her actually *murder* him, Sir. But she did dip the cloth in liquid and let him suck on it, more than once."

"And you swear there was salt in the water, enough to kill the infant?"

Molly begins to stutter. "Er—well, I don't know how *much* salt was in the water, Sir. Whether it was enough or not. I'm not knowledgeable about these things."

"Hmmn, exactly. Well Molly, Morag will be leaving Tarbert tomorrow. With no baby to look after, she has no work. I cannot think *why* she would wish to harm the infant, and lose her job. Have you spoken to anyone else about this?"

"No Sir, just my mother here, and my father."

"Very well. Well, I'll tell you what we'll do. I believe you have spoken to me in good faith, so I'm not going to punish you for false witness, this time. Now go back to work and don't mention this to anyone."

"Yes Sir, thank you." Molly leaves the room quickly. The seneschal glares at her mother who doesn't budge from her stance.

"You may leave now."

"What! You're not going to say *anything* to the Laird?" Molly's mother is in high dudgeon.

"You heard your daughter; she cannot swear to anything. Do you really want someone to die on a mere suspicion? Away with you!"

***

Fergus and Rhianna saddle up Thunderbolt and Starlight and roam the countryside above Loch Tarbert. It is a fine day, the sun shines and there is no suggestion of rain. They stop on a headland and look out at the splendid views across the sea and numerous islets. Fergus takes hold of Rhianna's hand and looks into her eyes.

"I love you," he says softly. "Since the day I caught you in the stables at Brodick, I knew you were the one. The day you married Ceredig was the darkest day of my life, and the day you ran away, my heart near burst with love and admiration. I think of you in the morning before the sun rises and in the black of night, I feel your presence." He leans over and kisses her long and tenderly.

"Oh Fergus, my heart, I love you with all my soul from the tip of my feet to the top of my head. I'm sorry if I've been dismissive of late, my grief for Eòghann…" her voice trails off.

"*Our* grief for Eòghann, a ghrá mo chroí, *our* grief, we will never forget him. We must try to be strong for the sake of our other children. Tomorrow we are to sail to Brodick, I have written to Tormey. He has three suitable ponies for our little ones."

"Oh Fergus! Please don't tell them tonight, we won't get a wink of sleep, and tomorrow they'll be as grumpy as an old bear awakened in the middle of winter!"

"I thought maybe you would also like to visit Beth? It seems to me she is more your friend than your servant. Maybe she would consider returning with us for a visit?"

"Oh Fergus, you have thought of everything! You are the kindest, most thoughtful person I know. Yes, I would love Beth to come, she will cheer me up no end!"

"That is good, because soon I must leave you alone again, duty calls I'm afraid, but I'll return as soon as I can."

***

The next morning at breakfast Fergus asks the children if they would like a trip to Brodick.

"To Grandfather Douglas, oh yes!" Tudwal says.

"Can we visit the horses, too?" Lisanda asks.

"I thought maybe the three of you would like to choose a pony." Fergus smiles.

"Oh *Papa!*" All three of them shout at once, jumping up from the table to hug him.

"Can I choose my *own*, just for *me*?" Lisanda asks, hopping up at down excitedly.

"Yes, you all can," Fergus assures them.

"Will you go hunting with me?" Tudwal asks.

"When I return from my duties, yes."

"That's not fair, I want to go hunting too!" Lisanda complains.

"Are you arguing already, young lady?" Rhianna asks in mock anger.

"No Mother," Lisanda answers demurely.

"Father, you will take *all* of us hunting, won't you?" Domangart asks.

"Of course my son." Fergus pats his head affectionately. "Have you grown again, *overnight*? You're taller than me now."

Domangart giggles. "Oh Papa, you're *sitting down*!"

"Ah, so I am, thank goodness for that, I was getting worried!"

***

When they return from Brodick, Beth accompanies them. The two women, best of friends, have been through much together. Rhianna talks of the loss of Eòghann. Beth is certain that there has been foul play, but she cannot imagine how or what. She doesn't speak out; she doesn't want to agitate Rhianna.

When Rhianna realises she is with child again, she frets and cannot sleep.

"I'm worried Beth, I'm terrified the baby might have some inexplicable disease and die again."

"The monk said you needn't be worried; you have two healthy children."

"I can't help myself, I brood on it, day and night."

"Well how about some distraction? Today is market day, shall we walk down to town?"

"That is a good idea."

The two women wander along the rows of market stalls, selling everything from foodstuffs and live animals to ribbons and knives. In one corner of the market, they see an old lady with just one small table and a few cheeses. She has a crooked back and is dressed in rags. Rhianna nudges Beth.

"The poor dear, we should buy a cheese from her."

They approach her table. She has prepared a plate with small pieces of cheese for people to taste before buying. She holds the plate out towards Rhianna and Beth, her hand shakes with the effort.

"Will you try a piece of wild garlic cheese, my Ladies?" she asks. Rhianna notices she has only one tooth left in her mouth.

They both take a small piece and chew it carefully. "Why it is absolutely delicious," Rhianna compliments the woman. "We must buy one, Beth."

Beth agrees and starts to pick a cheese up from the table.

"No," the woman says, reaching down below the table and retrieving a cheese from a box. "It has been in the sun, take this one!"

Beth puts the cheese in her basket and the women continue on their way. Birga-One-tooth keeps a sharp eye on them. Once they are out of view, she packs her things up quickly, and goes to the harbour where a boat is waiting for her.

"I told you Rhianna would come to the market sooner or later," she tells Cartan.

They had come to the market for five weeks running and today finally been rewarded with Rhianna's presence.

"I hope that the whole family eats from it," Cartan replies. "Soldiers hiss the sails! We must depart quickly."

Back at the castle, Rhianna and Beth put their basket of shopping on the table. Rhianna cuts some bread, whilst Beth pours them two mugs of ale.

They sit down and have just begun to eat, as Lisanda runs in screaming, "Mother, Mother come quickly, the boys are fighting again!"

Rhianna sighs, stands up and follows her. Tudwal is pulling Domangart's hair and Domangart is kicking Tudwal.

"Stop it, the two of you, stop it at once!" she tells them off. Suddenly an agonising pain rips through her body. She grips her stomach and falls to the floor.

"Mother!" The children stop fighting and run out of the room to find help, a monk, a healer, an adult, anyone. Racing through the kitchen they see Beth lying on the floor in a pool of vomit. They hold their breath a second, then run outside screaming.

Rhianna drifts in and out of consciousness. Sometimes she thinks she hears someone speaking to her. She tries to open her eyes, but her vision rotates and her head thumps.

Fergus holds her hand.

"Will she recover?" he asks the monk tending to her. Rhianna has lost her baby and has a high fever. She has been hallucinating for two days now.

"If we can reduce her fever, yes. I have tried to give her elderberry juice, just a drop at a time, but she cannot hold it down."

"What can I do?"

"Nothing. Luckily, she didn't eat as much of the cheese as Beth."

"And it was poisoned with lily of the valley?"

"It might have been an accident; the leaves are very similar to those of wild garlic."

"My men questioned every stallholder. Nobody knows who the woman is, she had only just started selling her cheeses at the market. But the strange thing is that she hasn't been seen since."

"It is lucky no one else has been harmed."

"That is what makes me suspicious."

Rhianna's eyes flutter open. "Fergus?" she asks.

"Yes, I'm here, I'm with you," he says.

"I'm thirsty," she says.

The monk gives her a sip of water. She keeps it down.

Chapter twenty-one
474 A.D. Death of Erc, Dunseverick

Erc goes out; he is caught in a storm. He returns home, drenched to the skin and freezing.

"What do you think you were doing out there in such weather?" Mista tells him off, as he removes his wet clothes. His teeth chatter. Servants bring mulled wine, and he sits in front of the fire.

"Stop fussing, Mista, I'll be fine."

Erc burns with fever and his breathing rattles. Lupus comes with several fellow monks.

"It is his lungs," he says. "We cannot help him; we should give him his last rites." Erc dies.

Angst creeps amidst Mista's grief. Her own sons still in Argyll, she doesn't know how her stepsons will react. The younger ones seem to accept her, but Cartan is very dominant and will no doubt influence his brothers to her disadvantage. She doesn't so much fear for her own life, she worries about her sons'. Taking the key to Erc's iron chest, she puts it on a chain and keeps it always around her neck.

***

Cartan is the first to arrive at Dunseverick. He has a last will and testament, drawn up for him by the druids, in Erc's name and in his skilfully forged handwriting. Now he just needs to exchange it with the real one. He notices immediately that Mista wears the key to the iron chest around her neck. *She's smarter than I thought,* Cartan thinks, *but no matter, I was going to have to deal with her anyway. She will be informed about the real will.*

***

Fergus, Loarn and Angus hear of their father's death and set sail immediately, home to Dunseverick. When they arrive, they are told that their mother, Mista, has died also.

"How? That's not possible," Angus cries out. "She was perfectly well!"

"She was poisoned." Tigernach, their second-eldest half-brother tells them. "She ate some game pie with venison and mushrooms and the mushrooms—well they were poisonous."

"Who did this?" Fergus asks angrily.

"We don't know. The cook says she would never make such a mistake. Then she noticed that there were eleven dishes with pie remains, and she made but ten pies. She has no idea where the extra pie came from."

"Cartan!" Fergus cries out enraged.

"Nothing can be proved," Tigernach answers.

***

Mista is laid on her bed. Cartan removes the key from her corpse and unlocks Erc's iron chest. He replaces the legitimate will with his false one. Then he throws the real will on the fire and watches it burn to cinders. He relocks the iron chest and places the key back around his stepmother's neck. He doesn't want to be the one to 'find' it.

***

The three brothers say their farewells to their father, and again, tragically to their mother. They meet in their father's study to grieve.

"We've been robbed of our parents," Angus sobs. "And all because of that villainous dastard!" He clenches his fists. Fergus and Loarn stand next to him and they all embrace each other.

"Tomorrow they will be buried," Fergus says. "We should all leave here immediately afterwards, before Cartan arrests us."

"Arrests us? What for?" Loarn asks. "And how come Cartan? He's not king—" his voice trails off. "Oh no, I hadn't thought of that! You think the Roydammna will elect him as Father's successor?"

"Well, he is the eldest, I expect it's his right."

Angus' jaw drops.

Recognising the truth in Fergus' words and the looming danger, he closes it again quickly and says, "I'll get our men to have the boat ready and waiting. We can use the souterrain if necessary."

"Are you sure Cartan doesn't know of it by now?" Loarn asks.

"I doubt it. Father would have no more to do with him after Lorcan's death and all his other evil doings. He was certain that he murdered Mongan."

"Don't worry. We have friends here too, looking out for us," Fergus reassures his brothers. "They will be present at the roydammna's announcement and make sure that we can leave unscathed."

"I don't believe it!" Loarn shakes his head. "What is the world coming to?"

***

Tigernach has taken the key to Erc's chest from Mista's neck before her funeral. Now, in the presence of a judiciary, three monks including Patricius, and all of his brothers and half-brothers, he opens the iron chest. He removes the testament, a scroll of parchment sealed with wax, and gives it to the judiciary. They all sit at a table and the judiciary breaks the seal.

"Are you sure this is his *last* will and testament?" he asks. "It is dated from 430."

"*Before* he married our mother? No, that can't be right! Our father was always very conscientious about keeping his papers in order. There must be another one somewhere." Angus is convinced.

"Maybe he saw no need to make a new will." Cartan sneers superciliously. Cartan's remark casts all doubt from Fergus' mind.

"He's stolen it!" he says flatly.

"How dare you!" Cartan springs up from his chair, ready to pounce.

"Calm down!" Tigernach intervenes. "Fergus I'm sorry, but we all opened Erc's chest together, and I took the key from your mother's neck. Cartan couldn't have stolen anything. I think you should apologise."

"No!" Fergus refuses. "No matter how impossible it seems, he found a way, of that I am certain."

"Well, please let everyone present take notice of the fact, that you have absolutely no proof whatsoever."

"They should leave," Cartan says. "And the monks also. Father's will was written *before* they were born and before he changed his faith, they cannot be included."

There is a stunned silence. Before Fergus and his brothers can get up and leave, Patricius speaks, "Your father gave our cause a generous annual allowance, will it continue?"

"My father had little enough as it is," Cartan says. "And we are seven surviving sons. Let us hear what his last will is, before we decide."

The judiciary reads the false testament that Cartan has provided. "I, Erc, son of Eochaid Muinremuir, being of sound mind and disposing memory, do hereby declare this to be my last will and testament. I bequeath all my properties and all my earthly goods to be divided in eight equal parts between my eight sons, Cartan, Mongan, Tigernach, Becc, Lugh, Naoise, Odhran and Ailill. Should a son of mine be chosen by the Roydammna to be king of the Dalriada, then I bequeath this above-named son, Dunseverick and its properties and all within. The rest of my properties should then be divided in seven equal parts between my remaining sons. This is affirmed to be ye last will and testament of Erc."

Fergus, Loarn and Angus stand up and leave the room. Patricius and the monks follow. They enter the kitchens and see Fionn there. His face is drawn, he looks old and haggard.

"Fionn!" Angus hugs the white-haired man, now in his seventies. "You heard about Mista."

"Yes."

"The funeral is tomorrow. The 'so-called' last will of our father has just been read."

"I know. I also know he wrote a new will after his marriage to Mista, and yet another one after he was elected king."

"Did you see it?"

"No, but he told me."

"I don't want his properties, but the injustice annoys me. Cartan is always one step ahead of us," Fergus says.

"I would've liked some memento," Angus says. "Some small thing to remind me of them."

"None of us will ever forget them, but our lives are in Argyll now. After we leave tomorrow, I shall never return, there are too many bad memories here," Loarn states.

"You must await the roydammna's decision," Fionn tells them. "And pledge your loyalty to the new king, whoever it is."

"No! I refuse to kneel before Cartan, I would kill myself first!" Fergus is adamant.

"Who says Cartan will be elected?" Fionn asks.

"Well, he's obviously banking on it. The clause in the will about Dunseverick was a giveaway."

"What did the will say?"

"Everything is to be divided into eight equal parts, *but* should one of them be elected king, that son gets Dunseverick and all within."

"Ah, he wants to appear fair to his brothers. And the monks?"

"Nothing."

"Well, I know for sure that's not right. In fact, as far as I remember Erc telling me, Cartan was the only one to get nothing. He had already received farms when he married. I have friends who belong to the Roydammna. They tell me that Cartan has bribed many people to vote in his favour, but there are also many people against him. There were numerous guests at your wedding, Fergus, and Lorcan was well liked. His murder hasn't been forgotten. Cartan dictates with blackmail and bribery, one day it will be his downfall."

***

The Roydammna have knocked the prospective candidates for the throne, down to three: Cartan, Tigernach and Fergus.

"Erc never even mentioned Fergus in his will," one of Cartan's cronies argue. "He can't have had a very high opinion of him."

"He wrote the will before Fergus was born, so it doesn't count. His mother was a daughter of Laeghaire, the high king of Ireland. Her grandfather too was high king. Marca was not of such Royal blood. And anyhow, look at how much Fergus has already achieved in Argyll."

"Cartan is a good and loyal warrior. He has served the high king for what, forty years now. Fergus wasn't even here."

"Tigernach served the high king also."

"Cartan is the eldest."

"Cartan murdered Lorcan, and he is surrounded by scandals and rumours."

"Lorcan was an accident, and the so-called rumours are just that."

"He is still the eldest."

"Tigernach is second oldest."

It is taken to the vote. Cartan and Tigernach lead. The Roydammna argue and vote again. The result is not unanimous but clear. Tigernach is elected king.

***

Cartan is seething. He feels cheated of his rightful claim to the throne and inheritance. The worst-case scenario has at least been prevented, and Fergus thwarted, thanks to his cronies. Tigernach could, thank goodness, be directed. Maybe he would die soon.

***

Erc's sons, resenting the expense of supporting Patricius, and desiring to keep the money themselves, decide to stop the payments.

"That is not right, it would have been our father's wish for the annual grant to the monks to continue," Fergus objects.

"You have no say in the matter," Cartan overrules.

"He is right," Tigernach agrees, although he himself was for continuing the stipend.

Fergus goes to Armagh and visits Patricius. "I cannot give you as much as my father," he says. "But I wish to help."

"My son," Patricius answers. "Although your brothers do not respect thee today, it is *you* that shall be king. The kings of this country and over Alba shall be from thee for ever."

Chapter twenty-two
474 – 479 A.D. Retribution. Argyll and Ireland

Mac Arthur dies, and Angus acquires his shipyard. He employs over a hundred men, joiners, and carpenters, to work under his command. Wood becomes scarce on Islay. Angus sails to Dalriada and buys wood from the thickly forested slopes of the luscious glens. Oak trees, five hundred years old, are felled. The trunks are stripped of bark and sliced into planks, ready for transport across the twenty miles of sea separating the north-eastern tip of Ireland and Islay. More and more Dalriadans follow Angus. He gives them work and they build homes. They buy land, cultivate fields, and intermarry with the native peoples of Islay.

Angus falls in love with, and marries a woman from Armagh. They have a son, whom they name Muredach. Angus has no need of a fortress. He builds a large wooden, two-storey home for himself and his family, behind the shipyard on Islay.

His vessels, fast-oared warships, can carry thirty armed men at a time. Angus, Fergus and Loarn, together with their fearsome warriors, rule the seas. They fight battles with their fleets of warships, and take possession of the Mull of Kyntyre up to the river Add, thus substantially embracing southern Argyll.

***

Tudwal is sixteen years old. He is a solid, reliable boy. He can read and write, do simple maths and his Latin is passable. He is good fighter and is interested in how mechanical things work. Although not overly astute, his heart is in the right place, and Fergus begins to consign small duties to him.

"He needs a little more time," Fergus tells the nobles in Strathclyde. "He will learn."

Domangart, a year younger than Tudwal, is a born academic. He can read and write Latin fluently at the age of six, and then progresses to learn Greek. He loves reading anything that he can get hold of, particularly the Greek and Italian classics. Fergus makes sure he can fight too. Along with Tudwal he spends a part of every day with sword practice.

"I want to be a cleric," he tells his parents. "I would like to study in Armagh under Patricius."

Patricius and his monks had set up schools of learning all across Ireland. Originally meant to educate young boys suited to become clerics and spread the word of the Christian faith, these centres had become famous. Nobles across the continent sought to send their sons to a Gaelic school. Armagh was the largest school and monastery. Patricius had made it his see. Built on a hilltop, it was enclosed by a circular ditch and bank.

"Oh no!" Rhianna cries out alarmed. "Not Armagh! Cartan will pounce on you immediately, and plunge his greedy claws into your heart. I cannot allow it."

"Mother! I cannot spend my life hiding away from Cartan. Anyway, Patricius and his monks are discreet, how would Cartan find out if I'm there?"

"He has his spies everywhere. Think of Beth and your unborn sister."

Domangart presses his lips together and looks stubbornly at his feet. He had known his plan would meet with opposition, and he wasn't ready to give up.

"I haven't forgotten Beth, Mother. Nor my unborn sister, nor any other of Cartan's misdeeds, that you and father have told me about. But I feel it is my vocation to become a cleric. Armagh is well protected."

"What about Tarbert and our extensive properties?" Fergus intervenes. "You will be my successor one day."

"One day yes, but hopefully not for many years, Father. You are not yet forty. In the meantime, I wish to study. The one does not exclude the other."

“I think we must let him go a chroi,” Fergus tells Rhianna. “But one thing you must promise me Domangart, you must wear the two enchanted rubies at all times.”

“Father! You know I don’t believe in *magic* rubies.”

“Neither I, my son, neither I. But the important thing is, that Cartan *does*. He was brought up by the druids and never became a Christian. He chooses his close advisors and commanders from amongst the pagans.”

“That may be, but I am not going to wear gems on a chain around my neck, nor a fox stole.”

“I was thinking of a sword, similar to your brother’s. We have the best smith in the whole of Argyll, right here in Tarbert. He can work the rubies into the hilt.”

Domangart sighs and gives in. “Very well Father, if you insist.”

***

Cartan is over sixty years old and embittered. His life hasn’t turned out as he had hoped. He had served the high king loyally but since turning sixty, he had been dismissed and sent home, without even a feeble ‘thank you’. His brother Tigernach had been elected king of Dalriada. His father-in-law had died. His brother-in-law, a *Christian* of all things, was now king of the Ui Neill and didn’t want Cartan in his inner circle. In fact, he was barely tolerated. His wife, Mairead, was of no importance; he had enough mistresses. The one thing he had wanted from her however, an heir, she had failed to give him. Well, she had given him a son, Caelan, an effeminate imbecile who spent all day on his mother’s lap, but he didn’t count. He would prefer to leave his properties to one of his mistress’ sons; but the Ui Neill wouldn’t stand for that. Well, he wasn’t sure that they were *his* sons anyway.

Cartan drinks some more wine and continues to reminisce morosely. There’s a knock at the door and Morag enters without waiting for him to call out.

“Birga-One-tooth wants you to visit her,” she says.

“What about?”

“If she’d told me, yer wouldn’t need to go.”

"Oh, get out of here!" Cartan dismisses her impatiently with a wave of his hand. He is too tired to argue with her. *Birga-One-tooth*, he thinks. As a child she had appeared old to him, like a grandmother. She had had grey hair and just one tooth as long as he could remember. *She must be ancient now, at least a hundred. Her mind is still sharp though.* Oh well, if he wants to find out what she is up to, he supposes he must visit her.

He gets up from his chair by the fire, and dons a warm cloak. Then he goes to the stables and tells a servant to saddle up a courser for him. While he waits, blood surges into his face as he remembers Lorcan deceiving him with Lockwood. He had tried to remedy the crumbly hoof by getting leather boots made especially for the horse. But they were ridiculously expensive, and only lasted three to four weeks before the leather wore through. Then he needed new ones. Here on Ireland, where there were no proper roads, the situation was borderline. In Argyll, with Roman roads leading everywhere, the horse would have been worthless.

The stable lad brings him a courser. He mounts and rides off to Birga-One-tooth's humble abode.

"You've come then," she greets him.

He thinks that that is pretty obvious, but seeing the pain on her face as she tries to stand up, bites down a sarcastic reply. He goes to her quickly, pushing her gently back into her chair.

"Hello Máthair, of course I came. I will always come if you send for me, you know that."

"His boy is here, in Armagh, *studying*."

Cartan needs a second to connect the dots.

"You mean, Fergus' son? In Armagh?"

"Aye, with those foreign *imposters*." Birga-One-tooth spits onto the floor. Cartan doesn't need anything spelling out. He has grown up knowing how much the pagan Druids hate and despise the Christians.

"If I attack Armagh and take the boy hostage, Fergus will come here running. We'll finally entice him onto our home ground!"

"Yes."

***

A messenger gallops up to Tarbert castle, jumps from his horse before it halts, and runs up the steps, losing his cap on the way. His cloak flies horizontally behind him like a magic carpet. He bursts into Fergus' study without knocking.

"Cartan's attacked Armagh and taken Domangart hostage!" he blurts out.

Fergus springs up from the chair behind his desk. "How long ago? Where has he taken him?"

"Yesterday, we don't know where—yet."

"Is he harmed?"

"We don't know."

"We must leave immediately. Send messengers to Loarn and Angus, we must rally all our troops together. I'll sail immediately to Dunseverick and speak to Tigernach. Don't mention this to Lady Rhianna, hopefully we'll find out where he is, before she finds out that he's been taken."

***

Tigernach is surprised when Fergus marches into the grand hall at Dunseverick.

"Fergus! I wasn't expecting you, welcome!"

"Cartan's taken Domangart captive!"

"Your son was in Armagh? Oh, I'm sorry, I had no idea!"

"What do you intend doing?"

"I was just discussing a plan of action with my commanders. Obviously, we cannot allow the Ui Neill to invade our territory and take our land. We have sent a delegation to their king to protest."

"*Protest*! Look, Loarn and Angus are on their way here now with as many men as they can muster. We mean you no harm Tigernach, but we shall regain Armagh from the Ui Neill and rescue my son, or may the devil fetch me! An attack against monks! I ask you, how deep can a man sink?"

"Fergus, I understand your anger, it is his most dastardly deed yet. However, we have reason to believe that Cartan was acting alone, without his king's approval. If that is the case, then the king of Ui Neill may support us. That would save unnecessary bloodshed. We should await the return of my delegation, and not rush into things."

"Tell me what you know."

"Cartan and his army, about four hundred men, supported by two hundred armed druids, surrounded Armagh. They burnt down the monastery, the school and all the other buildings. They stole plunder and killed many. About twenty monks are still in the enclosure, chained together as hostages."

"Six hundred men against maybe eighty monks!" Fergus shakes his head in disbelief.

"When will your brothers arrive?"

"Tomorrow morning at the latest."

"By then our delegation will have returned from Ui Neill. You, your brothers, and your men are welcome, Fergus, on one condition: you are under *my* command and will undertake *nothing* without my approval."

"I must find out where my son is and if he is well. Let me at least go to Armagh and scout the area."

"Very well, you may go with two men, but you must do nothing to antagonise the enemy before we are fully informed and ready. Come back tonight and report to me personally."

***

Fergus, Bram, and Sean ride to within a mile of Armagh. They tie their horses to a tree, and then bend down and dirty their hands with earth, damp from the night air. They rub the mud over their faces to camouflage themselves. Then they creep through the woods stealthily, keeping their eyes and ears wide open, for any unusual sounds or people. Slowly they sneak up nearer to Armagh's defensive ditches. The tree line ends two hundred yards from the earthen mound surrounding Armagh. The fertile land has been cultivated, but the crops trampled upon and ruined, by hundreds of soldiers.

Crouching down behind some dogwood, the men wait. They see trails of smoke rising into the dark sky from within the enclosure, and hear voices. It is hard to venture a guess as to how many men could be there. Sean nudges Fergus silently. A group of five guards are circling the outside ditch from the right. A minute later another group appears from the left. The two groups meet, exchange a few words, and then continue on their respective ways.

"I want to climb up the embankment and see what the situation is inside the enclosure," Fergus whispers.

"How? They'll see you," Bram replies.

"Not if I wait until the guards pass and then make a run for it," Fergus says. Another group of guards pass.

"They're not far apart," Sean says. "You heard what Tigernach said, if they catch you, well—"

"I could creep on my belly through the trampled down crops," Fergus says. "When there's a gap in the guards, I could dash up the mound and then lie down flat. If I'm quiet, they won't notice me. They're not looking for me."

"I don't know Fergus—"

"It's my son."

"Then I'm coming with you."

"Me too," Bram says.

Wriggling and writhing on their bellies and elbows, the three men advance slowly forwards through the mud furrows. Suddenly Bram gags and vomits. Fergus and Sean inch up to him. A monk lies on his back in the mud, his eyes have been gauged out, and left in the dirt besides him.

"Sadistic monsters!" Fergus mutters under his breath. "Are you all right now, Bram? Come on!"

Twenty yards from the mound, they flatten themselves between the crops, and wait until the guards pass. Then they jump up and run in a crouched position up the embankment before flattening themselves again. Raising their heads slightly they gaze at the scene in front of them. The monastery, as indeed all the buildings have been burnt down; the ashes are still smouldering a little, and wisps of smoke waft into the night air. About twenty monks are sitting on the ground in the centre of the compound. Fergus recognises Patricius. They are bound in chains, forty soldiers guard them. A further two hundred soldiers are in the enclosure eating, drinking, and resting. Fergus scans every last shadow desperately, there is no sign of Domangart.

"What have they done with him?" he mutters.

A Herculean man with biceps the size of a python that has just swallowed a deer, starts to walk towards them. His thigh muscles stand out like thick cords of rope, his hands are the size of frying pans. The three intruders bury their noses in the dirt. The footsteps stop, they hear a slight brushing movement, then a long stream of urine that never seems to stop. Relieved, the mountainous man turns back to re-join his comrades.

The three friends let out a collective breath of air.

"We must leave here, *now*!" Sean says.

The men swivel round on their stomachs and leave as they came.

***

Back at Dunseverick, Fergus reports to Tigernach. His brothers have already arrived and listen too.

"It won't be a problem to win back Armagh," Tigernach surmises.

"But where is Domangart?" Fergus asks desperately.

***

The present king of the Ui Neill, a man called Ultán, Cartan's brother-in-law, listens to the delegation from Tigernach. Unlike his father, he has no quandaries about destroying Cartan, in fact his sister would probably be better off without him. But land was getting scarce. If he dealt with Cartan, thus admitting his guilt, he would be forced to return Armagh to the Dalriada. Good fertile land that they could well use; his second oldest son was getting married soon and needed a livelihood. He orders his servants to bring Tigernach's men refreshments, he needs time to think.

A messenger arrives and tells him that Loarn and Angus are sailing towards the northern coastline with over a hundred currachs, carrying a force of one and a half thousand warriors. Ultán could muster a thousand men. *If Tigernach and his three half-brothers join forces? No that doesn't bear thinking about*, Ultán concludes. He returns to Tigernach's men.

"Tell your king that I will deal with Cartan, and return Armagh to Dalriada," he says. Ultán sends scouts to Cartan's home and is astonished to hear that Cartan has already returned from Armagh and was presently resting in his keep. He had taken a prisoner.

***

Cartan's home is a stronghold. A ditch, a mile in circumference, has been dug out and the earth piled up to form a dyke. The dyke is topped by spiked wooden palings. Inside this area is a second ditch, the earth from which has been heaped up on top of itself, to form a motte. Cartan has built a wooden castle on top of the motte and a keep, a square tower forty feet high. Cartan's family live in the castle, his army is quartered between the inner and outer ditch.

Ultán marches with his army to Cartan's fortress and orders his warriors to surround the dyke. Cartan cannot escape. Riders from Dalriada come galloping up to the Ui Neill King. It is Fergus, Loarn, Angus, Bram, and Sean. They dismount.

"He's holding my son hostage," Fergus tells Ultán breathlessly. "We must get him out alive."

"My sister and nephew are there too; I will do my best to save them."

"It's me he wants; we could offer an exchange."

"First we must pressurize him."

Ultán orders his archers to shoot burning arrows into the thatched rooves of the castle, the keep and all the other buildings in the bailey. They dip their arrow heads in tar, light them, and on commando, fire. The sky lights up with a barrage of hundreds of burning missiles. The majority find their targets, lodge into the thatched rooves of the buildings, and immediately set the dry reeds into a roaring furnace. Cattle bellow from within the bailey, followed by human screams.

Cartan's warriors begin to exit through the single entrance. They are unarmed, and have their hands folded behind their necks. Ultán signals to his men to lead them aside. A few pigs run out squealing between them. Ultán waits. A minute, then two. Silence. Then Caelan appears. His hands are folded behind his neck, and he is unarmed. His clothes are soiled, and he is in obvious distress.

"He's holding my mother hostage," he cries, looking at Ultán. "*Please*, you have to save her!"

"And Domangart? Is he there also?"

"Yes."

"Alive and well?"

"Yes." Caelan hesitates slightly.

"How many warriors are with him?" Ultán wants to know.

"Five, he wants Fergus and free passage to Gwynedd."

"Well go back inside, and tell him I'm here!" Fergus roars. "He can have me just as soon as he frees my son!"

Cartan rides out on Lockwood, his head held high, his countenance brazen. His warriors follow; two are holding a knife each, to Domangart's and Mairead's throats.

Fergus steps forward. "Dismount, you scum! Let Domangart go and fight me to your death!"

"What makes you so sure you will win?" Cartan sneers and removes his sword from its sheaf. It is Domangart's sword with the enchanted rubies. "If I win, I want free passage to Gwynedd," he tells Ultán. "I will release your sister when I get there."

Ultán wishes he could kill Cartan on the spot, but he is not sure whether the warrior will slit his sister's throat. He decides to let Cartan and Fergus fight, it could be amusing.

As Cartan dismounts, Fergus strides purposefully towards him. He holds his sword shoulder high with both hands, ready to strike. Cartan raises his sword, and with all his weight behind the blow, brings it thundering down and slashes it against Fergus'. Fergus' sword catches the blow, but is forced from his hands and tumbles to the ground. The crowd gasps, Cartan grins and raises Domangart's sword, relishing the pre-moment of striking the fatal blow.

"I'll cut your heart out and send it to your whore of a wife!" he threatens.

Fergus clucks with his tongue. Lockwood, standing proud just two paces behind Cartan, rears up and brings his front hooves pounding down on Cartan's back. Cartan flies forward headfirst into the dirt. His hands and arms lay spread-eagled out in front of him; his sword, thrust from his hand, lies four feet away. Fergus clucks anew. Lockwood rears again, and this time his hooves make a sickening crunch as they connect with

Cartan's spine. Blood trickles from Cartan's mouth and he dies, a look of surprise on his face.

The spectators are rooted to the spot, there is a stunned silence. They have never seen the like before. Fergus feels deflated, as if suddenly all the tension pent up in his body for more than twenty years, has been released abruptly, like a burst keg. He picks up the two swords and weighs them in his hands thoughtfully. Cartan's warriors let their hostages go. Fergus cuts through Domangart's ropes and hugs him.

"Father, I'm sorry!" Domangart says.

"Sssh a chroi, I love you. None of this is your fault."

Caelan runs to his mother. Ultán signals to two warriors to bring them away. He is absent-minded, in a stupefied trance. He has never witnessed such a deadly weapon as Lockwood before today.

Pulling his shoulders back to snap out of it, he orders, "Forward to Armagh, our work isn't finished yet."

Chapter twenty-three
479 – 498 A.D. Fergus King of Dalriada

Fergus and Domangart accompany Ultán and his warriors to Armagh. As soon as Cartan's warriors hear of their master's death, they surrender. Patricius and his monks are freed.

"Cartan handled on his own, without consulting me," Ultán assures Patricius. "I will pay for wood and stone to rebuild your monastery, and if you wish, I can assign twenty joiners and carpenters to come and help you build everything up again, bigger and better than before."

"I thank thee," Patricius says. "Your men will be welcome."

Fergus gets ready to leave Ireland with Domangart.

"No, Father, I wish to stay here," he says. Fergus looks at him considering what to say.

"Your mother—"

"Will miss me, as I her," Domangart interrupts. "Just one more year, then I will have completed my studies. Cartan is no longer here—"

Fergus claps his son on his shoulder. "I'll miss you too, son, but stay here and finish your studies, we're proud of you, know that."

***

Fergus takes Lockhead from the stables at Dunseverick and leads him to the harbour. Angus has prepared a ramp for the horse, onto the ship. Once aboard, they row out of the port and hitting the open sea, heave the sails for Aran.

A small crowd gathers at Brodick harbour as Sea Hawk Two docks. Lockhead is led from board and the crowd cheers. Fergus grins from ear to ear. He strokes Lockhead's forelocks.

"You've become quite a legend!" he tells the horse. Lockhead whinnies as if he's understood. Recognising where he is, he pulls towards the castle.

Hamish meets them, and immediately makes a fuss of the animal. Tormey and Mahon are also waiting there proudly.

"And to think we thought you were worthless!" Tormey shakes his head in remorseful dismay.

"I'm glad *he* was the one who killed Cartan; Lorcan would've liked that," Mahon, his twin, says.

"Well Hamish, have you got a paddock ready for him?" Fergus asks. "It's time the old boy is put out to rest."

"Aye, the best field with the greenest grass."

"Sounds just about right, here you are then!" Fergus hands Hamish the reins. "I think I should visit Douglas, whilst I'm here."

"He's not well," Mahon tells him. "You may want to warn Rhianna."

"That bad!"

"Aye, not good at all."

Fergus finds Anna at the castle; she cares for Douglas.

"He's taken to his bed," she tells him. "It won't be long now."

"Then I must return to Tarbert with haste, and fetch Rhianna."

"Will you bring Tudwal with you?"

"Yes Anna, of course."

***

Laird Douglas dies. His family and the village of Brodick grieve. Douglas leaves small legacies to his loyal servants. The castle and all his properties go to Rhianna and Fergus. The immediate family sit around a cheerful fire; Rhianna's face is long, drawn, and sombre.

Domangart takes her hand. "Grandfather wouldn't want you to grieve, Mother, he lived to a good age."

"I know a ghrá, but I'm missing him already. Don't worry, I'll be all right in a while."

"I have some news that might cheer you up a little." Domangart looks at the faces around him. "I've fallen in love with a young lady from Tara, her name is Fedelm the Fair, and we want to get married."

Everyone stands up to congratulate Domangart, nobody had had the slightest notion. Rhianna hugs her son.

"That is the best news in a long time!"

***

Fergus' kingdom is expanding rapidly. He decides to build a large, prestigious fort; a seat, a royal centre from which to rule his lands. He chooses the site carefully at the heart of his kingdom. An isolated hill stands ninety feet high amid an expanse of marshy bog, which carpets the southern end of the glen of Kilmartin along the River Add. A series of natural terraces lead to the top of the rocky outcrop. Fergus recognizes the defensive potential of the site and designs a formidable, multivallate hill fort to make good use of the natural barriers.

Entry is at the lowest level through a natural cleft in the rock, sealed by wooden gates. A massive outermost stone wall is constructed to encircle the hill. A water spring is blocked and a basin made of stone slabs form a trough to collect water. Beyond the gates, houses and workshops for smelting iron and gold are built. Leather workers, toolmakers, gold and silversmiths, weavers, and all kinds of skilled workers live and work here. A second drystone wall is erected around a second natural terrace. Entrance is through a second gateway. A bakery, kitchens, stables, and storage rooms are clustered together. Finally, on the summit, Fergus builds a citadel, a central stronghold. This is where he lives, in safety, with his family. Immediately in front of the citadel is another small enclosure, quarters for guards, and below this is a ravine.

Fergus, a trader at heart, doesn't just want a mere fortress, he builds an important trading point and a major production centre. He calls it Dunadd.

***

Loarn and Angus, accompanied by a large band of followers, ride alongside the River Add. Dunadd rises proudly from its rocky throne.

"An impressive sight!" Loarn says, and Angus can only agree.

They enter the fort, riding in single file past busy craftsmen. Angus decides to dismount to look closer; Loarn follows suit. Skilled workers are making a range of high-status weapons, metalwork, and fine jewellery. The brothers see rare minerals from the far east being crushed to powder, for scribes to illustrate and colour manuscripts. There are barrels of wine from southern Europe and a large range of pottery. They find Fergus in the keep, in his private study, discussing business with several wealthily dressed, foreign-looking men. Fergus dismisses the men and turns his attention to his brothers.

"Well, what do you think?" he asks.

"I'm at a loss for words," Loarn says. "It's breathtaking."

"I'm blown away," Angus concurs. "How did you manage to put this all together?"

"Oh, I didn't do it all by myself," Fergus replies modestly. "I had a few ideas and spoke to skilled workers, masons, and joiners; they told me what was feasible and what not. Then they drew up plans, I looked at the sketches and well, it was team work."

"But still! All the ideas! I'm completely flummoxed, it's absolutely spectacular," Loarn continues.

"Well, I wanted a trading centre, somewhere safe for goods to flow through. There's gold from Ireland! But it's also a production centre, did you see the artefacts?"

"Some of them," Angus answers. "I've never seen quality the like anywhere else before."

"Tell me what *you've* both been up to," Fergus enquires.

"I'm going to be a grandfather!" Angus grins. "Muredach's wife is expecting a child in spring."

"Congratulations! A cousin for Domangart's boys, Comgall and Gabran."

"Laird Mc Dougall died," Loarn says. "He left a small parcel of land to Stuart. He bequeathed the rest to me. You know, I heard someone the other day referring to us as 'the Second Dalriada'!"

"Aye, I've heard that too," Angus says. "Loarn and I have discussed this with each other, Fergus. Our entire kingdom together encompasses a vast area, and although each of us have separate settlements, they are related to each other and form one united dominion. We wish you to be our ruler."

"You honour me." Fergus is moved. "Then we shall form a single community, inside of which there are three cenels, divisions with their own local governments. I shall spearhead this community with honour, and Dunadd will be our capital."

***

Fergus knows how important ceremony is to his people, the Gaels. He asks his masons to chisel two footprints into the rock surface. During the coronation of himself and future kings, one of the procedures will to be to step into the two footprints, and swear an oath to serve the country honestly and to the best of their ability.

***

In spring 498 Tigernach dies and the Roydammna elect Fergus as king. The vote is unanimous. The Dalriada now consists of two halves: the territory in the utmost north-east of Ireland and a territory across the western sea from Loch Linnhe to the firth of Clyde including many of the western Isles. It forms a maritime province, united by the sea and separated from Pictland by the mountainous range, Druim Alban.

"I shall move the throne to Dunadd," Fergus tells the Roydammna.

"In that case, I shall lend you the Lia Fáil," Muirceataigh, his grand-nephew and high king of Ireland tells him.

"I am deeply honoured." Fergus bows his head towards him.

"It is only right that you, as the first Gaelic king to expand his Kingdom to Alba, should be crowned on the Stone of Destiny."

The Roydammna clap and cheer to show their approval.

***

Setna, Domangart's five-year-old daughter, sits on Rhianna's lap and asks, "What is the Lia Fáil, Grandmother, and why is it an honour to borrow it?"

Rhianna strokes Setna's long fair hair and looks into her granddaughter's large, blue eyes. An astute child who could read at the age of four, she was forever asking questions and usually two or three at once.

"The Lia Fáil is part of our heritage. It is used in the coronation ceremony of our high kings in Tara. So, if Muirceataigh lends it to your grandfather, it is a great honour."

"But what *is* it? What does it look like?"

"It is a large and very heavy oblong brick of red sandstone. On the surface there is an incised cross and at each end an iron ring to lift it."

Setna looks disappointed. "That doesn't sound very special."

"Ah my sweet, let me finish, it is special because the stone is magic."

"Magic?"

"Yes, when the rightful high king of Ireland puts his feet on it, the stone roars in joy."

"Oh, like a dragon?"

"Yes, but much louder. That is why some people call it 'the Stone of Destiny'. It has other powers too; it makes the king younger, and ensures him a very long reign."

"So grandfather will live to be a hundred? I'm glad about that! But how did the Stone of Destiny get to Tara, it must have come from somewhere."

"Well, once upon a time, more than a thousand years ago, there lived a prince called Eochaidh. He was the son of the high king. Eochaidh went on a long voyage to Jerusalem and there he met a young princess, Scota. They fell in love with each other. Whilst they were in Jerusalem, warriors came from Babylonia and invaded the city. Eochaidh rescued the sacred stone and boarding a Spanish ship, fled across the seas. On board there was also a Princess Tea, and a scribe, named Simon. The Spanish ship brought them to the old port of Carrickfergus. These three good people brought the Stone of Destiny to the Hill of Tara. Later, Scota arrived, and she and Eochaidh married. When Eochaidh's father died, he became high king. At the inauguration ceremony he stepped onto the Stone of Destiny and it roared out in approval. Since then, all our high kings have been coronated on the Stone of Destiny, or Lia Fáil, as it's called now."

"And did Eochaidh live for a long time, Grandmother?"

"Yes, but now young lady, it's time for bed."

***

Coronation day arrives. The streets of Dunadd have been decorated with colourful flags and the bakers have made special buns with sweet-candied fruit. Fergus wears his finest green linen ionar, the hem embroidered with geometric designs. His leíne is embroidered with golden thread and over all, he wears a white fur brat, clasped together at the shoulder with a golden brooch inset with large gems. Several gold chains hang around his neck. Thousands of people try to catch a glimpse of Fergus and his entourage as he strides towards the coronation site. He steps into the carved footprints, symbolising the new ruler's dominion over the land, and onto the Lia Fáil. Music plays, poems are recited, food and drinks flow. The celebrations last well into the night.

***

The next morning Fergus wakes up with a headache and groans.

Rhianna has little sympathy for him; Fergus takes one look at her face, and before she can speak says, "I know a stóirín, I know. Don't be angry. I need to sail to Dunseverick today, the brisk breeze will cure me."

"Today? Can't your business wait one more day? There is so much to be done here."

"Now I'm king of the Dalriada, I'm afraid you must get used to me travelling more than ever. Our kingdom is an archipelago, I shall sail constantly across the straits of Moyle back and forth. It's only twelve miles from the tip of Kintyre to Dalriada, I'll be quicker than other kings who have to travel overland."

"I suppose so. What will you do today?"

"You know Ireland has no roads, well now I'm king, I intend building one: from Dunseverick past Emain Macha and all the way to Tara. I must speak to builders."

"A slighe?"

"Yes, a great highway like the ones the Romans built in Britannia. I've already spoken to Muirceataigh, he has agreed. He said if it turns out well, he will even build it further himself, to the ford on the River Liffey!"

"Then you do good for Ireland, a stór."

Chapter twenty-four
501 A.D. The Storm

Fergus' sea kingdom expands. With travel by sea by far the easiest means of moving any distance, not only local trade but also long-distance trade is booming.

"Domangart, what do you think?" Fergus asks him.

"We need to spread out more and gain arable land for our folk. Shall we establish our presence further on Kintyre?"

"It is a prized area for settlers, Father. The coastal areas are rich and fertile. It would certainly boost our power, but the natives won't just hand it over to us."

"No, we must persuade them to, if necessary, with force."

Fergus concentrates on establishing his kingdom in Kintyre. Gradually the Dalriada share their language with the western coast of what is becoming known as Scotland, 'the land of the Scoti', as the Romans called the Gaels. This area speaks Gaelic, whilst east of the mountain ridge known as the Druim Alban, which serves as a natural border to Pictland, the Picts speak Brittonic. Fergus becomes known as Fergus Mór, Fergus 'the Great'.

In summer 501, just a couple of years after Fergus' coronation in Dunadd, he and his inner circle set out from Dunadd towards Dalriada in Ireland. It has been unusually hot for three days now. They board Sea Hawk Three and look to the sky, the wind stands still.

"I don't know," Sean says. "I don't trust the weather somehow. It's been too hot and humid for three days now; a storm is bound to break sometime."

"Hopefully," Bram says. "We need rain, or the crops will perish."

"It's been so dry this summer, that they haven't grown properly at all. It will be a poor harvest this year if the weather doesn't change soon," Fergus adds.

"Aye, we need rain, but not a violent storm or hail that destroys the corn. Then we'll have to buy grain from elsewhere," Sean agrees.

The men continue to study the sky. "Not a cloud in sight," Fergus says. "Come on then, we'll row if necessary."

They row out of the port and into the open sea. The waves roll lazily across the gentle waters. The men groan at the lack of a breeze and the heat. They heave up the rectangular sails, but their ship rests on the water's passive surface, scarcely moving. They remove their upper garments. They sit on their benches and pull on the oars. Their tanned backs glisten with sweat and their muscles ripple. Then abruptly, out of the blue, five miles out to sea, gigantic cumulus clouds billow up on the horizon. Scarcely have they appeared, then the clouds turn from snow white to thunderous black, and the blue sky takes on a strange yellowish hue.

"Where did they suddenly come from?" Sean asks.

"I don't like the look of those!" Fergus points at the clouds, shouting against a ferocious wind that has whipped up within a second.

"No, me neither, pull harder, make haste to reach the coast!" Sean cries.

As he speaks, streaks of lightning flash one after the other across the sky, and peals of thunder seem to shake even the sea and the whole world to its very core. Suddenly it becomes as dark as night. Fergus observes a large ball of blue fire about three miles distant from them.

"Lower the sails!" he screams, but the fire ball comes up so fast upon them, that before they can move, the mast is shattered into pieces and crashes onto the deck.

The boat is thrown back and forth, rocking wildly on the now turbulent waves. The ball of lightning hurtles itself along the railings, discharging a strong, sickening smell of sulphur. The ball of fire appears to be the size of a millstone. It bounces off a deck cleat with a loud explosion as it smashes the benches into smithereens. Sean is knocked down and Bram, going to help, screams as his hand is struck by the ball of lightning, and severed from his arm, falls to the floor. The blue ball of fire whirls around the deck, rises then, almost perpendicularly, and hits Fergus, alighting his whole body into an horrific, fiery silhouette. Then it passes backboard, along the deck, splitting the boat in two. Torrential rain follows the rare phenomenon, as the boat sinks and the crew plunge into the stormy sea and drown.

***

The Dalriadians witness the storm at sea from land. They take shelter in their homes as the freak storm reaches their coast. Tempestuous winds tear at the thatched rooves, fencing gets blown down, trees are bent in half and cattle sheds destroyed. A deluge of rain hurtles down from the sky, turning small streams into voluptuous rivers. Small lakes appear in the fields; the crops are ruined.

The following morning, the sun shines once again from a clear, blue sky. If it weren't for the damaged buildings, waterlogged fields and torn down branches from the trees, one could think that the storm had never occurred. As the natives begin to tidy up after the storm and repair their houses, Rhianna walks up and down the ramparts at Dunadd, wringing her hands together and waiting for a messenger to come and tell her that Fergus is safe.

She waits a day, then another day. Her friends and family gather around her. Her common sense tells her that there is no hope. Her family and friends realise this too and stand by, ready to comfort her when certainty comes. Rhianna cannot sleep nor eat. She is restless. Whenever someone comes to Dunadd, she runs to them breathlessly, her heart hopes for a miracle. But the messengers shake their heads. There is no sign of Fergus, nor any of his crew, nor their boat.

For seven days she hovers between an unreal state of neither wake nor sleep, not alive nor dead. Finally, two messengers come. They carry the carved oak sea-hawk figurehead of Sea Hawk Three.

"I'm sorry," the elder messenger speaks. "We found the figurehead washed ashore on the beach."

Rhianna sinks to her knees and weeps. Her daughter, Lisanda, helps her rise and brings her to her chamber.

"Come mother, you should rest now," she says quietly.

***

The Roydammna elect Domangart as Fergus' successor.

"Mother, we will never forget my father, I'm afraid I am not worthy to follow in his footsteps."

"Oh yes, my son, you are. Your father would be proud of you, as I am too"

"I will do my best and try to do everything as he would've done."

"Nobody can demand more, a stór."

Epilogue

Fergus, son of Erc, was king of the Dalriada from about 498 until 501 A.D. Up until his reign, Dalriada was a Gaelic kingdom in the utmost north-east of Ireland, covering part of the historical province of Ulster and corresponding to parts of the counties Antrim, Down and Armagh today.

Only twelve miles of sea separates the Mull of Kintyre from Antrim. Fergus, together with his brothers, Loarn and Angus, and their followers, crossed the Straits of Moyle, traded, intermarried, and sometimes fought. They spread over the islands of Islay, Jura and Aran, the coast of Argyll up to and beyond Dunollie (at present-day Oban). Fergus established himself as king over this area, which came to be known as the Second Dalriada. The kingdom thrived for a few centuries, and formed a springboard for Christianisation of the mainland. At its height in the sixth and seventh centuries, it covered what is now Argyll, (Gaelic: Earra-Ghàidheal means 'Coast of the Gaels').

Fergus and his men were known as Scoti. The Scoti spoke Irish Gaelic, which differed from the Celtic language of the Picts, and they gave this name to the whole country. Fergus chose, as the centre of his kingdom, a site on a hillock known as Dunadd. Dunadd was the capital of Dalriada for about 345 years. This was the seat of Fergus Mac Erc, and it is said that he brought with him from Ulster the Lia Fáil, later to be known as the Stone of Destiny. Their kings were enthroned at Dunadd, using the Stone of Destiny. St Columba crowned Aidan here in 574 A.D. using the Stone of Destiny as the throne. Some historians believe that the Lia Fáil, or Stone of Destiny, is the same as the Stone of Scone in Scotland. It is said that all future kings of Scotland, and British Monarchs, were inaugurated by the Stone of Scone. The stone remained in Scotland which is why Muirceataigh is recorded in history as the last Irish king to be crowned upon it.

From 1308 to 1996, the Stone of Scone rested in the Royal throne of England at Westminster. The Stone of Scone was last used in 1953, for the coronation of HMR Elizabeth II of the United Kingdom of Great Britain and Northern Ireland. In 1996, the British Government decided that the stone should be kept in Scotland, when not in use at coronations. It currently remains alongside the crown jewels of Scotland, in the Crown Room at Edinburgh Castle.

Fergus Mór is ancestor of all subsequent kings of Scotland and many members of the British Monarchy. The Gaels gave Scotland its name and its language. Fergus is widely recognised as the founder of Scotland. He was succeeded by his son Domangart.